P9-DNO-702

"What are we doing?" she whispered.

But she didn't move away.

"I think I'm kissing you," Tony said, leaning closer.

Their breaths merged, the heat of him seared her.

"Stop me now," he warned in a hoarse voice.

Their lips almost, almost touched.

And she couldn't speak, didn't want to deny him, found herself deep in the past, where Tony had been the only boy, then the only man, who'd drawn her, who'd made her desperate for his touch, who'd made her lose herself.

Their mouths explored as if in homecoming, as memories swamped her of laughing kisses, tender kisses, urgent kisses. Tony was still all of that for her, and no one had ever made her feel like this but him.

That made her break off the kiss and stare at him, wide-eyed. His eyes smoldered as they watched her mouth. He didn't look like he could stop, and for a moment, she wondered if she could, if Tony once again could create a passion that made her forget everything but him.

ATTENTION: ORGANIZATIONS AND CORPORATIONS
HarperCollins books may be purchased for educational, business,
or sales promotional use. For information, please e-mail the Special
Markets Department at SPsales@harpercollins.com.

Sleigh Bells in
VALENTINE VALLEY

EMMA CANE

A VALENTINE VALLEY NOVEL

AVON

An Imprint of HarperCollinsPublishers

This is a work of fiction. Names, characters, places, and incidents are products of the author's imagination or are used fictitiously and are not to be construed as real. Any resemblance to actual events, locales, organizations, or persons, living or dead, is entirely coincidental.

AVON BOOKS
An Imprint of HarperCollins*Publishers*
195 Broadway
New York, New York 10007

Copyright © 2014 by Gayle Kloecker Callen
ISBN 978-0-06-232340-8
www.avonromance.com

All rights reserved. No part of this book may be used or reproduced in any manner whatsoever without written permission, except in the case of brief quotations embodied in critical articles and reviews. For information address Avon Books, an Imprint of HarperCollins Publishers.

First Avon Books mass market printing: November 2014

Avon Trademark Reg. U.S. Pat. Off. and in Other Countries, Marca Registrada, Hecho en U.S.A.
HarperCollins® is a registered trademark of HarperCollins Publishers.

Printed in the U.S.A.

10 9 8 7 6 5 4 3 2 1

If you purchased this book without a cover, you should be aware that this book is stolen property. It was reported as "unsold and destroyed" to the publisher, and neither the author nor the publisher has received any payment for this "stripped book."

This book is dedicated to my great-uncle Francis "Budd" Theobald, who loved to write, though I never knew it until long after he died. I like to think that we shared the gift of creating our own worlds—and that he passed those writing genes on to me.

Acknowledgments

I had lots of research questions; so many people—and places!—were of enormous help with this book: Larry Brown, Kris Fletcher, and Justice Snow's Restaurant and Bar in Aspen, Colorado. My cousin Nicholas Perino was instrumental in figuring out Kate as a lawyer. And a special thanks goes to my son, Jim Callen IV, who spent hours on the phone with me discussing the details of his life in Colorado. For me, that was the best part of writing this book. Any mistakes are certainly mine!

Sleigh Bells in

VALENTINE VALLEY

Chapter 1

Valentine Valley, Colorado, was decorated for Christmas, twinkling lights lining nineteenth-century brick or clapboard buildings, wreaths hung on shop doors, greenery wrapped around every old-fashioned lamppost. The sight used to fill Kate Fenelli with happiness whenever she came home for the holidays. But now, as she drove down Main Street the day before Thanksgiving, the decorations only reminded her of her big Italian family and how she was going to break the news to them. Humiliation and anger crawled inside her like snakes, but once again she forced them down. She had to stay in control, and she'd been reminding herself of that all through the nearly two-hour drive from Vail. She'd soon be seeing her thirteen-year-old son, Ethan. Her embarrassment would only confuse and worry him.

But the closer she got to her parents' house, the more dread built up inside her, making it difficult to swallow past the constriction in her throat. She found herself taking a turn she hadn't meant to, the Range Rover sliding a bit on the snow. Like a coward, she was circling back, away from her family, trying to find the words that would reveal enough to satisfy them but not so much that her standing with her law firm would be jeopardized.

And then she saw Tony's Tavern, a squat, plain building close to Highway 82, neon signs blinking in the windows. Three pickup trucks were parked outside, but then it was only late afternoon. She felt drawn to it by a compulsion she didn't want to acknowledge. Deliberately keeping her mind blank, she got out of her Range Rover and walked up to the door with determined steps, packed snow crunching under her boots, her breath a mist in front of her. She opened the door, and the warm air surged out at her, smelling of beer and French fries. SportsCenter was on several flat screen TVs between mounted animal heads. Two middle-aged men, looking remarkably alike in matching Carhartt jackets and cowboy hats, turned their heads the same way to glance at her. And then they each did a double take. She might have overdressed a bit today in her "I'm a professional lawyer" double-breasted wool coat and leather boots, trying to give herself confidence when she faced her family.

And then the bartender looked up at her. Tony De Luca, owner of the tavern. Her ex-husband. His brown hair always looked like it needed to be trimmed, and there was a hint of lines fanning out from the corners of his brown eyes, but then he was thirty-three, like she was. Yet . . . thirty-three looked good on him. He wore a black buttoned-down shirt, probably over jeans, although she couldn't see behind the bar. His shoulders were as broad as ever on his tall, lanky body. He'd always been an athlete, and she had a sudden memory of playing the trombone in the marching band and meeting his laughing eyes when he took off his football helmet after a big win. Back then there'd been a spark of happiness and desire and endless possibilities.

From childhood, they'd been attached, knowing what each other had been thinking, sharing the same emotions, the same bond. Tony had never been one to hide his feelings or play it cool. But all that was gone—had been gone through the nine years since their divorce. Even the sad ache of regret and bewilderment she used to feel had faded into the past. Now he was just her son's father, and since he was great at that, he had her gratitude. He had Ethan through the school week, when he could be more of a full-time parent, and she had Ethan most vacations and every weekend, when Tony always had to work. She thought it gave Ethan full-time parents for the whole week.

By the lowering of Tony's brows, Kate could tell that her appearance was unexpected; it wasn't the weekend. She'd totally forgotten that she'd told Tony last week that she was just going to stay in Vail and prepare for an important court date over the holiday.

She gave a halfhearted smile as she approached the end of the bar. "Hi, Tony."

He nodded. "Kate."

His deep voice had once made her shiver all over;

now all she heard was the wariness, and it made her even sadder on this sad day.

He put down the glass he was polishing and approached her, lowering his voice as he said, "What're you doing here?"

"Can't a girl want a drink?"

His frown intensified. He poured her a glass of the house red and slid it in front of her. "If you changed your mind and decided to come for Thanksgiving, shouldn't you have rushed right to your parents' to bake pies or something?"

She grimaced. He knew she didn't bake—hell, she didn't like to cook much either, which was a sin in her family. Her parents owned Carmina's Cucina, the Italian restaurant on Main Street. She'd grown up in the business. Having served at the restaurant through her teenage years, she'd always sworn she would never be a waitress again. Why Tony had wanted the tavern, she could never understand.

She took a sip of her wine. "Tastes good."

He put both hands on the polished wood of the bar and leaned closer. "Kate, what's going on?" he demanded.

To her horror, a tear slid down her cheek, and she quickly brushed it away.

Tony's brown eyes, always the mirror of his emotions—but no longer where she was concerned—went wide. "Is something wrong? Is it Ethan?"

"No, nothing like that. I didn't mean to scare you." And then she had to wipe away another tear. "I've screwed everything up, Tony. I—I couldn't face them all at home. Not yet." She gestured bitterly to the wine-glass. "Guess I needed a drink to find my courage."

"You always had courage, Kate, maybe too much of it."

She winced. Of course Tony wouldn't want to hear her complaints—he was convinced it was her fault their marriage fell apart. Oh, she shared the blame, but certainly not all of it. She should leave. She had no right to dump her problems on Tony.

"My firm put me on two months' sabbatical," she blurted out.

He crossed his arms over his chest, still frowning. But he was watching her with those deep brown eyes, the ones that had once shown her the sympathy and understanding that had made her confide everything in him.

She rushed on. "I shouldn't tell you all the details—I'm not supposed to tell anyone. I certainly won't tell my family or Ethan. But it was wrong, Tony," she insisted earnestly, her voice a hoarse whisper. "I mean, what the partners are doing is wrong, and no one will listen to me! I discovered a report my client hadn't meant to include in some papers, a report that affects their filing with the FDA—hell, it could affect the public health. In this report, people exposed to a cattle growth hormone in the research phase were having severe flu-like symptoms. But there was no proof that *that* hormone was the one my client was presenting to the FDA. I wanted more information—I thought we have a duty to the public to ask for more info, you know? But since we're not certain it specifically relates to our case, they told me to forget about it."

"And you don't take orders easily."

"Tony, that's not true. Well, not where work is concerned, anyway. So . . . I kept bringing it up to the partners, and they finally told me I could scare away this big client—or others. I never considered breaking attorney-client privilege. I could lose my license for that! But the partners don't care. They said I need to take some time and get my priorities straight, when I was just doing my job!"

Kate took a sip of wine, her hand shaky. The two men farther down the bar—who had to be twins—were making no secret of their interest. She'd kept her voice down, but now she prickled with heated embarrassment. At last she snuck another glance at Tony. His eyes were downcast, and he absently wiped a smudge on the bar. She felt a bit deflated by his attitude, but the lump had eased in her throat, at least.

She sighed. "There's nothing you can do, I know that. I'm sorry to have unburdened myself like that. You probably wish I'd leave."

It was his turn to sigh. "No, I don't. I'm a bartender; people talk to me all the time. It makes them feel better."

She winced. "You think that's the only reason I spilled my guts?"

He met her gaze, and for a moment, everything seemed to still until it was just the two of them, looking at each other across a distance of years. Had she been looking for the comfort only Tony had once given her, the security, the reassurance? There hadn't been another man like him in her life—she'd never allowed it. There had been dates and the occasional couple-month relationships, but that was it. The pain she'd felt when their marriage had crumbled . . . she'd sworn she never wanted to feel that again.

Yet here she was, telling Tony everything, like he could make things better, just because once upon a time he'd made every bad situation look golden. But they weren't married anymore, and it looked like the casual friendship they'd shown for Ethan's sake must have been more of an illusion than she'd thought. Like she needed to be more depressed. . . .

He cleared his throat. "So what's next? How will this affect Ethan?"

She sighed. "I'll try not to let it affect him at all. I'll tell him I'm on sabbatical, but I can't tell him the confidential details I just . . . spilled to you."

"So you'll be here for Thanksgiving?"

"I guess so. Is that okay?"

His hesitation was almost invisible. Almost.

"Of course it's okay. It'll be strange for Ethan to have us both on a holiday. Just so you know, I've been invited to your mom's for dinner tomorrow."

She winced. "It's been a while since I missed a holiday; I'd forgotten that little tradition. When I'm not home for a big day, it's like you take my place with my family."

He leaned toward her, and his glance was suddenly solemn. "You know I could never do that. And if you'd rather I stay away—"

"Of course not!" she interrupted earnestly. "My family adores you."

Maybe more than they adore me, she thought with a twinge of regret.

"What about after Thanksgiving?" he asked.

"After?" she repeated, bemused.

"What do you plan to do on your . . . vacation?"

She snorted, then coughed to try to cover it. The two men down the bar grinned at her, and she gave them an awkward smile.

"*Vacation.* That's not a word I associate with this," she said through gritted teeth. "I'm being punished."

"So what are you doing for your punishment? Staying here or going back to Vail?"

Vail had once seemed a punishment to her; now it was home. She'd been made junior partner a couple years ago and been asked to open a branch of the law firm there. She'd felt like she was being thrown out of the big city of Denver, but it had been an interesting challenge. And it made seeing Ethan so much easier. But go back there, where people might ask questions when they saw workaholic Kate just hanging around? No.

"I—I don't know where I'll go," she finally admitted. "I hadn't thought that far. I just . . . couldn't stay in Vail for Thanksgiving after . . . everything that's happened. And all that trial prep I had to do? Pfft. I don't even know how I'll explain things to my family, let alone my friends."

"Or—what's his name, Keith?"

She blinked at him, watching as he picked up a glass

and started polishing with deliberation. "Keith? I had a few dates with him. How did you know?"

"We do share a talkative kid."

"Oh, right." She waved a hand. "We dated. It never went further." But inside, she felt a little disturbed. Had Ethan volunteered that information—or had Tony asked him about it? She didn't know which was worse.

And suddenly, she felt more vulnerable than she had in a long time, she, who'd always prided herself on being in control. She wasn't in control of much of anything these days.

"I guess I should go," she said, sliding her wallet out of her purse.

He frowned and put his hand on hers. "Put that away. You own a piece of this bar, remember? I'll never forget it."

She stared into those serious eyes. "Tony, it doesn't bother you, does it? You know I wanted to help."

"And I'm grateful," he said shortly.

She'd fronted the loan for him to buy the tavern a few years back—not that he'd asked, and not that he'd accepted easily. But then she'd reminded him that he'd supported her in college, helping her make her dream career come true, and she wanted to do the same for him. Tony never missed a payment to her, and he'd insisted on interest.

She hoped bringing up the loan didn't add a new layer of awkwardness to their already strained friendship—if you could call it that. She'd always wanted it to *be* a friendship, didn't want to be one of those couples who couldn't see past their anger or see what it was doing to their families. That had never been Tony and her.

But friendship? She looked at his closed-off, polite expression and suddenly knew she was kidding herself. They'd broken each other's hearts and would never recover from that. And the ache she thought she'd long ago buried suddenly made it hard to breathe.

One of the guys at the other end of the bar signaled for Tony, and he glanced at Kate.

"Go do your job," she said, forcing her voice to sound mild rather than strained with unshed tears. "Thanks for listening."

He nodded. "See you tomorrow."

She walked out of the tavern, straightened her shoulders, and prepared to face her family.

Tony closed the cash drawer, letting his stiff back loosen when he heard the front door close. He glanced over his shoulder to see that Kate was really gone, and he felt a sense of relief, as well as a sadness so old he could blow dust off it. An older man and woman had entered in her place, wearing the more expensive coats and boots that you'd usually see up in Aspen rather than in his tavern, at least this early in the season. But even the rich liked the occasional low-key night. He saw that Rhonda, his daytime server and a mom in her forties, was gathering menus as she watched them take a seat at a table.

What the hell had Kate been thinking, coming here? He remembered his flash of surprise when she'd walked through the door, and then the momentary appreciation of her beauty, the same beauty that had been kicking him in the gut since he was a kid. She'd cut her blond hair short, and though it had been windblown when she'd walked in, he guessed she could make it look professional and neat when she wanted to. But it was her eyes that always lured him in, their purple color that was indescribable, lavender or amethyst or—thank God he wasn't still the lovesick boy who'd once composed mind-poems about her eyes. But today they'd been full of an anguish he hadn't seen in years. She could still move him to worry, and he'd had to work hard to appear disinterested. And it had hurt her, he knew, not that he took any pleasure in it, although once he might have. It was simply self-preservation.

Ned and Ted Ferguson, identical twin plumbers, glanced at each other with smirks, then back at him. They were always a day behind shaving, and their whiskers were as shot through with gray as their hair was.

"Wasn't that your ex?" Ned asked.

You could tell it was Ned, because he'd once cut his chin on a pipe, leaving a scar.

"Yep," Tony answered. "Another beer?"

Ted glanced down at his half-full bottle and eyed his brother. "He doesn't want to talk about her."

Tony sighed. "There's nothing to talk about. She's home for Thanksgiving. Our kid'll be happy."

"But not you?" Ned prodded.

"Guys—"

"I don't like to see my ex," Ned continued as if Tony

hadn't spoken. "And she don't look anywhere near as good as yours. Yours has done good for herself."

"Classy," Ted added, the twin who always agreed more than instigated. "But then, Ned, your ex could give a horse a run for its money."

Tony sighed and walked away. The twins bantered but never took offense, and as Ned shot back a good-natured retort, Tony found himself staring unseeing at SportsCenter on the closest TV.

Kate had certainly been flustered, but she'd never met a situation she couldn't conquer. She had a fierce will to succeed. It had attracted him to her, but it had also been one of the causes of their breakup. They'd been in the same class in kindergarten, but she'd just been another girl then. It wasn't until fourth grade, when she'd developed a friendship with his sister, Lyndsay, a year younger than them, that Tony had come into contact with Kate outside school. He'd found himself playing the role of annoying older brother for a while. Only in hindsight had he realized he'd been trying to get Kate's attention even then. She'd been like the sun shining on his world, vibrant and happy and so driven—always so driven, he thought, shaking his head. She'd wanted to be the smartest student, the best trombone player, the fastest cyclist, and being around her and all that energy had been exciting. He hadn't even minded that she liked to be in charge all the time.

By high school they were a couple. He accepted his sister's teasing, Kate's brothers' protectiveness—none of it mattered. The future seemed far away; he lived for his moments with her, kissing her, touching her. He even got a part-time job bussing tables at her parents' restaurant so they wouldn't have to be separated. During the summer, he hung around at the end of each day at the local law firm where she interned, hoping to buy her ice cream or walk her home. And when Cal Carpenter, one of the lawyers, said she could always work for him after she graduated, Tony started deceiving himself about their future.

Together they went off to college in Denver, though she'd landed a full ride at the best university. He played down how much he loved her, how she was the center of his world. He knew that scared her, and he was willing to let her go for her dreams, never wanting to stand in her way.

And then she got pregnant the summer after their freshman year, and everything between them changed. She was panicky and scared, but he wasn't. He'd always meant to marry her, to be a family. The thought of their baby just thrilled him. They were young, but they'd have all the time in the world to be parents, unlike his mom, who died before she was even fifty.

But their marriage only lasted four years—four years during which the pressure of college and jobs and a baby stressed their little family. It didn't break it, though, until the final realization that he and Kate didn't want the same kind of future together after all.

"You look like crap."

Tony looked up to see Will Sweet taking the seat Kate had just vacated. Will was a tall cowboy with sandy hair, hazel eyes, and a cleft in his chin that set the girls' eyelashes fluttering. Of course his devil-may-care attitude and constant flirting helped.

"Nice to see you, too," Tony said dryly.

Will parked his cowboy hat on the stool beside him and eyed Tony. "Was that Kate Fenelli I just saw looking as grim as death as she drove off in that fancy Range Rover?"

Tony nodded. Without being asked, he poured a draft beer and set it in front of his friend. "She's got some time off, so don't be surprised to see her around."

"You okay with that?"

Tony's eyes widened. "Why wouldn't I be? This is her hometown, same as mine. And Ethan'll be glad."

Will snorted before taking a sip of beer and smacking his lips. "Good stuff. Yeah, the kid's always happy to see his mom, which says good things about her, I guess."

Tony grinned. "That compliment was dragged out with reluctance."

Will shrugged. "She's always been gorgeous, but I never thought she was your type."

"I have a type?" Tony countered, glad to be feeling amused again.

"She might have been born here, but she's a city girl at heart, and you're, well, you're practically a rancher, you're so small town."

"*You're* the rancher—I'm just a simple barkeep. And she lives in Vail now, remember."

"But I bet she misses Denver. To think she tried to force you to live there. Like you or Ethan would have been happy."

Tony kept his smile in place, although it was strangely difficult. "That's old news, Will. And it wasn't just her wanting to live in Denver, and me here, that ruined our marriage."

Will harrumphed, even as he took another sip of beer. "Then what was it? You don't exactly talk about it much."

Tony hesitated, then spoke softly. "It's hard to talk about the biggest failure of your life."

Will eyed him, then looked around. "I'd like to listen."

Tony chuckled. "It's my job to listen." There weren't many people he'd unloaded his problems on, and he wasn't going to start now. "Thanks, but it's in the past. I've moved on."

"Really, with who?"

"Hey, I've dated."

"I can't think of anyone who lasted longer than three months. I think you're way too loyal to a memory."

"I haven't met the right girl. And I have Ethan, you know. I have to be careful. I really don't intend to marry again until he's an adult. Why traumatize him that way?"

Will's only response was a snort.

But inside, Tony was worried that he'd met the *only* girl for him and, since their relationship was ruined, he'd never have another. Their breakup had shattered him. She'd seen the real person inside him—and hadn't wanted him.

More and more lately, he was reminding himself how good his life was, with family, friends, and the best son in the world. More and more he was trying to prove to himself that everything was as it was meant to be.

But he was trying too hard.

Chapter 2

Kate arrived at her parents' home on Grace Street around dinnertime. Not having called ahead, she knew she'd be alone. Her parents would be at their restaurant, and so would her youngest brother, Joe, who was seventeen and worked there part-time—just as she and all her brothers once had, she thought with a wince. Serving at Carmina's had convinced Kate she was never going into the restaurant business, much as her parents had wished otherwise.

She let herself into the dark kitchen through the back door, then turned on the light over the sink. It gleamed on maple cabinets and stainless steel appliances. The kitchen island held a cornucopia, complete with tumbling fruits and vegetables for the Thanksgiving season. The long tablecloth had cartoon turkeys all over it. She remembered how her parents had proudly displayed on their refrigerator every handprint-turkey Ethan had made when he was little, just as she had.

Now her little boy was almost fourteen, an eighth-grader taller than she was, although still shorter than his dad. Suddenly, she felt old.

"Barney?" she called, even as she heard the clicking of claws on the tile floor.

Her parents' dog, a beagle mix, came toward her, tail wagging. He went right through her legs so he could have his hips scratched. He had a bit more white on his snout, and she thought she detected a faint limp, but her mom told her Barney was holding his own, even though he was as old as Ethan. Barney had been bought as a playmate for Joe when the boy was four, but it was Ethan who loved him the most. At last the dog tired of Kate's attention and agreeably went outside to the fenced-in yard, before coming back in to curl up on his bed in the corner.

She reheated the morning's coffee in the microwave, then sank down on a stool at the island. Finding the semidarkness almost a comfort, she warmed her hands around the mug. She didn't want to think any more, still feeling ridiculously vulnerable after spilling her newest secrets to Tony. What had *that* been about? How the hell had she just looked into his eyes and fallen back into her need to tell him every important thing, as if nine years hadn't gone by?

She glanced out the window into the backyard next door—Tony's backyard. He'd bought the house for Ethan's convenience, she knew, so the little boy would always have family nearby; if not her family, then the widows of the Widows' Boardinghouse, three elderly ladies who knew everyone, and every secret, in town. When Ethan was little, the widows had taken turns sleeping on Tony's couch when Tony had had to work evenings. Everyone had coordinated together so that Ethan never felt bad about the divorce or both parents working.

Not that Ethan had all that many memories of Kate and Tony together. Kate had been a busy student by day, doing her homework in the evenings while Ethan had slept and Tony had worked at a Denver bar. She'd once thought that love would get them through the temporary rough patch of opposite schedules, but she'd been naïve.

She rose and went to the window, looking at the swing set in Tony's backyard, which Ethan never used anymore. It was covered in a couple inches of snow, and the swing moved gently back and forth in the breeze, as dusk began to obscure the view. Frosted with snow, the Elk Mountains now shadowed the valley, rising high above the town. It was a beautiful view, and part of why living in Vail was so easy. It was just like home.

She'd enjoyed Denver, too, although not in the first years of her divorce. But big-city life and the endless entertainment of clubs and restaurants, shows and museums, had proven a good distraction on her rare evenings without work. She hadn't had many of those, since she'd tried to get her work done during the week and save her weekends for Ethan.

She heard the jiggle of the knob before the back door

burst open and Ethan entered, his eyes narrowed with concern. "Mom? I saw your car. Why are you here? Is everything okay?"

She put her mug down on the island and opened her arms wide, feeling a rush of love and gladness. "Can't I have a hug first?"

He actually had to bend to hug her, and it was over too soon. His cheek was chilly from the outdoors and pink with the cold. His hair, once blond like hers, was now sandy, perhaps on its way to darkening to his father's brown. He already had his dad's brown eyes, which now looked at her like something terrible must have happened to make her change her schedule. Was she teaching her son that change was a thing to be dreaded? That made her feel guilty—but she should be used to guilt by now.

"Nothing's wrong," she said, patting his cheek like she used to.

He ducked his head away and absently reached down to pet the adoring Barney. "Mom—"

"You must have just come from ski club? Oh, sorry, I mean snowboarding."

"Same difference."

"Is that a new jacket?"

He nodded to both.

"Did you have fun?"

"Yep—it's always fun when we have a good base this early. But Mom, I thought you had plans this Thanksgiving?"

She sighed and sank back down on her stool, pointing to the one beside her. He glanced around first, looking as if he could eat the whole kitchen, then went immediately for the cookie jar, a giant turkey for the season. Her mom was old-fashioned that way. Ethan took a handful of chocolate chip cookies and set them on a napkin, pushing it toward Kate. She helped herself, grinning her thanks at him. He was a thoughtful kid. She and Tony had done something right. Barney waited patiently at Ethan's knee, and soon he gave the dog a piece, after making sure there was no chocolate in it.

She'd thought she'd be explaining her problem to her mom first and hadn't considered what she'd say to Ethan. Now she took a deep breath. "Well, I've taken some time off, E. It's called a sabbatical. I've been having trouble with a case, disagreeing with the partners, so . . . I've got some time away."

He frowned and swallowed a mouthful of cookie. "Sounds like a punishment rather than a vacation."

"Well, I'm choosing to see it as a much-needed vacation. I haven't had much of one since that Disney cruise we took a couple years ago."

"That was four years ago, Mom."

She winced. "Really? Time flies."

He studied her with those eyes that echoed his every emotion, and once again, she was startled at the resemblance to Tony. She was thinking too much of her ex since unwisely revealing her problem to him. Now Ethan looked at her with a son's worry, and she knew she had to put him at ease.

"This is nothing, E., I promise you," she said, touching his hand. It was still chilly, so she gave his hands a brisk rub between her own, like he was still her little boy coming in from building snowmen. "People disagree all the time and work out their problems. I wish I could tell you more, but—"

"Client confidentiality. I know." He took another bite of cookie. "You and Dad didn't work out your problems."

He spoke guardedly, not bitterly, and she was surprised he'd even brought it up.

"That's true, but marriage is very different from business. Hearts and emotions are involved in a marriage, two people's beliefs. You have to be perfectly in sync to be married, and work hard at it. That just didn't happen for us. I think it's because we were too young and didn't know what we really wanted in life."

He accepted that with a nod, since it was her standard explanation for something that was far more complicated. But their youth had surely played its own role.

"What did you want that was different from what Dad wanted?" he suddenly asked, his voice squeaking on the last word.

"Has your voice started to change just since last weekend?" she asked, forcing a laugh.

He cleared his throat and gave a chagrined shrug, but she was only distracting herself from his pointed question.

"Well, E., your dad and I made the mistake of never really talking about where—or how—we wanted to live once I finished law school. We both made assumptions and never had any deep discussions. For instance, since you and your dad moved back to Valentine during my last couple years of law school"—a horrible, heart-wrenching decision made in desperation—"he just assumed I wanted to move back here, too. And I assumed he knew I was working hard to earn a job at a big law firm, which meant Denver or another city. When I got that job offer, we were forced to face the realization that neither of us would be happy settling for what the other wanted."

And there had been so many other things wrong, including the ways they'd disappointed each other.

"What's wrong with Valentine Valley?" Ethan asked almost conversationally, picking up another cookie.

"Absolutely nothing. I grew up here, after all, and this is where my family is—where you are. But . . . the job opportunity I wanted nine years ago wasn't here. I wanted the chance to represent large companies in major cases, to test my skills and grow as a lawyer."

"I get that," he answered. "Sort of like if I wanted to move up to the first snowboarding team instead of the developmental team."

She smiled with relief. "Exactly. And you haven't seemed to mind living in two different towns."

"Nope, it's kind of cool." He poured a glass of milk, looking up at her to ask, "So if you're on a break from work, what are you going to do?"

She found herself blinking at him. "Uh . . . I don't know. I haven't thought that far. Any ideas?" she joked halfheartedly, unease feeling like a weight in her chest. "I guess you could finally teach me to snowboard."

"Uh . . . I don't know, Mom. You probably couldn't keep up."

"Hey, I'm not *that* old! At least I'm ready to take you on in Xbox."

"Sure, we'll do that." He grabbed the backpack he'd left by the door. "Gotta go, Mom. Dad's expecting me home."

"Of course," she said, even as he shut the door, leaving her and Barney alone again.

She sighed and took another sip of coffee. Ethan was growing up so fast.

Not ten minutes later, just as she was bringing in her suitcase, her parents showed up, bustling through the back door, snow falling from their coats and hats as they took them off. Barney took turns leaning against their legs for the adoration he was due.

"Ethan texted us," Christina, Kate's mom, said. "He felt bad that you were hanging out alone."

Christina Fenelli was a chubby woman in her early sixties, with dimpled cheeks and blond hair several shades darker than Kate's, which curled around her shoulders and often drove her crazy.

"You cut your hair!" Christina exclaimed.

Kate wasn't sure if her mom was disappointed or envious. She patted her shorter cut. "Yes, but I'm not sure yet if it's worth the work."

"Well, you look beautiful, as always," her dad said.

Tom Fenelli was barely taller than his wife, only Kate's height, with a stocky, slightly overweight build and dark brown hair going silver at the temples.

"Thanks, Dad," Kate said, giving him a hug as he kissed her cheek. She kissed her mom, then took a step back and waited for the interrogation to begin.

"We're so glad you decided to join us for Thanksgiving," Christina said, going to the fridge and looking inside. "I'll see what I can whip up for dinner."

Kate blinked in surprise. No questions about her last-minute schedule change? "Mom, don't worry about me. You must have pies or something to bake for tomorrow. Let me help."

Both her parents eyed her as if she'd spoken another language.

She gave them a mock frown. "I can follow directions, you know."

Christina grinned, flashing her dimples. "Of course you can. And I'm happy for your company."

"As if that's all I'm good for?" she shot back in amusement.

Her dad studied her, his smile fading, but to her surprise, he didn't ask any questions. "We had meatballs last night. Unless your brother Joe polished them off after school today, we should have leftovers."

"Where is Joe?" Kate asked, taking the containers her mom passed her.

"Basketball practice," Tom answered.

"On Thanksgiving eve?"

"He has a tournament this weekend. If you're staying around, you can watch him play."

"Sounds great, and . . . yeah, I'll be staying around—if it's okay with both of you."

"How nice that you were able to take some vacation time for the holidays," Christina said, slipping on an apron.

Kate took a deep breath. "Well, it'll be longer than

just the weekend. I'm on sabbatical for the next two months."

Both her parents froze, her dad pulling a beer from the fridge, her mom reheating a pan of sauce.

"I know you're curious," Kate hurried on, wondering how many times she would have to explain this to her large extended family tomorrow, "and I can't really say much, since it's the firm's business, but . . . at least I'll have some extended time with Ethan, right?" Her voice sounded weak by the end, and once again, she felt the rise of tears. Hadn't humiliating herself in front of Tony been enough for one day?

Her dad surprised her with a hug. "Looks like you need one of these, Katie."

Only her dad called her by her childhood nickname, and for a moment, she clung to him, overcome by the feelings of failure she'd felt only once before, because of her divorce. She'd promised herself never to fail again, but now she'd disappointed the senior partners. And she was disappointed in them, too, and so furious at the whole situation.

"I-it's not as bad as it seems," she said when she finally broke away and gave her parents a wobbly smile. "We disagree about a client, and they just want to re-think some things and . . . it'll be okay."

"Will it?" Christina asked softly. "If you disagree with the partners on something so fundamental that it's causing you this kind of anguish, maybe you need to rethink your future—"

"No," Kate said quickly, firmly. "I work for a great firm. We'll find a middle ground and compromise.

That's what we do." But she felt a renewed stab of disappointment that the partners hadn't seen her side, hadn't *wanted* to see her side. And the thought of doing all the compromising frustrated her. "Now really, what can I do to help?"

"Well . . . I'll let you in on a little secret, but you can't tell anyone," her mom said conspiratorially, sharing a wink with her dad. "We're not baking pies—I ordered them from Sugar and Spice."

Kate gasped with appropriate melodrama before repeating, "Sugar and Spice?"

"The new bakery in town," Christina answered. "Well, not so new—two years old now. The owner, Emily, moved to town, fell in love with Nate Thalberg, opened the bakery, and now they're married."

"I'm really happy for Nate," Kate said. She remembered him from school, a big, handsome cowboy from the Silver Creek Ranch family. "If I can't bake pies, and I confess I'm not too disappointed, can I pick them up for you?"

"That would be great," her mother said, beaming. "Let's eat a quick meal so you can get over there before she closes at seven. The bakery is right on Main Street."

When Christina wasn't looking, Kate studied her face, wondering if she was imagining that her mom looked more tired than usual. Of course her mom was tired—she helped run a busy restaurant, and tomorrow was Thanksgiving. But to give up baking the pies, when she'd always been so proud of her homemade crusts? It was a little strange . . .

Kate's brother, Joe, came home in time for dinner,

and the four of them enjoyed a good meal and lots of laughs, the tension Kate had anticipated being mostly absent except for her brother's occasional curious glances, which she ignored. Joe was blond like her, a guard on the high school team, since he was only a little taller than their dad, and beginning to fill out from the gangly stage that Ethan was just now entering. The two boys were only four years apart in age, and toddler Joe used to pipe up that Ethan wasn't his brother but his nephew, shocking and delighting everyone who'd asked.

Kate silently admitted to herself that she was a little disappointed Ethan hadn't called to see if he could join her for dinner. But this was Tony's holiday, not hers, and she would never dream of interfering.

Christina wouldn't let Kate help with dishes, sending her off to the bakery and even trying to slip her money to pay for the pies.

"Mom!" Kate protested, firmly handing the money back. "I may not be working at the moment, but I'm still getting paid. I can afford some pies. And I'm happy to contribute to Thanksgiving."

Christina kissed her cheek. "And we're so happy to have you—for as long as you want. You know that, right?"

Kate nodded, slipping into her coat and heading out into the falling snow before she could embarrass herself by tearing up again. She would have walked the few blocks to Main Street, but she needed her car to carry the pies. Still, parking was difficult, and she ended up around the corner from the bakery. Standing just outside the colorfully decorated front door, she took a moment to enjoy the beauty of her hometown. Now that she'd crossed some of the initial hurdles of her return, she was more able to appreciate the twinkling lights outlining the buildings and the wreaths on so many doors. No town did Christmas like Valentine Valley.

At last she entered Sugar and Spice, and the aroma of cinnamon and vanilla wafted over her in a wave that made her mouth water. Unlike the Christmas-focused Main Street, Emily Thalberg had decorated for Thanksgiving, with stalks of hay in the corners and little lights that looked like turkeys strung along the front windows. Ten people stood in line along the glass-fronted display case. Kate slipped in line behind the last person and examined the brownies, cookies, and cakes, trying not to salivate.

"Kate Fenelli?"

Kate looked up to see Mrs. Thalberg, one of the three widows she'd just been thinking about earlier. She still had unnaturally red hair, and her makeup made her look years younger. Her jeans and turtleneck were covered by a Sugar and Spice apron that read, WE PUT THE HEAT IN SWEET. Behind her crowded her two housemates, Mrs. Ludlow and Mrs. Palmer. Mrs. Ludlow was your typical grandma, with her white hair and walker, blouse and slacks, but Mrs. Palmer had only gotten wackier as far as Kate was concerned, her blond wig towering above her forehead, her makeup exaggerated, her dress patterned with tiny Pilgrims.

"Hello, ladies!" Kate answered cheerfully, for regardless of what had happened in her marriage, these women still treated her fairly, rather than as the selfish "career woman" who'd broken Tony De Luca's heart.

"How wonderful that you're in town for Thanksgiving!" Mrs. Thalberg said.

"It's kind of a last-minute thing," Kate admitted. People ahead of her in line frowned as she distracted the employees, so she said, "You go ahead and work. We'll talk afterward."

For the next ten minutes, Kate enjoyed watching the ladies work. They knew everyone's name and asked questions about relatives and friends. How could anyone mind chattiness, even on the eve of a busy holiday? Every so often, a pretty woman roughly Kate's age came out of the kitchen, her strawberry blond hair bouncing in a ponytail, her apron matching the ones worn by the widows. Kate wondered if this was Emily Thalberg, who'd been the one to snare the most eligible bachelor in Valentine Valley.

When it was Kate's turn to be waited on, the widows fussed over her, asking about her job (she changed the subject) and Ethan, whom she was happy to gush over. These ladies had taken care of him as if he'd been their grandson, and Kate could never repay their generous gifts of time and love. Her five pies were produced from the kitchen by a blond teenage girl who looked Kate over with a frown, as if she recognized her. Come to think of it, she did look familiar.

Mrs. Thalberg saw Kate glance a second time at the girl. The widow leaned over the cash register and said quietly, "Don't mind Stephanie. She's young and only hears old rumors."

"Stephanie Sweet," Kate said as the lightbulb went on in her head. "Her brothers are good friends of Tony's. Makes sense. She's all grown up, isn't she?"

"She's home from college," Mrs. Palmer added, eavesdropping, her Western twang pronounced. "Business and pastry arts. She wants to work with her sister here."

"Sister?" Kate said blankly. "Last I knew, she only had brothers."

"The bakery owner, Emily, is her long-lost half sister," Mrs. Palmer eagerly explained.

Mrs. Ludlow frowned. "No need to speak of such personal things at work, Renee."

Mrs. Palmer stuck out her tongue. Kate bit her lip to keep from laughing at their antics. She always loved running into these women.

"Have some coffee, dear," Mrs. Thalberg said. "We'll introduce you to Emily when the line shortens."

Much as Kate didn't look forward to answering more questions, it was good to just sit and people-watch. The coffee was excellent, the décor relaxing, and for the first time, Kate let go of her worries and just vegged.

Twenty minutes later, Emily turned over the CLOSED sign in the window and breathed a sigh of relief. Kate wasn't the only customer still sipping her coffee, but she felt guilty regardless and slipped her purse onto her shoulder.

"Don't go running off," Mrs. Thalberg said, leading Emily to Kate's table. "Kate Fenelli, this is Emily Thalberg."

Kate stood up, and they shook hands. She figured

that Emily knew Tony, who was good friends with Emily's husband. Usually people who knew Tony first looked at Kate like she was the Wicked Witch of the West, but Emily only seemed politely curious. People's hostile attitudes weren't Tony's fault, Kate knew—he'd never speak unkindly about her. But when a man was a single father, sharing custody, women just felt sorry for him.

"It's so good to meet you, Kate," Emily said, pulling up two chairs, one to rest her feet on. "Ethan is such a wonderful boy. You and Tony have done a great job with him."

"Why, thanks," Kate said. "Now that he's a teenager, we'll see if it's still smooth sailing, but so far, so good, thanks in large part to these ladies."

Mrs. Thalberg waved a hand dismissively and walked briskly back to the display counter.

Emily smiled as Stephanie brought her a coffee, but after a brief nod at Kate, Stephanie left in a hurry.

Emily frowned. "I'm sorry, that was really rude. I haven't seen that side of her since . . . well, since she first heard about me!"

"It's okay, I'm sort of used to it. I'm the ambitious lawyer who divorced wonderful Tony De Luca."

Emily winced, though her smile didn't dim. "And I was the new sister coming in to take some of Daddy's attention. Don't worry, Steph's pretty open-minded, even if it takes a little while."

Kate shrugged. "It's okay. I live in Vail now, so I don't run into it too often."

"Home for the holiday?"

Kate nodded, but she only sipped her coffee rather than explain more. She was going to have to come up with a better explanation of her extended time off. She felt rootless and uncertain, things she *never* experienced.

"We've got to be close to the same age," Emily said ruefully. "It's so weird that you have a teenage son, and I'm only just getting started."

"Having kids soon?" Kate asked politely.

"We've started the adoption process." Emily leaned forward, blue eyes shining. "It's very exciting!"

Kate grinned. "I bet it is. We were young and scared when we had Ethan. It must be very different to plan and prepare."

"Both paths have their advantages, I bet. Do you think—" Emily stopped and blushed. "Oh, never mind."

"Go ahead," Kate said. "I don't offend easily—I'm a lawyer."

"It's just that . . . I find myself more and more worried about how adding the strain of adoption and a child will change our marriage."

"Do you worry because having a child changed things for Tony and me?" Kate asked.

"Well . . . gosh, it's not my place to even assume . . . I can't believe I'm asking you such personal questions."

"No, it's okay, really. Sure, a baby changes things, but in the end, having Ethan didn't cause our divorce. We just . . . didn't talk enough, both too busy to think beyond our own noses."

"That's good to remember, thanks."

In Kate's mind she saw the little apartment with baby toys everywhere, the way she and Tony passed each other in a hurry as one came through the door and one went out. She used to think back a lot and wonder what she should have done differently, but she was trying to concentrate on the future now rather than mull over what couldn't be changed.

The door jingled as it opened, and Emily glanced at it, her eyes alight with expectation. In walked her husband, Nate, cowboy hat perched on his wavy black hair, dimples revealed as he spotted his wife and smiled with his whole face. Kate withheld a sigh. It had been a long, long time since a man had looked at her that way, and the only one who ever had was—

Tony. He followed Nate into the bakery even as she thought his name. When he saw her, his brown eyes widened only a fraction. His naturally friendly expression remained the same, though, and she found herself releasing a breath she hadn't known she was holding. They'd worked hard to be at ease with each other for Ethan's sake, and she didn't want that to change just because she might be hanging out in Valentine for a while—and just because she'd automatically gone to Tony with her problems, as if she still had that right. It made her uneasy.

The last in line, Ethan closed the door behind him. "Hey, Mom," he said in surprise. "Thought you'd be with Grandma."

"She sent me on an errand," Kate said, resisting the urge to hug her son in public. "Where are you guys off to?"

"Tony and I are playing hockey tonight," Nate said. "Our team's called the Valentine Massacre." He gave Kate a hug. "Good to see you."

That was nice of him to say, but she never quite believed it. He was Tony's staunch friend, though they'd all gone to school together. She wondered what Nate would tell Emily about her later. Emily might not be so friendly the next time they met. Kate felt sad, before mentally kicking herself for worrying about something that hadn't even happened. It was one of her flaws—she overthought everything. Of course, it worked in her job, or it had until she'd overthought too much for the partners' comfort.

She found herself watching Tony as he strolled to the counter to greet the widows. He had the same irrepressible smile he'd had since childhood—maybe since birth—one that made a person feel the center of his thoughts. He bantered with ease, making the ladies blush and chuckle. He had such a way with people.

Nate turned to Emily. "You sure you still want to come the night before Thanksgiving? You've been having such long days this week leading into the holiday."

"You couldn't win without my cheerleading," Emily insisted. "Just let me get my coat. Steph said she'd lock up."

After Emily hurried into the kitchen, there was an awkward pause, as if Nate and Tony didn't know what to say to Kate. Ethan just looked at his phone. Maybe it would just have to be up to her to make things easier.

"I remember when you guys used to play on the pond at the Silver Creek Ranch," she said.

Nate and Tony exchanged an amused glance, and she was glad to see Tony think about the past in a happy way. But his expression faded to politeness when he looked at her.

Nate said, "Yeah, I seem to remember you insisting you could play, too. Sprained your arm good from a simple fall."

"You bodied me out of the way," she protested.

Ethan looked between them all, his expression curious. "Mom, you played with the guys?"

"Sure I did. After I was knocked over, your poor dad insisted on carrying me all the way to the pickup, like I'd broken a foot."

Tony's lips pressed together in a line, and she hoped he was restraining a smile rather than a frown. She remembered feeling safe and loved because of his concern. And being held in his arms always left her breathless—at least it had in those early days. She wondered if he was thinking the same thing, because he looked away, his expression neutral. Toward the end of their marriage, she hadn't had time for many hugs, and soon Tony had stopped trying to give them. It was a little thing but something that caused her great regret. She had a lot of regrets.

She wasn't sure if their silence had grown awkward, for Nate cleared his throat and seemed almost relieved when his wife emerged from the kitchen.

"Ready!" she called cheerfully. "Kate, are you coming?"

She felt Tony's gaze on her and quickly said, "No, no, I haven't even unpacked, and my mom is expecting me.

But thanks for the invitation. Have a good time." She turned to the stack of pie boxes, only to find Tony picking them up before she could. "You don't have to—"

"Be right back," he called to Nate and Ethan. "Where'd you park, Kate?"

She almost wished Ethan had helped as well—and that was a baffling thought. Why would she not want to be alone with her ex-husband? After wrapping her scarf back around her neck and buttoning her coat, she held the door for him. "To the left and around the corner," she said, catching up to walk at his side.

The snow crunched under their feet, sounding loud in the stillness of a town closing down for the night. Somewhere in the distance, Christmas music played.

"I'm sorry if that was awkward for you back there," Kate said, her breath a mist in front of her.

Tony glanced at her from beneath the brim of his cowboy hat. "What are you talking about?"

"Emily seems really nice, and she doesn't realize . . ." She trailed off, but Tony said nothing. "You know, that Nate's your friend, and Emily doesn't know me and—"

"Kate, this is your town, too."

She nodded, glad he couldn't see her red cheeks as she unlocked the Range Rover and opened the rear door. Of course it was her town. She'd never been self-conscious about this kind of stuff before, so she shouldn't start now. What was wrong with her?

Tony set the tall stack of pies down, and together they rearranged them so they wouldn't be damaged. Then she pressed the button to close the door.

"Thanks," she said.

He nodded. "See you tomorrow."

"Score some goals," she called as he walked away.

He lifted a hand but didn't turn around. She found herself watching him walk, his hips narrow as they moved rhythmically, his shoulders broad beneath his thick, tan Carhartt jacket. She caught herself and whirled around before anyone could see her gawking at her ex. Her job situation must really have been messing with her head. Or she'd been without any intimacy for too long, or—she was staying at her parent's house, however briefly, right next door to Tony, bringing up all the old memories. She started the car and told herself her mom would keep her busy. For the tenth time that day, she wondered what was wrong with her.

Chapter 3

At dawn, when she heard her mom get in the shower, Kate escaped her childhood room to go for a run. Barney used to know it was running time just because she was putting her hair in a ponytail. It was too short for that now, but he still got excited when she put her tennis shoes on. She was used to the cold; she didn't even need a scarf over her mouth. It wasn't that running was fun, but it took up less time than the traditional winter pastimes of skiing or snowshoeing. She hadn't skied since childhood. Outside, she quickly shoveled the sidewalk first, then put a leash on Barney, who'd been waiting patiently at the back fence. She turned away from Tony's house and began to run, keeping her pace slow for the dog. He kept up for a while, but after a mile, she took him home to his doggie bed and returned to her run at a quicker pace.

She was trying to brace herself for the day, when

she'd face her four brothers, aunts, uncles, and cousins. It had taken a long time to get over her feelings of failure after the divorce, and it was as if this sabbatical was a way of letting her family down all over again. The very presence of Tony and Lyndsay, along with Kate herself, would remind everyone about the past. All the old bleakness was resurfacing, when Thanksgiving should have been a joyous day. She ran harder, reminding herself that she was in the right where the firm was concerned, and she'd prevail in the end. As for the divorce, she and Tony were certainly better off apart than married and unhappy.

Back at home, she showered and made herself useful through lunchtime, moving tables with Joe, carrying plates and silverware from the kitchen to the dining and living rooms, where the tables were lined up. Barney watched serenely from the couch—although once upon a time, they'd have been tripping over him. One by one, her brothers began to arrive midafternoon, their hugs making her relax—although she reminded herself they didn't suspect anything was wrong. They brought casserole dishes and brimming salad bowls, which she schlepped to the kitchen while they took off winter coats and boots.

"This is a surprise," Jim said when he entered the kitchen. He was two years older than Kate, dark-haired like their dad. He owned Mirabella's, an upscale Italian restaurant in Aspen, and was still happily single.

"Yeah, strange, isn't it?" she answered vaguely.

Jim eyed her but held off on questions as Walt came in, carrying his one-year-old. Walt was blond like Kate and Joe, and though he was only thirty, he and his wife already had three kids under the age of seven. Kate could just see Diana, her frizzy red hair practically standing on end, wrestling the other two kids out of their jackets and boots in the front hall, while Barney waited to be petted. There was always a sense of friction between Kate and Walt. Even as a teenager, he hadn't understood why she'd abandoned the family restaurant; she'd always had the nagging sensation he still felt the same way. Her parents never questioned what she wanted—only Walt did.

Kate reached for Walt's little boy, who promptly cringed back against his father.

"It's the age," Walt said apologetically.

"I remember." Kate tried to laugh it off, but today she was feeling a little too vulnerable to banish the brush of uneasy sadness.

Dave was the last of the brothers to arrive, and he'd brought a date. He worked for the family restaurant as a sommelier, and though he knew his way around wine, he specialized in beer. He was dating a waitress from Carmina's, and she seemed almost embarrassed to be at the family dinner, although Kate's parents quickly put her at ease. Dave looked more like a surfer dude than the small-town boy that he was, with his sunburnished curly hair and tanned good looks.

The three grandkids descended on Kate's parents, leaving her to face her brothers. "What?" she asked, faking innocence as they eyed her.

"Okay, what's going on?" Jim put his hands on his hips. "You weren't scheduled to be here, and if you were anyone else, we'd think it a lucky coincidence. What's wrong, Kate?"

She let out an exaggerated sigh and told them what she'd told her parents—that the law firm had put her on sabbatical because she and the partners had disagreed about a case and the partners wanted her to rethink some things. "It's okay, really. It's probably for the best. Cool heads and all that."

"*You* argued with the senior partners?" Dave asked, sipping his beer and looking at her like an alien had taken over her body.

Jim and Walt sported earnest frowns.

"The case is complicated, and we could go several different ways." She gave an exasperated shrug. "You know I can't talk details." But she'd revealed more to Tony, she thought uneasily.

Diana stepped close and gave her a hug. "You know we're here for you, Kate."

Kate blinked at her in surprise, then slowly smiled. "Thanks, Diana. I appreciate that." She and Diana were friendly, but they'd never had the chance to be close, with Kate's work/Ethan schedule and Diana being busy with her three kids.

Walt acted as if his wife had silently prodded him to speak. "Well, of course you can count on us. I'm concerned with how they're treating you. Is it harassment?"

Walt, with his business degree, was always practical.

"I appreciate you assuming it's all their fault." Kate was certain he used to believe she shouldn't have gone into the law in the first place. But it wasn't just about her supposedly turning her back on the family business. Didn't he ever think there wouldn't have been room for the both of them at Carmina's? Hell, she'd probably done him a favor!

"Of course it's their fault," Jim said, smiling. "*You* couldn't do anything wrong."

He and Dave elbowed each other, and suddenly Kate felt like a girl again, being gently teased by her overwhelming number of brothers. She let her breath out, surprised to feel a little shaky.

"We don't need to go into details with everyone, okay?" she said. "It's . . . too hard to explain, since I can't discuss it."

"I'm pretty curious," Joe said, coming to standing beside all his older brothers, speaking around a mouthful of bread.

Dave took his teenage brother around the neck with one arm. "Hey, you get to eat and not the rest of us?"

"Oops, I was supposed to set out the appetizers," Kate said, tapping her head with the palm of her hand as she hurried toward the oven. "Oh, I hope the pastry around the Brie didn't burn."

"Will we be able to eat her cooking?" Jim asked Dave.

She ignored their laughter because it felt absolutely normal, which was what she needed.

Soon her parents' siblings began to arrive, along with cousins and their kids, and the house was overflowing with people. Kate was so busy taking coats and organizing boots that she didn't notice the next pair of boots handed toward her was Tony's until she looked up and met his eyes. She paused for a moment, and he gave a faint grin. He was wearing jeans and a t-shirt under an open flannel shirt.

She straightened up as Ethan came through the door, threw his snow-covered coat on a pile, gave her a brief kiss on the cheek, handed over his boots, and sped on past, all at the speed of light. Barney gave a joyous bark, and they collided in a petting, wagging frenzy.

"So you're the welcome committee?" Tony asked.

Flakes of snow were melting in his dark hair. He put his hands in his pockets and rocked on the balls of his feet, eyeing her a little too closely. She felt flustered, knowing there was flour on her sweater because she'd refused to wear an apron, and there'd been so much to do that she'd only put on half her makeup.

"Everyone has a job," she quipped, setting both pairs of boots on a throw rug nearly overflowing with footwear.

Why was she feeling nervous around Tony? Was it still because she'd gone to him first, out of instinct, and didn't know how she felt about it—or how he felt about it, except awkward?

She offered a bright smile. "Where's the rest of your family?"

"Dad's picking up a couple of the widows, who had midday dinner at the Silver Creek Ranch but still wanted to join your parents. As for Lyndsay . . ."

To her surprise, he avoided her gaze, looking past her to the holiday mayhem of kids running around, arguments over the Xbox, and someone calling that they needed more forks for the tables.

"Lyndsay?" she prodded.

"She's feeling under the weather, or so she told me."

"Oh."

"Me, I think she wanted to see her new guy but didn't want to share him just yet."

"Of course, that makes sense." But Kate felt like Lyndsay had very different reasons for staying away, and they all centered on her. She lowered her voice. "Tony, I didn't plan on being here. She knows that, right? I feel terrible if she felt like she had to avoid me."

"Kate—"

"Just call her and say we have over thirty people."

"Kate—"

"We can stay on opposite sides of the house, and—"

He caught her elbow, and she stopped her rambling to stare up at him in surprise. She didn't remember the last time he'd deliberately touched her. His fingers were surprisingly warm, though he'd just come from outside.

"She makes her own decisions," he said. "I think she's an idiot. Just because you two aren't close anymore. I mean, damn, doesn't she realize she's making me feel bad, like I was the cause of the wreck of your friendship, a friendship which started long before me?"

"You?" she cried in disbelief, then lowered her voice when she saw her mom staring with interest from the kitchen doorway. "Tony, you can't possibly believe she feels that way. It's me she's angry at, and very defensive on your behalf. You're her brother."

He shrugged. "It doesn't feel that way to me."

She groaned. "Trust me. I know Lynds—okay, I

used to know her as well as you did, maybe better. She doesn't blame you for anything."

"Well, she should. The marriage wasn't one-sided, after all, so neither was the divorce."

Now it was her turn to shrug. "Tell her from me that I wished she'd have come. It would have been good to see her."

He gave her a doubtful look, then started to move past her. It was her turn to catch his arm, then quickly let go.

"You think I wouldn't want to see her?" she asked.

"It's been a long time. Not sure why you'd want to revisit it when you've both moved on."

"So you're saying you wouldn't try to fix a friendship with Will if you'd had a problem?"

"But that's Will."

"And you're saying that's not me?" she asked sharply. "Or not your sister?"

He opened his mouth, blinked, and only said, "Never mind. You do what you want. You always do."

It was her turn to gape as he went past, and she felt herself heat with a blush. She turned away, struggling to make her expression serene. He'd spoken casually, not meanly, but she felt pricked just the same. Was he referring to the past they shared, or just to her friendships? It was maddening and defeatist to worry about such things, especially coming from a man she'd divorced nine years before. But she'd loved him once, and she shouldn't have been surprised that his opinion still mattered.

She turned and saw the moment when he greeted her

brothers, their easy acceptance, how they handed him the beer he liked best. There was no mild disapproval from Walt, like she always vaguely felt from him. Nope, Tony might be divorced from her, but he still fit right into her family—maybe better than she did.

Okay, *that* thought was a little childish and unnecessary, but she wasn't feeling herself. And just to prove that theory, she had a brief time-travel thought, wondering what her life would have been like if she'd stayed married. Maybe she'd have been in town for Walt and Carmina's Cucina after all; maybe she'd have had more kids, and Ethan wouldn't have been an only child. Life was full of maybes, and she usually never second-guessed her choices. But this Thanksgiving wasn't her usual holiday—it was the start of her exile.

Reluctantly, her gaze was drawn to Tony, and she had the sudden memory of a weekend morning in bed reading the paper to each other, he, the sports section, she, the local crime report, then him pulling her newspaper away and pressing her down into the pillows.

She turned her head away, as if someone could read her thoughts from her flushed face and wide eyes. Oh, she really was losing it. She hadn't let herself think of Tony sexually in years. They'd never had a problem once they'd gotten into bed; it had been finding the time for it. Toward the end, their timing had always been horrible, and for that, she'd been mostly to blame.

She gave herself a mental shake. This was Thanksgiving—time to be with her family in the present. She went to the kitchen island, where the appetizers were laid out and a dozen shoulders bumped each other as hungry appetites were fed. She watched her father, his face red as he laughed at something a cousin said, before he took another bite from his plateful of appetizers. She couldn't imagine him being skinny, of course, as the owner and sometime chef of a fantastic restaurant, but she thought he'd put on a little weight recently. Maybe she could get him to go for a walk with her . . .

There were other dads present, of course, and she found her gaze sliding to Tony, who stood with Ethan. Their son wasn't yet as tall as his dad, but they could almost look each other in the eye. She wasn't sure what they were talking about, although she thought she heard the word *snowboard*. They shared a love of sports, which kept Ethan active, and woodworking, which made her boy handy, and she was grateful. She was the homework and video game specialist. But it wasn't the conversation between Tony and Ethan that mattered to her, it was their close relationship, for which she was truly grateful. With Ethan, Tony looked like the man she remembered—genial, easygoing, lighthearted, without the wary, distant look he reserved for her. Over the years, she hadn't had much opportunity to see their relationship in action, but she'd always known that he was a wonderful dad; he had been from the beginning. She'd been scared to death on discovering her pregnancy. Rather than backing off or getting angry, he'd stared down at her stomach with the silliest, most tender smile growing wide on his face as he'd touched her. "Our baby?"

She'd told him it would change everything, that she was scared, that everyone would be upset with them—

and weren't they too young to be parents? But Tony, as usual, had been so calm, so sure it would all work out. He'd been at her side, ready to get married—when she'd been dazed and frightened and worried about how she could be a mom and study at the same time. Though she'd been right in her fears, she'd never regretted the choice, and she loved Ethan more than she'd imagined possible.

Taking a deep breath, she stepped forward to join Tony and Ethan's conversation—the three of them together was such a rarity—but Ethan just gave her a quick nod, waved at a cousin, and left, Barney at his heels. She watched them walk away.

She wasn't sure what her expression showed, but Tony cleared his throat and said, "The kids are having a pool tournament in the basement. It's nothing personal."

She sighed. "I'm telling myself that a lot lately."

She caught Jim's frown as he passed, and he paused, saying, "Is everything okay?"

But he was looking pointedly at Tony—as if Tony had been the cause of her bad mood.

"Of course everything's okay," she hastened to assure Jim, surprised and touched at his protectiveness.

Tony lifted his beer toward Jim as if in a toast. Jim nodded, but he wasn't exactly smiling as he moved away.

"Sorry," Kate said awkwardly.

Tony shrugged. "Nothing to be sorry about. At least Jim and I speak to each other since the divorce—unlike you and my sister," he reminded her mildly.

She winced, but she didn't want to talk about Lyndsay. "I'd like to hang out with Ethan more while I'm here, but I'm getting the impression he'd rather things didn't change."

"I don't know about that. He's not rigidly fixed on a schedule."

"Unlike me?" she countered.

He sighed. "I didn't say that."

"No, you didn't," she said with her own sigh. "Don't mind me, I'm not feeling like myself."

He nodded, dipped a cracker in the artichoke dip, and pointed it at her. "It's not just you, you know. Ethan's pulling back from me, too. When we go snowboarding, he usually goes off with friends and leaves his old man to fend for himself."

She reluctantly smiled, looking at Tony out of the corner of her eye. *Old man?* He was self-deprecating, but to her, his looks had only improved with "age." There was strength, masculinity, and confidence to Tony that always made female heads turn. Even after all these years, she wasn't immune to it. He had prominent brows and a square jaw that seemed all manly, not to mention a mouth that—

Enough of that. "Do you remember when Ethan was three, and he wandered away from us at the park?"

Tony gave an exaggerated shudder. "How could I forget? He wanted to play on the swings but didn't bother to tell us. Those were the worst five minutes of my life, as we ran around the pond and looked for little footprints at the water's edge."

"Mine, too." They'd had other bad moments, like

when Ethan had broken his arm snowboarding, but nothing compared to that moment of terror when they'd looked into each other's frightened eyes and thought they'd lost the heart of their family.

She'd let her family go not a year later, she thought starkly, sadly. She met Tony's eyes, and with an unspoken agreement, they moved off in different directions.

Tony told himself he felt relieved to get away from Kate—it was unsettling to spend time with her, after nine years of passing Ethan from car to car on weekends. What he most noticed was how he had to fight an incredible feeling of sadness, mixed in with a lingering trace of anger he just couldn't let go of. Every time he thought he'd put the past behind him, something happened to make him realize he might as well be stuck there.

He munched on shrimp and pretended he was listening to conversations around him, but he was really watching Kate. He wondered if part of his anger was a lack of forgiveness. He'd once thought her career had been more important to her than their marriage, but he wasn't so certain of that now. His own parents had struggled for years to have children, and his mom had died of cancer when he was only ten. He knew life had to be enjoyed each moment for the precious gift it was. That's why the miracle of Ethan, though unintended, had been so easy for him to accept and appreciate, whereas for Kate, their baby had changed her carefully planned life. Life wasn't about schedules, but she hadn't seen that. She hadn't been there when Ethan had cried for his mom—

And then he took a step back from the anger he thought he'd buried. To be honest, Ethan had probably cried for him on the weekends, too.

Just when the turkey was coming out of the oven and Tom Fenelli was preparing to carve it with elaborate ceremony, the front door opened again and Tony saw two of the widows enter, with his dad following behind. He felt a moment of relief. It wasn't as if he'd been in a wilderness of enemies, but seeing his father put him back in the holiday mood, especially after his sister had chickened out.

Kate hadn't chickened out. She'd come home and faced everyone with her work problems, the job that had defined her life. She might have been humiliated and furious, but she was taking the questions and side-long glances. He had to give her credit for that.

"Hey, Dad," he said, giving the old man a hug.

His father, Mario, was tall, and bald above a gray fringe of hair, with a working man's belly and the big shoulders of his plumbing profession. Though he was semiretired now, he'd always had his own business, so when Tony's mom had died, Mario had been able to schedule his appointments around his kids' school activities. He'd attended every one of Tony's football and hockey games, each of Lyndsay's marching band competitions. He'd even served on the PTA. They hadn't had a big house or lots of money, but they'd been happy, and Tony had learned to take things as they came, with the patience his older parents had shown him.

Mario grinned at him, even as Tony greeted Mrs. Thalberg and Mrs. Palmer. Mrs. Ludlow was having dinner with her own family—not at the White House this year, though they'd all hoped. Mrs. Ludlow's granddaughter had married the son of President Torres just last May in Valentine Valley, but the president was traveling this November.

Kate came over to take their coats. "Hello, everyone." She smiled a bit cautiously at Mario. "Mr. De Luca, Happy Thanksgiving."

Tony's dad returned her smile. "Thanks. You, too, Kate."

Kate turned to the ladies. "Let me show you where the appetizers are. How was Thanksgiving lunch at the Silver Creek Ranch?"

When she moved away, the widows chattering as they trailed behind her, Mario took the beer Tony offered and spoke softly.

"I didn't know she was coming."

"I thought Lyndsay would run to you with the news."

"Nope." Mario frowned. "Where is my baby girl?"

"Not here. Said she was 'under the weather,'" Tony said, emphasizing his sister's excuse.

Mario sighed. "Subtle, isn't she? I would have thought that if you were fine having Thanksgiving dinner with your ex-wife, your sister should be, too."

Tony shrugged. "I guess a girlfriend bond is even more sacred. Break it and . . ." He ran a finger across his neck.

With a chuckle, Mario said, "You're a good boy, Tony. All these years, you've never made it hard for Ethan to be with his mom."

"And she's done the same for me, remember. And I

like the Fenellis. They're a great family." After the divorce, he'd thought he'd lose them as his second family, but that hadn't happened. He was still like another son to Tom and Christina, and eventually, even Kate's brothers had recovered enough from their defensiveness to treat him as they always had. Obviously Jim, being the eldest, was still keeping an eye on his little sister.

How they found places to sit for all of their guests, Tony never knew. He ended up on the couch with a tray table in front of him, along with a lot of cousins. Ethan had invited him to a table, but he hadn't wanted to make waves with Kate there. To his surprise, even she avoided the main table and was sitting cross-legged on a pillow near the big fireplace, her plate in her lap, Barney waiting patiently beside her. The dog knew a sucker when he saw one. More than once, Tony found himself glancing at her, at ease in a loose sweater, skinny jeans, and polka-dotted socks, a scarf looped around her neck. She looked happy and carefree, chatting with her brother's wife, but he knew how good she was at disguising her feelings—she was a lawyer after all, and a good one.

A toddler crawled into her lap, almost upsetting her plate, but she positively beamed her happiness, bringing him up onto her knee and blowing kisses deep into his neck until he giggled.

The flash of memory caught him by surprise, and he suddenly saw a much younger Kate in their tiny apartment, bent over her school books, as always. About to leave for his bartending job, he hadn't been able to get

Ethan to bed on time. The little boy had been crying when Kate had picked him up. Though she'd obviously felt frustrated, the look on her face had been just as happy, just as full of love as he saw now. Long-ago Kate had looked at him over Ethan's head, her expression one of sorrow and worry. He'd known that they couldn't go on much longer the way they were.

After dinner, Ethan invited him to play Xbox with him and Kate on the basement TV; Tony almost turned them down. He knew it was their thing, and the thought of all those educational puzzles and mazes didn't exactly interest him, but he didn't want to disappoint his son. To his surprise, Kate and Ethan were playing Diablo, and she was killing demons from hell like a pro. She was almost at the kid's level, and Tony couldn't hide his shock.

She eyed him, her amusement tinged with triumph. "You knew we played Xbox together."

"Yeah, but I thought . . . I don't know."

Kate elbowed her son. "Guess you didn't want to confess to your dad how often I kicked your butt."

Ethan winced. "Mom, come on," he said in a low voice, looking around at his amused cousins.

"Oh, sorry," she said, taken aback, but not exactly upset.

Violent video games, Tony mused. Should he play the offended parent? Naw, the kid was thirteen.

She'd changed a little bit, he realized, then kicked himself for imagining she'd stayed the same for nine years. Her life wasn't all about school and studying, as it had seemed during their marriage. Kate was a different person, who could let loose with silly games or tell off her bosses instead of toeing the company line.

And suddenly he realized he had to be very careful. He wasn't going to get caught up in her again, not after everything that had happened, everything she'd done to ruin their marriage—to hurt him. He wasn't going to become friends with her—there were walls he'd built to protect himself when he was twenty-four, and he was going to reinforce them.

While Kate played another game with Ethan, Tony went to look for the bathroom. The first-floor one was occupied, so he headed upstairs. When he heard his name called as he passed one of the bedrooms, he ducked his head in and found Kate's three oldest brothers in their mom's office and craft room, where fabric drooped from a sewing machine to the floor.

"Tony, come on in and shut the door," Jim said.

Considering Jim had been suspicious of him just a few hours ago, Tony was surprised, but he did as he was asked. He put his hands in his jeans pockets and regarded the Fenelli brothers.

"So what did Kate tell you about her law firm problems?" Walt asked.

Tony frowned, feeling wary. "Is this a trap?"

"A trap? Hell no," Dave said. "We're just worried about our sister. This job has been really important to her—you know that better than anyone."

Tony let his faint smile return, but he was starting to feel cornered.

"So she tells us she's on sabbatical," Jim said, "that she disagreed with the senior partners, and they wanted her to 'think'—whatever that means. Is that what she told you?"

"Pretty much." But Tony realized she'd told him more than her family, about an undocumented client report that couldn't go to the FDA, and how the partners wanted to bury it, worried that she'd scare away their clients with her nosiness. There was a lot more involved than just thinking things over. She obviously had to decide who she had a duty to—the public, her client, or the senior partners. But if Kate thought her family didn't need the details, it wasn't up to him to provide them.

"'Pretty much'?" David echoed suspiciously. "That's all you got?"

"Look, don't you think you guys should be talking to Kate about this if you're so worried? It's not like she's your little sister on the playground anymore."

"Well, since she hung out with you on the playground, it's pretty obvious we didn't do such a good job protecting her before," Jim said with faint sarcasm.

Walt and Dave eyed their brother in surprise.

"Now, Jim," Walt began, "aren't you going back a little far into history?"

Tony didn't say anything; he just rocked once on his heels and thought with longing about the beer he'd left downstairs.

"Yeah," Jim said grudgingly. "Sorry."

"I have a sister," Tony said. "I get it. But I don't understand what you want here. Either ask Kate for details or live with what she told you. Me   I don't want any details. She doesn't owe me any." But she'd supplied them anyway, which made him feel uneasy. Why him? "Now, if you'll excuse me, I need the bathroom, and then another beer."

Dave smiled at him knowingly. "Been kind of a long day for you, Tony?"

"Something like that."

Chapter 4

When the last guests—including three of Kate's brothers—had departed, she leaned back against the door and blew her bangs out of her eyes. On the boot tray and wet rugs next to the door were two pairs of boots that didn't look like Joe's or her parents'. Someone would have cold, wet feet when they got home.

Even Ethan had gone back to Tony's before she had had a chance to ask about the weekend. He was always with her on weekends, their special time together. Even the car trips, which she'd first worried would make him hate being with her, had turned into their special time together. They played games and sang songs, and Ethan reveled in seeing if he could find questions about the world to stump her.

Would he still think those car trips were worth it when he was seventeen and missing out on high school parties?

She couldn't let herself think about that now. She

was in Valentine Valley for who knew how long, and Ethan had his own bedroom right next door. It seemed crazy to keep him with her, but . . .

With determination, she went back into the kitchen and found her dad sorting leftovers into plastic containers, Joe still eating two pieces of pie at once, Barney looking starved at his side, and her mom unloading newly clean dishes from the dishwasher. Kate helped her mom with the plates, then started loading the third dirty batch of the day.

Christina eyed her. "So . . . was Thanksgiving better or worse than you expected?"

Kate grinned tiredly, then patted her stomach. "I had too much pie. I'm having a food baby, I think."

Christina laughed. "Well, if that's the worst of it, count yourself lucky."

"It was okay. Kind of strange with Tony here, if that's what you're asking. Probably not strange for you, of course, considering he lives next door."

Her mom glanced over her shoulder at Tom and Joe, who'd begun to fold chairs and line them up near the basement door. She lowered her voice. "Did it bother you when he bought the Parsons' old house? You never wanted to talk about it."

"His decision made perfect sense, and believe me, I admire how fair he is about Ethan, everything he does to make things easy for him. Did it bother *you* when he moved next door?" she teased.

Christina's smile faded. "I won't assign blame for your failed marriage, but I'll admit it was hard seeing him all the time at first, knowing how hurt you were, knowing that you were alone in Denver, without your family, and he was here."

"Those were my choices, Mom," Kate said quietly.

"I made peace with that, peace with Tony. Ethan is more important than any of us. And obviously you've both done an excellent job with him."

"Both of us? What about all of you? The widows? Everyone has helped raise him—the whole 'it takes a village' idea, you know."

"I appreciate that, of course." After adding detergent, Christina closed and started the dishwasher, then leaned her hip against the counter. "So what's going on with your custody arrangement this holiday weekend?"

"You went right to what I was thinking," Kate said ruefully, then sighed. "You know me too well, Mom. It's Tony's holiday, and I wasn't supposed to be here. It doesn't seem fair to change things at the last minute." She gave a lopsided grin. "And can't you hear the conversation now? 'Ethan, have a sleepover at Grandma's with me.' Yeah, he's not too cool for that at all."

"If you miss him and want to be with him, he'll appreciate that."

"Someday," Kate clarified.

Christina smiled. "Okay, someday."

"I guess I'll wait to see what happens. I—I don't even know how long I'll stay, after all."

As her mom covered a pie with foil, she glanced at Kate with somber eyes. "I've already told you you can stay as long as you want. Why go back to your empty condo? You can see Ethan every day while you're on vacation."

"I'm not on vacation, Mom," she said, bitterness coloring her voice. "I'm being exiled for standing up for my beliefs."

"Well, you haven't exactly explained . . ."

"I know, and I'm sorry." *But I told Tony.* "I'll tell you what I can, soon, I promise. But right now, I just want to forget about it."

"Then stay here, where we can distract you." Christina took her daughter's hand and squeezed it. "Unless you have a boyfriend you haven't mentioned, of course."

"Subtle, Mom. No, no boyfriend to speak of. I date, of course."

"Naturally. You're beautiful."

That made Kate laugh aloud. It was good not to take herself seriously. And her mom was right—she needed to be distracted.

When they got home, Ethan ran upstairs to his computer and Tony walked into his kitchen, only to find his sister at the kitchen table.

"I didn't see your car," he said warily.

"I parked down the block. Any leftover pie?"

Frowning, he handed over several containers, and she spread them out on the table eagerly.

Lyndsay was a year younger than he was, with brown hair she kept highlighted because she said it made her look younger. She was hardly old at thirty-two, but he'd sensed her restlessness lately and didn't want to rile her up by contradicting her. She'd spent her life wanting to be a teacher, and she now taught math at Valentine Valley Middle School. There was a boy-friend, of course—she never went long without a guy, one at a time—and he mostly approved of her choices. But none of them had been long-term guys, and Tony was starting to wonder if that was more her fault or the men's.

"You look remarkably better," he said dryly, sitting down opposite her and reaching for a fork. "Not sick very long?"

"Nope." She slid a container of pecan pie toward her, then pushed his fork out of the way with her own. "Hey, you already had some."

He swiped a forkful anyway. It could have ended up a tussle over the food, but she too easily backed down.

"Ethan missed you," he said.

She made a face. "That was unfair."

"But true. Dad, too. And me."

"Next you'll be saying Kate missed me."

"She asked about you, seemed disappointed you weren't coming."

She eyed him skeptically. "You're lying."

"I'm not. It's been nine years since the divorce, Lyndsay."

"And yet you still had to spend Thanksgiving with her."

"We'll always be connected through Ethan. It was awkward, but we managed. You could have done the same."

Lyndsay leaned over her pie. "Look, it's not like I spend my days ruminating over what she did to our family."

"Wow, that's a broad stroke."

She ignored him. "But . . . we haven't talked in a lot of years, and I just wouldn't know what to say. I was thinking of Ethan by not going. Why would he want to see his mom and his favorite aunt at odds?"

"I won't tell Diana you called yourself that," he said, his smile temporary. "Look, you lied to me about why you wouldn't go instead of just saying the truth. Which means it's obviously a bigger deal to you than you let on. Why?"

She took a bite of pie and chewed it slowly, not meeting his eyes. He waited.

With a sigh, she said, "I don't know. I don't know about a lot of things anymore."

"Then why don't you talk to me?"

"Donning your bartender hat?" she asked with faint sarcasm.

"Donning my big-brother hat."

Her shoulders slumped. "I'm just not . . . happy. I thought I'd be happier in my thirties, with a good job and a steady guy and maybe kids."

"Your thirties have barely begun," he said gently.

"Stop acting so perfect," she grumbled, forking the pie but not eating.

"Stop ruining my pecan pie." He pulled the container back. "And you know I'm not perfect. I'm trying to make the best of things, which you usually do, too. You're just having a bad day."

She reached across the table with her fork, and after some sleight of hand, he let her stab a piece.

"And you do have a good job," he reminded her.

She shrugged.

"What's that supposed to mean?" he said, reacting to her dismissive gesture. "You wanted to be a teacher, and you made your dream come true."

"It isn't what I thought it'd be. But I really don't want to talk about it."

"Lyndsay—"

"So how did your Thanksgiving go?" she asked, after swallowing a bite.

He shrugged. "Pretty good. Kate and I talked a bit, mostly about Ethan. Did you know, all this time she's been playing video games with Ethan, I thought they were educational—you know her focus on school—but she's been killing demons. She beats him sometimes, too."

Lyndsay eyed him. "And this is earth-shattering because . . ."

"I didn't say that. It was just surprising. And a reminder that we all change."

Lyndsay groaned. "You're sounding like a self-help book."

"Bartender class."

She tossed a napkin at him.

Kate woke up Friday morning when Barney jumped up into her bed for a cuddle then curled himself into the bend behind her knees. Outside the window, she could see the deep blue Colorado sky, no snow clouds in sight. She thought she could smell coffee, but she didn't hear a sound. Taking a deep breath, she tried to force herself to feel peaceful, but it wasn't happening. This was the first non-holiday weekday she'd had nothing to do in . . . forever.

This was obviously proof she needed to take more vacation time. If she had, she'd at least have had some practice. But her parents had never taken many vacations while building their business, so she came by her work ethic naturally. She could exercise more, of course, maybe get Ethan to teach her to snowboard. She could Christmas shop; her mom had told her that Josh Thalberg had married the owner of the new lingerie store, Leather and Lace. And she could read, something she hadn't done much of in a long time.

What she wouldn't have to do was drive hours to see Ethan. She could walk next door—not that she'd be doing much of that. She'd call him. Easier on everyone.

Not for the first time she felt like a noncustodial parent, and it was an awkward, guilt-inducing feeling. It was so easy, as a woman, to blame herself for not being able to do more.

So she went running, did some more post-Thanksgiving cleaning, checked her almost empty e-mail inbox—had the firm taken her off the loop already, or was it simply the holiday?—then had lunch at Carmina's Cucina. Her parents were thrilled to see her (as if they hadn't just shared breakfast that morning). She oohed over a new cluster of canvases depicting spices, recently hung on the wall, met a new employee, and teased Walt by following him around as he managed the restaurant. He was by turns grumpy and good-natured. Didn't he realize that if she'd come into the business, too, there might not have been enough work for them both? Hell, even Jim had gone his own way—but the family saw a restaurant in Aspen as an extension of Carmina's. Surprisingly, Walt invited her to Valentine Valley's traditional tree-lighting ceremony at town hall with his family that night. She found herself wondering eagerly if Ethan would join her, and when she called, he agreed without too much hesitation.

"Can I bring a friend?"

"Sure," she said brightly, hung up, then resisted a pout at having to share him. He was thirteen, she kept reminding herself.

She spent a few hours and a hundred bucks at the Open Book, browsing the shelves on two floors of a nineteenth-century brick building. She relaxed in an overstuffed chair as she read, and even bought a few Christmas gifts. She'd have lots of time for Christmas shopping, she realized, and tried to feel some enthusiasm. She wasn't used to her hours dragging. She could only imagine how she'd feel next week, when her law firm was open again and her clients were being told they'd been assigned a new lawyer. Dread and frustration were warring inside her, and she actually found herself looking forward to the tree-lighting.

That evening, Ethan came over so they could walk to the town hall together, Barney moving almost briskly in front of them in his excitement. They cut over to Main Street, where the old-fashioned lampposts were wrapped in greenery. There were single candles in most of the second-story windows, along with wreaths; candles lined the paths to some shop doors. Kate heard

sleigh bells and turned in surprise, because how could
there be a sleigh on Main Street? A horse and wagon
with SILVER CREEK RANCH on the side drove by, the
reins held by a wizened old man, who was all bundled
up. A couple dozen tourists sat on the benches inside,
their faces reflecting the Christmas lights.

Kate and Ethan walked the few blocks west toward
town hall, enjoying the Victorian carolers strolling
about in costume. She kept pointing out the
characters—someone in a Tiny Tim costume complete
with crutch, ladies corseted into gorgeous gowns, men
in top hats with long, bushy sideburns—until Ethan finally said with exasperation, "Mom, they do this every
year. So does Vail."

"Oh. Well, I'm enjoying it," she added in a more sub-
dued tone, tugging on Barney's leash to keep him from
sniffing under Victorian skirts.

"Then you can enjoy this stuff every weekend, because they've been going all out for Christmas the
last few years. There's even a Christmas market over
in Silver Creek Park, all these decorated wooden huts
with stuff for sale. I know we don't have a big Christmas skating show like they do in Vail, but we're doing
okay."

He grinned at her and she grinned back, knowing he
was trying to make her feel better.

"I'll buy you some roasted chestnuts," he said. "I
tried 'em a couple years ago—not bad."

While they blew on their chestnuts and tried not to
burn their tongues, Kate saw other booths selling hot
chocolate, spiced cider, pretzels, and Christmas cook-

ies. There were lots of people enjoying the evening, streaming in from the side streets—Bessie Street, Clara, and Mabel, all nineteenth-century names reminding people of the past. She heard ladies in three-part harmony and, to her surprise, saw the widows perched on stools outside the massive stone façade of the Hotel Colorado. They were seated beneath one of the arched columns, surrounded by poinsettia plants in the snow. They, too, were clothed in nineteenth-century dresses, shawls, and bonnets, but it was the perfect blending of their voices that brought Kate to a halt, made her breath catch at the haunting beauty of "Silent Night."

"Oh, Ethan," she murmured, squeezing his hand. "Aren't they wonderful?"

He nodded, watching for a moment, before his gaze began to roam the crowd again. She let go of his hand, and after listening to another few songs, she waved to the widows and continued to walk up Main Street.

The tree was a massive evergreen planted on the grounds of the town hall long ago. The hall itself had spotlights highlighting the stone clock tower and the wreaths on the doors. Crowds of people mingled there, but it didn't take Kate long to spot her brother, whose three-year-old was perched on his shoulders. Diana had the baby, and their six-year-old held Walt's hand. Barney moved among them eagerly, rubbing against legs as he begged to be petted.

Once reunited with family, Ethan seemed to take that as permission to start texting on his flip phone. Kate let it go on awhile, knowing he and a friend were supposed to meet up.

Ethan briefly glanced at her. "Dad's here. He got away from the tavern after all."

"Good for him," Kate said, though inside she winced. Tony was going to be sick of her after just a couple days. But then again, at least she didn't have to feel bad about depriving him of a holiday tradition with his son.

A band started playing Christmas carols, and she tapped her foot to "Joy to the World." She wasn't feeling exactly joyous this holiday, but maybe she could fake it until she really felt it.

And then she saw Tony, crossing First Street, head down against the wind. He was wearing a ski hat and snowboarding jacket that had obviously seen a lot of use; his jean-clad thighs showed a long line of muscles as he strolled. He looked healthy and tan, like a man who spent most of his time outdoors. It suddenly dawned on her that she hadn't dated many men like him since the divorce. She'd stuck to lawyers and bankers and doctors who wore expensive ski jackets and went to après-ski in wine bars at the base of the slopes. For the first time, she wondered if she'd deliberately steered clear of men like her ex-husband. And what was that supposed to say about her?

But she couldn't dwell on it, because she noticed Lyndsay at Tony's side. Kate's Christmas spirit kicked into overdrive in preparation. She and Lyndsay weren't enemies, after all—they were just no longer best friends. They could be polite to each other.

But they'd been the *best* of friends from the time Kate was in fourth grade. On the playground, she'd rescued third-grader Lyndsay from a bully when Tony had been home sick. They'd discovered they both liked to hand-sew Barbie clothes and make them little homemade houses. Kate had even gone through a phase when she'd sewed little beanbag frogs her aunt had once made for her, and Lyndsay had followed Kate's lead. They'd talked school and boys, and since both had only brothers, it had been a relief to talk to a girl. They'd competed in marching band together, kept each other company on long school bus trips to football games and band competitions, helped each other with their homework.

At first, Lyndsay had seemed leery of Kate's growing friendship with Tony, but Kate had just taken that as a girl not wanting her older brother hanging around. But Tony was Kate's age, in a lot of her classes, and he'd liked riding bikes on the trails of the Elk Mountains just as much as they had. Having him around had started to seem natural.

Dating Tony had actually been an easier hurdle to cross. Sometimes they'd all even double-dated, for Lyndsay was always dating someone or other.

The first thing Kate had had trouble talking to Lyndsay about? Her pregnancy. She hadn't wanted to confide in anyone at first, except for Tony, because she'd been so scared and upset that her well-planned life had taken a major turn. At nineteen, who knew antibiotics and birth control pills didn't mix well?

But Lyndsay had been thrilled when they'd gotten married, had wiped away tears as Kate's maid of honor, then Ethan's godmother. But the end of Kate's marriage had been the end of Kate's friendship with Lyndsay. The divorce had meant the loss of two of the most important people in her life. Lyndsay felt her brother's pain and blamed Kate for all of it. Kate certainly knew she'd been partly to blame for all the mistakes, but she'd hardly been in a position to ask Tony's sister for advice as the problems had piled up. So the marriage breakup had completely blindsided Lyndsay, since Tony hadn't exactly been talkative either. Kate had lost her best friend, and she'd never really replaced her. Oh, she had friends, but they weren't—Lyndsay.

Lyndsay came to a stop next to Tony, her hands stuffed in the pockets of her ski jacket. She wore tight jeans tucked into knee-high leather boots, her wavy brown hair pulled into a ponytail, a winter headband protecting her ears. She was even wearing bangs now, feathery ones that looked good with her highlighted hair.

"Hi, Lyndsay," Kate said cheerfully.

Lyndsay gave her a perfunctory smile. "Kate." She bestowed a more natural smile on Walt and Diana, who were pointing out the Christmas decorations to their kids and trying to get the littlest to say "tree."

Lyndsay glanced at Kate again. "I bet Ethan's glad to have you home for Thanksgiving."

They both turned to see Ethan looking down at his flip phone, as if he really didn't care if his mom was there or not. Kate exchanged a glance with Tony, who rolled his eyes. For just a moment, she felt like they were on the same side.

"Ethan, who are you texting?" Tony asked.

"Brad," Ethan said absently, head still bent. "He's here somewhere with his girlfriend." His voice sounded a little sour as he said the last word.

"Girlfriend?" Tony and Kate both echoed at the same time, then gave each other a surprised look.

It was Lyndsay's turn to roll her eyes before looking toward Mayor Galimi, who was getting ready to speak at a podium on the raised steps of town hall.

"Yeah, they're dating," Ethan said irritably. "It's a pain. It's not like anybody can drive yet, but they have to do everything together now."

Ethan wouldn't be driving for three more years, but he made it sound like it was only next week. And it might go by that fast, too, Kate thought balefully.

"Be nice about it to Brad," Tony said. "He can't help it."

"Sure he can," Ethan mumbled, but then he waved to someone.

Kate turned and saw a tall, lanky boy holding the hand of a girl whose braces glinted in the lamplight. "Do they want to join us?" she asked, giving a wave.

The two kids looked at each other and the girl waved back, then they bent their heads together and laughed. Kate knew she wasn't being thought of as "cool" at the moment.

"They just got away from their parents . . ." Ethan began. "Do you mind, Mom?"

"No, of course not. Just listen for your phone."

He brightened, nodded, and hurried to join his friends.

"They seem awfully young," Kate said wistfully.

"You two were practically dating at that age," Lyndsay said. "Guess you guys know the kinds of mistakes they could be making."

Kate was only a little taken back. "Yeah, you're right, Lynds," she agreed. "It's a different world now that my son is almost in high school."

Tony didn't know if he should step between his sister and his ex-wife or let them fight it out at last. They looked at each other like strangers. In some ways, that was almost as bad as his ruined marriage. But they were polite to each other, and Lyndsay had a big smile for Walt and Diana and their kids. Yet when Lyndsay looked away, Walt glanced at Tony and gave him a raised eyebrow. Well, there wasn't anything Tony could do to make this reunion between former best friends less awkward, so he just shrugged.

He remembered how Kate had ducked calls from his sister when he and Kate had first started having problems. Or she would only tell Lyndsay about school stuff. He, too, had felt bad for not confiding in his family, but how would he have been able to tell them he'd made a terrible mistake, when he'd been so certain marrying Kate had been his destiny?

During the lead-up to the divorce, he'd had to deal with his own sadness and feelings of betrayal while answering his sister's endless confused questions at the same time. Once everything had settled down and they'd gone on with their lives, things had worked out fine, but now, looking at the invisible shield Lyndsay seemed to be wearing, he wondered what she could be thinking.

As the band played "O Holy Night," Kate offered a paper sleeve of roasted chestnuts. Tony helped himself while Lyndsay politely declined. Kate handed them off to her brother, whose middle child grabbed for it and almost knocked it to the ground.

"So what did you do with yourself today?" Tony asked Kate, just to fill the awkward silence.

She shook her head. "You'd think I'd be used to holidays, but it felt so unusual to have nothing to do. I went to the restaurant for lunch, I hung out at the bookstore. Barney and I sometimes kept each other company." She rubbed her dog's ears.

"I never thought to send Ethan over to you," Tony admitted. "And you usually have weekends, too."

She chuckled. "I didn't know how to handle it either. But he's right next door."

"It's not the same as having him with you twenty-four-seven," he said.

She met his gaze, her smile softening. "Yeah, thanks for understanding."

Lyndsay pointedly cleared her throat, but he ignored her.

"Mom offered the futon in her office if he wanted to spend the night with us," Kate continued. "I'd feel stupid asking him to stay, when his own room is so close."

"It does seem silly," Lyndsay agreed.

Kate's smile faltered.

"Mothers sometimes do that kind of stuff to be with

their kids," Diana interjected, then made a grab at her three-year-old's hand before he could chase after Father Christmas. "Or so I hear," she added dryly.

Tony saw his sister's eyes flicker with some kind of pain before they became simply polite again. What was that about? Diana hadn't tried to be rude.

The microphone at the podium suddenly gave a piercing whistle that made them all wince. Mayor Galimi, her short silver hair glimmering under the lights aimed at town hall, smiled broadly and said, "Happy holidays, Valentine Valley!" Her voice echoed and her breath misted.

People cheered amidst the muffled sound of gloves and mittens clapping.

The mayor spoke about the town councilpeople who'd help make the day possible, the Dickens actors, the food booths. She mentioned the Christmas market at Silver Creek Park, and open skating on the frozen pond in the Rose Garden. At last the band played "We Wish You a Merry Christmas," and Mayor Galimi threw the switch. The Christmas tree lit up with what had to have been thousands of lights. Tony glanced around for Ethan. He and his friends stared up at the tree, wonder still reflected in their bright eyes.

As Kate's smile deepened with contentment, Tony knew that she'd noticed their son, too.

"He's still our little boy," she murmured.

The multicolored lights played across her face and danced in her wide violet eyes as she stared at the festivities. For a moment, he found it hard to look away. Christmas Past briefly haunted him with memories of their first Christmas tree, when she was eight months pregnant, and Ethan taking his first steps the next year, arms wide as he tried to tackle the tree.

And then he noticed Lyndsay frowning at him, and he shrugged, mouthing, "What?"

His sister gave an aggrieved sigh and turned back to stare up at the towering Christmas tree. He didn't know what her problem was.

"Kate!" called a feminine voice.

They all turned to see Emily Thalberg approaching, bringing along her best friends: her sister-in-law cowgirl Brooke Thalberg; her other sister-in-law, Whitney Winslow-Thalberg, who owned the new lingerie store; Monica Shaw, owner of Monica's Flowers and Gifts; and Heather Armstrong, the new local caterer. Whitney carried her baby on her hip. Olivia had been born the previous May, making her big appearance at the wedding reception of the son of the US president. Things were always exciting in Valentine Valley, Tony thought, shaking his head.

Kate looked a little wide-eyed at the group of lovely women bearing down on her. Brooke had almost the same reserved look Lyndsay wore, and behind Kate's back, Tony gave his friend an exasperated frown. Dark-haired Brooke worked on her family ranch, along with her fiancé, Adam Desantis. She could hold a grudge, and Tony wondered why all his women friends felt like he needed to be defended from his ex-wife. At least Monica looked friendly and cheerful, her amber skin glowing in the cold, her curly black hair sticking out beneath a winter hat. Brooke and Monica were three

years younger than him, and the only two who knew
Kate, although not all that well. Whenever Kate came
to Valentine, she always focused on Ethan and the rest
of her family. Consequently, she didn't know a lot of
the newer residents.

He listened with hidden amusement as Emily introduced Kate to Heather and Whitney, the other newcomers in town. Whitney smiled as Kate leaned down to
grin at Olivia. Whitney was the only one not wearing a
hat or winter headband, obviously preferring the cold to
ruining her hair. She came from an extremely wealthy,
well-traveled family, and though she never came off as
obnoxious, you couldn't miss by her clothes or her hair
that she'd been raised differently.

"How come I haven't met you before, Kate?" Whitney asked innocently.

Kate glanced at him, and so did every other female
pair of eyes in the know. He sighed. "Because she's my
ex-wife, and she lives in Vail."

"Oh," Whitney said, eyes widening.

"I'll be in town for a while," Kate admitted. "I came
to the tree-lighting ceremony with our son."

"You must be having a nice holiday vacation," Whitney said.

"Something like that," Kate answered vaguely.

Tony saw Lyndsay studying Kate with narrowed
eyes, and he gave her shoulder a brush with his to jar
her out of her suspicious behavior. She shot him a look
but started making faces at little Olivia, who seemed to
be having trouble waving her arms inside her snowsuit.

Deciding a strategic retreat was in order, Tony said, "Well, I should get back to the tavern."

"We'll all see you there," Lyndsay called.

Tony sighed. Leave it to his sister to hint at a gathering Kate hadn't been invited to.

"Why don't you come with us, Kate?" Emily asked.

Tony saw Brooke and Monica exchange amused smiles. Emily was always the one to try to make everything better.

When Kate hesitated, Emily turned to Tony. "You don't mind, do you? There'll be lots of people there. What else does she have to do on a Friday night?"

"Look," Kate said, lifting a hand. "That's nice of you to include me, Emily, but . . . it would be awkward."

"So you won't know anybody there?"

"Well . . . I'm from here, so yeah, I'll know people. I think."

"Then you should come. Tony?"

Emily looked to him, Kate gave him a worried frown, and Walt's face was full of guy-to-guy sympathy. Walt's youngest started to cry, perhaps sensing the shifting emotions of the crowd.

Tony raised both hands and began to back away. "You guys do what you want. I'll be so busy it won't matter to me." Though he did feel uncomfortable, and he wasn't certain why. "Kate, tell Ethan I had to go back to work. Enjoy the festivities, ladies," he called to the group, very glad to be escaping.

Chapter 5

Once he got back to the tavern, Tony jumped into the well and started pumping out drinks for the holiday crowd. Some of his friends were already there, shooting pool in the back room as they waited for their wives, fiancées, and girlfriends. Tony stayed behind the bar with Lamar Cochrane, one of his evening bartenders. Lamar moved with smooth efficiency, a young guy able to banter and never lose track of what he was doing. It was so crowded that Tony might not even be able to join his friends until the festivities died down.

A long time ago, he'd been the only one married, and it had made maintaining guy friendships awkward, because he hadn't been able to do the weekend partying his friends had. After the divorce, he hadn't wanted to party, although it was his job to make sure people had a good time. Soon his child-free weekends gave him more leeway, but he was always labeled the single dad. Women in their twenties weren't exactly lining up to be with a man with a kid. But now, in his thirties, things were different. Women *wanted* kids, were rather fascinated that he'd had his so young. Dating was easier, especially since he no longer needed a babysitter. He'd just never found anyone to be interested in for long.

The rest of his friends began to trickle in, the Sweets and Thalbergs after working a long day on their ranches. Matt Sweet, in charge of landscaping at the Sweetheart Inn, looked particularly beat. Tony knew he'd been working on their new and upcoming "Christmas by Candlelight" event. He could only imagine how many strings of lights decorated the grounds of that old Victorian. Then the ladies trooped past his bar in a long line, and he noticed that Whitney had managed to find a sitter for Olivia. It wasn't difficult, with Olivia being the first grandchild in both families. And he'd heard that Whitney's parents were in town at their condo up in Aspen.

Kate came in last, minus Barney, throwing her coat over her arm as she stopped at the bar to speak to him. The neckline of her shirt was draped in loose folds across her chest, and when she leaned across the bar, he got a glimpse of the cleavage he hadn't seen in over nine years. And for a moment, it was difficult to look back into her eyes. What the hell—? It'd been a long time since he'd thought of her in any sort of intimate way— even though in high school it had been *all* he could think about. He found himself noticing her unruly short hair and the way it feathered on her cheeks and forehead, emphasizing her amazing eyes. She looked like she'd rolled out of bed—and not in a bad way.

"Hey, Tony, we were both kind of surprised by this invitation," she said earnestly. "Do you want me to head home? I can fake a reason."

More than one guy was checking out her jean-clad ass as she leaned over the bar. Even Lamar was eyeing her with interest. Lamar saw Tony notice and quickly turned back to his work.

Tony was surprised she'd offered to leave so easily. Years earlier, she would have been offended; after all, these had been her friends, too, once upon a time, before her ambition had made her want different things. "No, stay," he said, pouring a draft beer. *Go home,* he said in his head, deliberately avoiding looking at her again.

"Thanks," she said, her voice relieved. "It's still pretty awkward with all these people, but . . . it's weird being home for hours on end. I don't really feel like myself, you know, with nothing to do?"

He nodded.

She looked around, and a smile quirked one corner of her mouth. "Nice Christmas decorations."

A couple of poinsettia plants were scattered haphazardly, and silver garland draped from the deer antlers.

"Uh, thanks," he said.

"Don't go too crazy."

She turned away. Like lots of other guys, he watched her hips move as she walked.

Ned Ferguson whistled, and his twin, Ted, chuckled.

To Tony's surprise, Kate whirled and briefly walked backward, giving a little smirk and a wave before disappearing into the back room.

"That's some ex you've got," Ted said, shaking his head. "Wish I was younger."

Tony rolled his eyes, then focused on the next customer. Nicole rushed in and out of the back, taking drink and food orders, so in the weeds that Tony had to take a tray in himself.

"Tony!" came the rousing cheer from a chorus of voices.

As always, he laughed it off, though he was certain his face reddened. Travis Beaumont, Monica's ex-Secret-Service boyfriend of six months, turned back to his deep discussion with her brother, Dom, and Brooke's fiancé, Adam Desantis. Dom worked as an upscale food broker, and Adam was an ex-Marine and current cowboy. Though Tony didn't try to look for Kate, he saw her in a little group with Emily, Heather, and Whitney, dancing. He found it interesting that she was dancing with the newcomers to town and not the women she knew. Well, it would probably take time for everyone to get used to her being around, him included. Though he tried not to, he found himself glancing more than once at Kate as he handed out drinks.

Will Sweet approached and took a beer off Tony's tray. "In case you're wondering, your ex has turned down a couple offers to dance from various men, myself included."

"Why am I not surprised," Tony said dryly.

"You're surprised she didn't dance with men?" Will shot back, grinning.

"Maybe that, too. It's probably because this is my place. She must feel awkward. It's been a long time,

Will. I wish everyone would get over seeing her here. It's not like she hasn't been back in town many times a year visiting her family."

"But something's different, we all think so," Will said.

Tony delivered the last drink and headed back out to the bar. "And you insist on telling me," he said over his shoulder.

Will stood at the entrance to the bar, crossing his arms over his chest. "Don't you want to know?"

"Not really."

"Okay, then, never mind." Will ambled back to where he'd come from.

And Tony resisted the urge to call him back. No one had to tell him Kate seemed different. She'd become vulnerable with this job setback. That's all it was. She'd be her no-nonsense self again once she went back to work, and back to Vail.

"Hey, Dad, got a moment?"

Ethan shouldered his way between Ned and Ted, who chuckled and shouldered him back.

Tony smiled. "Sure, kid, come on back to my office. Lamar, give me a minute, will ya?"

Lamar nodded after waving at Ethan. Tony led the way into his small office off the kitchen corridor. The monitor of the POS, the computer system used throughout the tavern, took up a lot of room, and though Tony had a filing cabinet, his desk was still a mess. He shut the door, and the sound of country music faded a bit.

After sitting in his office chair, he swiveled to face the chair Ethan had dragged into the room. "Is something wrong? You looked like you were having a good time tonight."

"Sure, it's not that. It's Mom."

Tony frowned. "You know she's here, right?"

Ethan winced. "I forgot. She texted me, and I was talking to Brad, and—"

"Yeah, yeah, God forbid I ever miss one of *your* texts."

"I'm important," Ethan said loftily. "I'm your only kid. Just think how easy it would be for me to text on a smartphone like Brad's."

"You know the rule your mom and I set down. When you can afford one—and that includes the monthly plan and insurance—you can buy one."

"But you won't let me get a job!"

"Not during the school year. Let's not talk about this now. The bar is swamped, and they need me out there."

"Oh, right." Ethan shot a guilty look at the door. "I'm worried about Mom."

"She understands her weekends with you won't be the same as in Vail. Did you think she was going to try to force you to stay at Grandma's with her?"

"Well, that wouldn't be terrible or anything. I'll hang around a bit this weekend, but my friends and I are going boarding Saturday or Sunday."

"I'm sure your mom would understand." Tony started to rise. "If that's all—"

"No, there's something else. Mom's not like other moms, you know? She's not used to having downtime. And lots of days of it? Forget it. She's already going a little crazy, and she's only been here two days."

"Ethan, aren't you exaggerating?"

"She tried to hold my hand at the tree-lighting ceremony!" Ethan threw his hands wide.

Tony snorted a laugh and tried to disguise it as a cough.

"Sure, you can laugh," Ethan said, "but she needs something else to think about. Once her office opens Monday, she'll be trying to reach people there."

"That's probably not smart."

"Yeah, well, Mom has been mentioning leaving her clients hanging. Yeah, that might distract her from me, but . . . I don't want her in trouble with her bosses. She bought all these books today—some of them for me. Like I have time to read during ski season." He put up a hand as Tony opened his mouth to protest. "I have time for my homework reading, and that's it."

Tony hid a smile. "What do you want me to do, Ethan? Your mom and I only cross paths when it's about you."

Ethan rolled his eyes. "You could have fooled me. You've seen her a couple times each day since she arrived."

Tony swallowed and felt a little overheated in the small office. Of course he'd seen Kate; it was Thanksgiving, perfectly normal.

"Just . . ." Ethan began with exasperation, "just help me out, okay? Mom still thinks I'm eight years old. She doesn't need to babysit me, but she's bored enough to try. And it's the holidays, and I don't want her to feel bad and . . ." He heaved a sigh.

Tony stood up and put a hand on Ethan's shoulder.

"I'll keep an eye out if it looks like she's freaking out on you."

"Aunt Lyndsay might help. Maybe they'll be friends again, now that Mom's in Valentine Valley for a while."

"Don't get your hopes up, kid. Those are two stubborn women."

"Why did they fight in the first place?"

"It's probably my fault. Your mother and I divorced, and Aunt Lyndsay thinks no one should hurt me. Of course, a bad marriage has two people in it doing stupid things, not just one, but your aunt doesn't see it that way."

"She thinks you're perfect. A lot she knows."

As Tony opened the door, he grabbed Ethan around the neck with one arm, rubbing his head hard with the other hand while Ethan laughed convulsively.

And there was Kate, watching them from the doorway of the back room, her eyes full of love and happiness—and maybe even shining with tears. "Hey, E.," she said softly.

Ethan cleared his throat, glanced nervously at Tony, and said, "So you don't mind if I go to Brad's? I'll be home by eleven."

"Go ahead. But maybe you should check with your mom, since she has custody of you on the weekends."

Ethan turned worried eyes on his mom, as if he thought he'd offended her.

"Hey, we don't have to be so strict with me in town," Kate hastened to say. "Maybe we should just say that if you're going somewhere, text us both."

Ethan held up his flip phone. "It's really hard to text on this."

Kate didn't bat an eye. "I'm certain it is. Think what exciting technology you'll have when you can afford it. Say hi to Brad for us."

Ethan good-naturedly stomped through the bar and out the front door.

"Whatever mistakes we made when we were young," Kate said softly, "I think we've done a great job with our son."

"But apparently he's the last kid in the entire world with a flip phone. Which is why he wants a job."

Kate's smile faded. "A job? He's a little young. And his schoolwork—"

Lamar popped his head in the door. "Hey, Tony. Gettin' a little busy up here." And then he was gone.

"You go," Kate said. "I'll probably be saying my good-byes back there soon."

He looked up at the beer clock on the wall. "It's all of nine o'clock. And you don't have to work in the morning."

She winced.

"Sorry. I didn't mean to remind you."

"I know, but . . . are you sure it's not bothering you that I'm here?"

"Kate, go have fun. Unless . . . people aren't making you feel too welcome. They see me a lot and don't see you much, so—"

"I can handle myself, don't worry. You've always been one of Valentine's favorite sons," she added, shaking her head.

"Oh, come on . . ."

She just grinned and walked down the short hall, forcing him to look at her ass again.

She turned around and caught him looking, and in that moment, something . . . strange passed between them, a charged feeling that seemed resurrected from some deep pit of prehistory. He knew her well enough to see that she forced a smile.

"Hey, Tony, I keep hearing from people that the tavern needs to throw a party. A big event. Thought you might want to know. I'll keep my ear to the ground."

"No big events!" he called. Then he grumbled, as he headed out to the bar, "They end up costing more than they're worth."

Chapter 6

When Kate got home, she curled up on the couch in front of the fire, absently petted Barney, and told her mom all about the tree-lighting ceremony. Her dad had spent the evening at Carmina's, so he'd already gone to bed.

"I can't believe you went to the tavern!" Christina said, shaking her head.

"Well, Emily invited me. She's very nice."

"And Tony didn't mind."

"If he did, he didn't show it. He's still such a nice guy, Mom." She heaved a sigh.

Christina studied her. "What's the sigh for? You almost sound like you regret letting him get away."

"I didn't say that," Kate insisted, then turned to stare at the fire, the question surprising her. Her mom usually avoided discussing Tony, unless it was in relation to Ethan. For a long time after the divorce, her mother would have tears in her eyes if Tony's name came up.

Kate hadn't taken offense—she'd known her mom had ached for all three of them.

But suddenly she flashed back to what she'd felt earlier in the evening, when she'd seen Tony staring at her butt, as if she'd been teleported back in time to high school. She used to saunter past him in a flouncy skirt, hoping he'd look, wanting to turn him on. And then she'd meet him at his truck, and they'd steam up the windows.

Good God, was *that* why she'd gone to Tony's Tavern tonight? Could Tony think she was flirting with him? *Was* she flirting with him?

That was just wrong, after all they'd gone through. She had to be losing her mind, and this sabbatical had only just started.

"Kate? You've got a weird look in your eyes."

"Just shock, believe me. Mom, it's been nine years since the divorce, you know. We're finally able to be friendly rather than defensive. Isn't that a good thing?"

"Of course it is, especially for Ethan."

But Kate's worry that Tony might think she was flirting lingered for a few days. Being with Ethan, yet not twenty-four hours a day, made for the strangest weekend in a long time. Ethan came and went a few times, but he seemed perfectly content. Kate began to wonder if going back to the regular custody schedule would make him resent her, especially if she made him sleep on a couch at his grandmother's.

As he got older, there'd be more events with his friends—how much longer would it be before he resented being away every weekend? She was afraid to think about it before she had to, or even more guilt and worry would consume her.

She got in some time with him by dropping him and his friends off in Aspen and picking them up at the end of the afternoon. That was a few hours in the car for her, but for half of it, she could listen to them talk. She stayed silent, trying to pretend she wasn't there as they discussed girls and teachers and an upcoming snow-boarding event. The sound of their voices lifted her spirits for hours afterward.

Her weekend went downhill from there. She worked up the courage to call Michelle Grady, a fellow lawyer at the firm, but Michelle didn't return the call. It was a holiday weekend, Kate reminded herself, but it made her feel nervous, and worried about her clients. She went to Joe's basketball game in Basalt and found her-self remembering the rec league they'd once tried to sign Ethan up for. Games had always been on Saturday, with practices during the week, so he couldn't partici-pate. He'd lost out wherever he'd been, making her feel like a terrible mom.

Watching his excitement at being in Valentine for the weekend didn't help. She knew it wasn't about her, but she was feeling particularly vulnerable. She used all the free time to catch up with some friends in Vail and Denver, but talking on the phone wasn't the same as being able to go out for lunch or a drink.

So she thought about Lyndsay—a lot. The woman's cool attitude Friday night hadn't been surprising after all their years of separation, but Kate was surprised that it had hurt. What had she expected? Just because she and Tony were friendly after years of parenting Ethan didn't mean that Lyndsay had to join the friends bandwagon. And hearing about Lyndsay through Tony just wasn't the same for Kate either. She remembered being shocked when Tony had told her that Lyndsay and her longtime college boyfriend had broken up by their midtwenties. Kate had thought they'd last forever. Now she and Lyndsay were in the same boat, never dating a guy for more than a few months. They'd probably have a lot to talk about. But with the way Lyndsay had reacted on seeing her—as if she'd stepped in a puddle of mud—well, Kate didn't think calling would get a response. Maybe if they kept running into each other. . . .

And that was when Kate realized she was already thinking of just staying in Valentine for the whole sabbatical. She kept telling herself to book a vacation somewhere warm for a week, but she couldn't take Ethan away from school—or snowboarding—and didn't want to go without him, not when she had the chance to see him almost every day.

But by Monday, she thought she'd go out of her mind. Everyone went back to work and school, and she was alone but for Barney, who kept her company at home, since the old guy couldn't exactly go for long runs anymore. She read a book. She baked the simplest cookies for Ethan after school like he was six, and he humored her, good son that he was. But she caught his worried looks just the same.

She called her lawyer friend Michelle again—no answer. The partners would never reveal details about her sabbatical, but she still felt paranoid. She kept thinking of that report she wasn't supposed to have seen, and she wished she could talk to someone about it. But obviously her firm didn't want to listen.

Tuesday, on her late-morning run, she passed by Tony's Tavern. Without planning it, she turned around and went inside. Compared to Friday night, it was pretty empty, just a couple people starting an early lunch. No one sat at the bar, behind which Tony stood at the POS computer, his back to her, his head bent, unruly brown hair touching the creased collar of his black polo shirt. She felt a momentary need to straighten it. The thought was so shocking that she was about to leave, when he looked up and saw her. She froze, wondering if she'd overstepped her bounds.

He frowned, but he seemed puzzled, not annoyed. It made her feel braver, so she sat down at the bar and pulled off her winter hat and gloves. She casually ran her hands through her hair to straighten it, and he watched her without saying a word.

"Is something wrong?" When his voice emerged with a husky tone, he cleared his throat.

"May I have a glass of water?" she asked lamely. Dammit, why had she come here?

He poured her one from the tap. "Tough workout?"

She nodded. "They always are. I hate running."

"Then why do you do it?"

"Quick and convenient, keeps me healthy, and holds down the weight." She held up a hand. "I know, I know, there are ways to have fun and exercise. But this works for me."

"Do you *have* any fun, Kate?" he asked softly.

For a moment, she didn't know how to answer that. "Every weekend when Ethan is with me."

"No grown-up fun?"

And then she blushed, though she assumed he didn't mean sex. "I had a pretty good time in here Friday night. I date occasionally at home, too. That's fun."

He nodded slowly, almost as if he didn't believe her. So she added defensiveness to her feelings of panic and desperation.

"I don't have anything to do," she finally said in a hushed whisper, her throat tight. "I feel . . . lost. The thing I'm best at—they won't let me do, won't trust my judgment. I'm not even the homemaker type, and I'm cleaning my mother's house every day. I'm running out of stuff to do. I think I'm driving Ethan nuts—and I don't mean to! And now here I am driving you nuts. I'm sorry, I should go."

He looked at her for a long minute, eyes narrowed in thought, but not anger. Still she didn't go; she only took a long swig of her water.

Then he reached beneath the counter and slid a crumpled apron across to her. "My lunch server, Rhonda— her kid had his appendix out. There's complications, poor little guy, but he'll be okay. She's going to be out a while. Wait tables if you're so bored."

She stared at him in shock. There was a faint smirk twisting his lips, as if he expected her to turn him down. He knew she hated serving. It was hard, demanding work, and people were difficult to satisfy.

But . . . she was alone all day, with not enough to do.

She lifted her head and met his gaze with a challenging one of her own. "Are you offering me a job?"

"A temporary one," he amended, then crossed his arms over his chest. "I don't think you'll last."

She straightened her shoulders. "You've gotta be kidding me. I've never left a job unfinished." And then she felt a spasm of worry as she remembered her law career, her marriage—the unfinished things in her life. He started to pull the apron back, and she suddenly grabbed it, looking him fiercely in the eyes. "You're on." She heard the words coming out of her mouth and couldn't regret them, although she wasn't sure why.

His brows lowered. "I'm not kidding around. I need someone right now. You'd need a crash course in the wine and beer we serve, and you'll have to memorize the menu."

"I remember that from my days at Carmina's. And I don't want to be paid."

"What? I don't know if that's legal."

"Then . . . then . . . put it in Ethan's college fund."

He sighed, nodded, and glanced at the only occupied table. The customers had set down their menus and were talking. "I'll take that order, and then you can watch me input it in the POS, the point-of-sale system."

"We had one back in the nineties." She looked down at her lululemon black track pants and purple zip-up, with another layer beneath. She could always go into the restroom and remove the ColdGear if she got too hot. "Do I look okay?"

"I don't compliment the staff."

She shot him a startled look, and he didn't smile.

"Sexual harassment," he explained.

"Oh."

"Wear jeans and a black shirt tomorrow, but for now, you'll do. Put on the apron."

Kate must really be desperate, because she was actually looking forward to proving to him that she could handle anything. He gestured her to follow him, and she listened as he took the customers' orders, his demeanor laid-back and pleasant as he remembered it all without writing anything down. Back at the POS, he was all business, maneuvering through the various screens and inputting the order. It would be printed out in the kitchen and hung on the line, she remembered.

"So let me introduce you around," he finally said.

He took her back into the kitchen, where a man and a woman worked the line. The kitchen was clean and tidy, just like at her parents' restaurant, everything in its place between the grill station, the sauté, and the fryer. There was an industrial dishwasher near the door and a walk-in cooler. The man who seemed to be in charge was a burly, tattooed guy with a couple-day-old beard, his long, graying hair pulled back in a ponytail beneath a ball cap.

"Chef Larry Baranski, this is Kate, our new server," Tony said.

Kate noticed he didn't give her last name.

The chef eyed her. "Is this a joke?" he asked gruffly. "This is your ex."

"I didn't say she wasn't." Tony's response was mild "She's in town for a while and wants to work."

"You're a lawyer," Chef Baranski said, speaking directly to her, his bushy brows low over his eyes.

He looked her over like she was a piece of steak gone bad.

"I'm on sabbatical, and I'm bored out of my mind." Kate tried to sound cheerful and confident.

"So you want to work for *him*?" Chef Baranski pointed at Tony with his thumb.

"It was his idea."

The chef looked between them for a moment, then shook his head. "I got food to cook. Don't bring your fights into my kitchen."

"We don't fight," Kate insisted.

"Uh-huh."

Tony spoke Spanish as he introduced her to the line cook, Valeria Tamez, who was small and dark and didn't meet Kate's eyes.

When they were back behind the bar, Kate sighed. "I don't think either of them liked me."

"Valeria probably heard the word 'lawyer,'" Tony said. "She understands more than you think. Her family has had some trouble, but she's perfectly legal, believe me. As for Chef, I thought he liked you right away."

Kate eyed him skeptically, but Tony was looking past her to the door, which jingled as it opened.

"Go seat your guests," he said. "We don't usually have a hostess."

"Yes, sir."

After years in a courtroom, Kate wasn't nervous talking to people, so she had no problem chatting up the young couple who'd just come from a winter hiking excursion. She seated them at a two-top (she remembered the lingo!), brought them ice water and menus, and felt Tony watching her the whole time. Well, at least he wasn't looking at her like he had on Friday night, with his eyes all hot and half-lidded. The memory of those eyes had made sleeping difficult that night, and she'd told herself she was going too long between dates. Obviously Tony was, too.

After getting Tony's table another beer and soda refill, she hung out near the wait station, wiping down bottles of ketchup and mustard, until her new customers seemed ready to order. She thought about Tony dating—obviously she knew he did. Ethan even mentioned it occasionally. She hoped their failed marriage hadn't ruined the way he focused on a woman without pressuring her, letting her know with his gaze and his manners that he was into her. Back in the day, he used to make her feel like the sexiest girl alive, the only one he wanted. After victorious football games, he'd take off his helmet, and their eyes would meet as he grinned at her like only she understood how fun a victory was. Because that's all sports had been to him—fun—and she'd had a hard time understanding that. He liked to win, but he was laid-back enough that he didn't take losses personally. He was so . . . different from her in every way, and she recognized that was once part of his appeal. Unlike her, he'd never talked about his future career or what he wanted to do—he'd just assumed it would occur to him eventually. That had shocked her, especially since she'd joined some clubs simply because she'd known they'd look good on her college applications. More and more during their marriage, his lack of ambition had gnawed at her. And now he was running his own successful business, making her rethink her old assumptions.

Her two-top looked ready to order, and she bluffed her way through the menu, writing everything down—unlike the expert, Tony. He was there at the POS when she entered the order, looking over her shoulder, guiding her when she needed help. She fumbled a lot, with him standing so near, and let out her breath in a rush when he finally stepped away to prepare her drink order.

The flare-up of her old physical attraction to him was going to be damned inconvenient.

The place got a little busier around noon, and Tony took a table or two himself, for which she was grateful. She saw his dad come in, begin to sit at the bar—then do a double take when he saw her. He went back to wait by the PLEASE ALLOW US TO SEAT YOU sign.

Kate smiled as she approached him. "Good afternoon, Mr. De Luca."

"Kate." He studied her cautiously, holding a cap in his hand that must have protected his balding head. "Are you helping out?"

"I am. I didn't have anything to do, and one of Tony's servers can't come in for a few weeks. I used to work at my family restaurant when I was a kid."

"I remember. Tony insisted clearing tables at Carmina's was the only job he'd have," Mr. De Luca said dryly.

"How could I have forgotten that?" They'd wanted

to be together so much that Tony had boldly asked her parents for a job. She'd been flattered that she'd meant so much to him. "Let me get you settled at a table. You must be thirsty. Is this your lunch break from work?"

He nodded, taking the chair she'd pulled out for him. "Couple houses with frozen pipes bursting this morning."

She winced. "That's awful. Hope it wasn't too big a mess."

She brought him water and a menu, remembering that, unlike Lyndsay, Mr. De Luca had never been anything but polite to her since the divorce. Not that they saw each other all that much. She noticed him glance at Tony over his reading glasses, but she couldn't understand the look.

While she had a moment, Kate retreated behind the bar and stood next to Tony, who was pouring a glass of wine.

"So does your dad come in often?" she asked.

"Couple times a week."

"I don't think he knew what to make of me."

"I think lots of people will have the same thoughts when they see you working here. You sure you're up for it? I know you're trying to pretend you're on a vacation—this won't help with that."

She made a face. "I know. But I was going stir-crazy. People who need to know why I'm here—I'll eventually tell them a bit more."

When she returned from delivering the glass of wine and taking Mr. De Luca's order, she stood at the POS and slowly inputted it.

Tony approached her. "You know my dad's going to ask me questions."

"Go ahead and tell him I've taken a sabbatical. That's what I'll tell anyone else who asks. Then . . . they can all imagine whatever they want." She sighed on finishing her order, then smiled up at Tony. "Your dad reminded me that you'd taken your first restaurant job at Carmina's. So I'm the reason you're still in the restaurant business all these years later." And then she remembered the loan, and her smile turned to an earnest frown. "Oh, Tony, I didn't mean—"

"I know what you meant," he said, his voice light and neutral.

She put a hand on his upper arm. "Really? Because I wasn't thinking about the loan. But now I'm wondering—did you offer me the job because you felt like you had to?"

He looked down at her hand, and she realized his muscles had gone tense. Could touching him be called flirting? She'd promised herself she'd never do that.

She let go, flushing. "Sorry. No sexual harassment of the boss."

His expression eased. "Right. As for the job—no, I didn't think about the loan either."

"Then why did you give it to me? I know I acted wild and desperate—"

"Not two words I normally associate with you."

She waved a hand impatiently.

"I thought you might drive our son crazy otherwise."

She smiled up at him. "If that's it, then I'll take it. You're not bad as a boss, you know."

"So that's the reason my employees don't quit?" He heard the bell signaling that an order of food was ready. "This is only the first day. You might totally change your mind."

Chapter 7

Tony wasn't surprised when his dad lingered longer than normal, waiting for Tony to find time to sit down with him. By three in the afternoon, Tony had a chance, so he left Kate polishing and rolling silverware into linen napkins.

"Hey, Dad." He slid into a chair and took a sip of the water his dad hadn't touched.

"Tony." Mario was still nursing the one beer he allowed himself at lunch. "It's an interesting day, I take it."

Tony's gaze went to Kate, who was bent over the silverware with all the determination she probably showed trial briefs. "Yeah, you can say that."

"Is this some new method of self-torture?"

Tony chuckled. "Honestly, Dad, people seem to think Kate and I must hate each other. That's not true. It's . . . awkward, yeah, but you didn't see her. She's really beat up about this problem at her law firm. She's on sabbatical until things get figured out."

Mario frowned. "Isn't that like getting laid off?"

"Naw, I think she still gets her salary. She just has to . . . think about stuff, I guess."

"You think she's thinking of moving back to Valentine Valley?"

Tony almost gaped at his dad. "Of course not! She doesn't want the kind of clients she'd represent here."

"She's in Vail, after all."

"They're a lot closer to Denver, and that makes a difference."

"There's Aspen . . ."

"Nope, trust me, that's the farthest thing from her mind. She's in charge of that branch of her law firm. She's not giving up that kind of power."

"But she's taken a waitressing job—"

"The PC term is *server,* Dad," Tony said with a smile.

"The point is, she's here. She didn't go to Cal Carpenter and ask to work at his law firm."

"She can't do that without quitting the other firm. She's just . . . passing time, looking at it as a challenge. She can't be with Ethan all the time. And Ethan's the one who was worried she had nothing to do."

"So he'll be fine with this."

"I think so."

"Good. I'll tell her."

"Tell who?"

"Who? Oh, nobody. Lyndsay."

But Tony got the feeling his dad wasn't talking about Lyndsay.

"What do you mean, Kate's challenged by working here?" Mario suddenly said.

Tony put his curiosity aside. "Well, she kind of took it as a challenge because I told her to work here, just to stop her desperate rambling."

"This was *your* idea." His dad sat back in his chair and stared at him.

Tony cleared his throat. "Well, yeah. So what?"

"Tony, don't get me wrong, boy, but . . . this might have been a bad idea."

"What harm could there be? So she'll drive me nuts, but in a couple weeks or so she'll be gone again."

"What if she doesn't drive you nuts—what if you *like* her being here?"

"Why are you emphasizing it that way? If she does a good job, I won't mind her being here."

Mario glanced again at Kate, and Tony saw that she was talking to one of her tables, smiling broadly, short blond hair dancing around her head as she gestured when she spoke.

"Tony, be careful. Don't let her hurt you again."

Before Tony could respond to that ridiculous statement, the door opened and Ethan walked in.

"Hey, Dad and Grandpa," he said, flinging his backpack on a nearby chair. "Dad, I've been texting Mom, and she doesn't answer. Where do you think—"

And then they all heard her laughter.

Relief crossed Ethan's face, then confusion. "She's waitin' on a table, Dad," he whispered.

"I know," Tony whispered back, trying not to laugh. "She needed something to do—you said so yourself. So she's working here." He didn't bother to point out that Mario thought he'd challenged her to a competition, like this *mattered*.

It couldn't matter to her, not really. She'd always been faintly dismissive of the restaurant business. He used to think it was because she'd wanted so much more, but toward the end of their marriage, he'd assumed she thought such work was beneath her—beneath him. Years later, even though divorced, he knew her better, knew that it was about the pressures of a family business and her need to escape. Sadly, she hadn't learned how to keep from pressuring herself.

Yet . . . he heard her laughter again. She'd taken this job even though people were going to gossip about her. It was pretty bizarre . . .

Ethan watched his mom work for a while, his eyes full of bemusement.

Kate cleared a table after a departing couple, then came over and pulled up a chair. "Hi, E. What are you doing here?"

"Looking for you. You didn't answer my texts, Mom. I thought that was the worst sin ever."

She blushed. "I'm sorry. I haven't looked at my phone since I started working." She leaned forward and fake-whispered, "Blame your father. He's a strict boss where phones are concerned."

"He's definitely strict about phones," Ethan said glumly. "Speaking of phones—"

"You don't mind me working here?" Kate cut in smoothly.

Tony exchanged an amused look with his dad.

"Naw, why should I?" Ethan asked.

"Well . . . people might talk about why I'm taking time off from the law firm. Gossip can be ugly. I'd prefer it if you just walked away from that kind of stuff. Don't try to defend me, okay? It's no one's business why I have time off from work."

"Uh . . . sure," Ethan said, his brow wrinkled in confusion. "I know it's your business, not anyone else's."

Kate grinned at him. "Good. And I promise to check my cell on breaks."

Ethan cleared his throat and looked around uncomfortably. "This isn't because of . . . money, right?"

Kate squeezed his hand. "No! Of course not. I'm perfectly fine, and I'm still getting my salary. This is just like a fun . . . project for me. Didn't I tell you I used to work at Carmina's?"

"I don't remember."

"Well, I did. I knew how important it was to my parents—that business put food on our table and a roof over our heads, as my dad used to say. They *had* to work hard to keep it prosperous. Problem for me was, I always associated the restaurant with taking care of my brothers. I was sort of in charge of them after school, and I didn't like making them do their homework and stuff. Don't tell Grandma I said that. We often did our homework at the restaurant, when they were all too young to be home by themselves. But now, serving here is just about me and the customers—and doing a good job," she added, glancing at Tony with sparkling eyes.

He didn't smile, thinking about her being in charge of all those brothers. He mostly remembered them as being in his way, now that he thought about it, but that was a lot of responsibility to put on a girl.

Kate looked past Ethan. "Are we okay, E.? I think one of my tables needs me."

"Sure, Mom. Have fun. Not sure this actually looks like fun."

"Work isn't always fun," Mario pointed out.

Kate nodded in agreement, still watching her table.

Ethan sighed. "Grandpa, you sound like Dad."

"Well, it *can* be fun if you choose work you enjoy," Tony said.

Ethan looked around. "Well, you own the place, so you must enjoy it."

Tony felt Kate watching him.

"Of course I enjoy it. I like being with people, making sure they have a good time. There's something about knowing that people can talk to me while they relax."

"Sort of like a psychologist," Mario put in.

"Yeah. And I like knowing that after they leave here, people are relaxed and happy and ready to start fresh the next day."

Kate gave him another glance before smiling at Ethan and rushing away. Tony wasn't sure what that glance was about—but then they'd separated when bartending had still been just a job that had let him be home with Ethan during the day. She probably didn't know why he'd grown to truly enjoy the hospitality business. She'd never seemed to care. When they were married, she'd been totally focused on school, with every hour she'd been able to spare for Ethan. Tony had understood and been patient. But the feeling that he wasn't respected, that what she was contributing toward their marriage, their future, was so much more important than anything he could do, had worn away at him after a while.

And then he had an interesting realization: Maybe Kate was working at the tavern partly because she regretted that. Maybe she was trying to prove she'd changed.

He suddenly noticed that his dad and Ethan were both looking at him intently.

"What?"

With a glance at his grandpa, Ethan shrugged. "You look sad."

"Memories, I guess. No point focusing on them, except to learn from them. Let's finish up here and get home."

At the end of her shift, Kate officially met Nicole, one of the evening servers, and had a hard time not staring at the woman's cleavage. Kate guessed that was the point of a low-cut black tank top in wintertime. Did that lead to better tips? Nicole's personality was nothing but cheerful, her black hair held back with bobby pins, emphasizing her freckles and bright green eyes. She showed Kate the side work she should be doing while Nicole herself took over the tables. Kate polished glasses, straightened the wait station, rolled more silverware, emptied trash. Tony called her into his tiny office to fill out employee paperwork and hammer out her work schedule. After handing her menus and beer/ wine lists to study, he sent her on her way.

"Ethan has Technology Club until five," he said. "Mind picking him up?"

"Of course not."

And then Tony went to talk to the other bartender, Lamar, whom Kate had already been introduced to. She felt dismissed, but what did she expect? She was an employee now. She picked up the chicken wings and salad she'd ordered for dinner, then headed home.

When she arrived, the house was empty but for Barney. She knew her dad was at the restaurant, and that her mom was attending a basketball booster club meeting at Basalt High School. Her mom had been president for two years. Kate had seen files open on the computer: flyers for a fund-raising dinner, the itinerary for an upcoming tournament, a database of club members. Her mom had always been an involved parent. Kate felt a stab of guilt, though she should have been used to it. She didn't live near her son's school, so she couldn't participate in the parent stuff. Hell, with the amount of work she did in the evenings, she didn't know if she'd have time even if she did live close by. Though she admired her mom, Kate wondered if this was why she always looked so tired. Christina was probably one of the older moms involved, since there was a nineteen-year span between Joe and Jim, Kate's oldest brother.

Kate and Barney went for a walk, then she picked up Ethan. When they got home, she settled down at the kitchen island to do her tavern homework while Ethan did his schoolwork.

"It's weird to see you doing work," he said, munching on a cookie.

Barney lay on his dog bed and gave Ethan soulful eyes.

"I worked at home all the time—you just never saw me, because I finished it up during the week so I could devote every hour to you," she teased, giving him a light punch on the arm. "And enough with the cookies—I have a big salad and chicken wings keeping warm in the oven."

Her parents eventually came home, bringing Joe from basketball practice, and the five of them sat down to dinner.

"Guess what," Ethan said, after they'd all satisfied their initial craving. "Mom got a job today."

Kate gave her surprised parents a lame smile.

"Did you quit your law firm?" Joe asked with interest.

"No, nothing like that. This is something to pass the time."

"Did Cal Carpenter need some law advice, Katie?" Tom asked with interest.

"Uh, no, I couldn't work for a different firm."

"I bet the widows talked you into volunteering," Christina said brightly.

Kate shook her head.

"She's working for Dad," Ethan said without regard for how her parents would react.

Tom frowned. "Law advice? Marketing?"

"Not exactly . . ." Kate began.

Christina bit her lip, obviously trying not to smile, but her dimples were giving her away.

"She's a waitress," Ethan said.

"Server," Kate corrected.

Her dad blinked at her in surprise and bemusement. "You hate serving," he pointed out.

"I did, I know, but I was young then, impatient, ready to see the world." She gave them a cheerful grin.

Christina cocked her head. "And what, now you're old, patient, and sick of the world?"

"Ha ha." Kate focused on a chicken wing, hoping she'd answered enough questions.

Joe looked between them all with interest, even as he devoured wing after wing.

Christina glanced at Ethan, then back at her daughter. "Really, Kate, is that wise?"

"Won't you two start fighting again?" Tom stated the obvious. "Tony'll be your boss."

"We never fought much," Kate insisted, nodding her head meaningfully at Ethan, who was bent over the various platters of chicken wings, choosing between garlic and teriyaki.

"You know we always have a place for you," Tom continued. "I would have loved to see your pretty face every day."

Christina said nothing; she just watched Kate too closely.

"Thanks, Dad. But you already do see me, right? You'd probably get sick of me. I didn't ask for a job, honestly. I was whining too much about having nothing to do and angsting over my law woes. Before I knew it, Tony was shoving an apron at me because one of his servers will be out a couple weeks. I accepted the challenge."

"The challenge?" Christina echoed.

Kate spread her hands. "Well, sure. He acted like I wouldn't be able to do it, and of course I can. Heck, I waited on his dad already."

"Mario didn't think it sort of odd?" Tom asked.

"Sure he did. Everyone will. But I don't care. I can't just clean and shop and read for two months, guys," she said with exasperation.

"Okay," Tom said, and turned to ask Joe when his next game was.

"You haven't checked the wall calendar?" Christina teased. "Joe's entries are in orange."

Tom and Joe rolled their eyes at each other, but Kate thought about how she'd learned to do the same organizational trick from her mom. Dinner resumed, but Kate knew Christina kept watching her.

"We girls can do the dishes tonight," Christina said. "You boys can have a turn tomorrow."

She shooed the boys away to their Xbox, and Tom to the computer. And all the boys, big and small, escaped.

Kate started loading the dishwasher. "I know what you're going to say."

"You do?"

"You probably think it's a mistake for me to work at the tavern."

"Only you can decide that, honey."

Leaning back against the counter, Kate said, "It's been nine years, Mom. I don't feel the same way about Tony. It's like . . . we can be friends again." When she wasn't looking at his body, she thought uneasily. He was still hot, and her insides weren't letting her forget it.

"But you were never 'just friends' for long. Be careful of that. You won't hurt only the two of you if something goes wrong."

"And our son is the biggest incentive for nothing to go wrong," Kate insisted. "Try not to worry, Mom. I'm thirty-three years old, and I think I've learned a thing or two."

Chapter 8

"**Y**ou're late."

Kate was hanging up her coat on the hooks in the dry-storage closet when she saw Tony standing in the doorway.

"I am?" She pulled her phone out of her pocket. "It's five after four. I'm sorry. At the last minute, I decided to walk instead of drive and misjudged. Won't happen again."

He nodded and gave her a look she couldn't read. It was a pause, barely a moment, but she could swear he looked at her mouth.

And hers went dry, and it took everything in her not to lick her lips. When he turned away, she let her breath out in a rush.

What was that?

She pushed it aside, reminding herself that there was no flirting. Besides being her ex, Tony was now her boss. He was never Mr. Punctual in his personal life, but apparently business was different. She got that—she even liked that. Everything she'd seen so far showed him to be organized, on top of things, and effectual. His employees liked him—okay, she wasn't sure about the chef, who didn't seem to like anyone.

But she certainly didn't want Tony to regret hiring her—hell, maybe he already did, and that was why he'd become the punctuality police. She was determined not to give him reason for regrets.

She took over tables from Erika, who was tall and skinny and anxious to go out on the town. As Kate went about her work, occasionally asking questions of Tony or Nicole (who wore a buttoned-down shirt with a healthy number of buttons unbuttoned), Tony treated her the same way he treated any other employee, pleasant and neutral, as if they hadn't known each other their whole lives. Then it dawned on her, as he mildly criticized the way she polished glasses or left some crumbs on the floor after serving a table with kids, that maybe he was being a bit more picky with her than was necessary. But as they got busy, she ceased noticing Tony and began to notice how some people looked at her.

Oh, Ned and Ted, the twin plumbers, teased her good-naturedly about coming down in the world, but all she had to do was spend a couple minutes bantering, and they were satisfied. But occasionally she waited on a table of her parents' friends or people she went to school with, and their sidelong looks and abruptly stopped conversations were very obvious. When anyone asked, she explained that she was on sabbatical, just enjoying being home with her son and helping

Tony out, but that hardly satisfied the gossips' curiosity. And if there were deeper reasons—no, she shied away from even the thought.

Though she'd told Tony that rumors wouldn't matter to her, she found the blow to her pride a little deeper than she'd imagined. After all, these people were right: She'd done something her firm had disagreed with—she'd questioned their decision one too many times. It weighed on her, and more and more she wondered if she should do some investigation of her own into her client. She'd been tempted to ask questions when Michelle Grady had called about another case, but she'd decided that might get back to the partners.

"Kate!"

She heard Will Sweet's jovial voice and turned to see him and Nate Thalberg hanging their beat-up jackets on hooks by the door. They were both cowboys, one fair-haired, one dark, and she watched many feminine heads turn as they replaced their cowboy hats after shaking off the snow. They advanced toward the bar, their cowboy boots hitting the floor hard.

"Hi, Will, Nate," she said. "Do you want a table, or will the bar do?"

"We'll take a table, thanks," Nate said. "We need sustenance before the hockey game."

"Is it Wednesday again?" That meant she'd been in town a week already. And Tony would probably be leaving soon for the game. "Do you guys want water with your menus?"

"Tony knows what we drink," Will said, sitting down and taking the menu, but not looking at it.

He eyed her casual uniform—or maybe he was eyeing her. It didn't bother her, but she saw Tony looking at them from behind the bar, his expression genial, but his brown eyes a bit more intense. She shot him a bemused look, and he bent to the reach-ins to grab a couple bottles of beer.

"So the rumors are true," Will said.

At the next table, the elderly town doctor and his wife stopped talking to listen.

Kate grinned. "Tell me the rumors first, and I'll confirm or deny."

"You're actually working in our favorite local dive."

"Don't let Chef Baranski hear you say that. His food is better than at any old dive."

"True," Nate said, scanning his menu. "Hope he's got the shepherd's pie today."

"He does."

But Will kept his gaze on her. "So you haven't confirmed or denied. You're officially working here?"

"Temporarily, but yes."

"Why would you want to do that? I hear you're on sabbatical, but that usually means you're still getting paid."

"Way to be personal, Will," Nate said, shaking his head.

Will chuckled. "Kate here knows I just have her best interests at heart."

She smiled. "My best interests? How's that?"

"Well, someone needs to look out for you, to make sure the gossips don't have the wrong story."

"And what story do they have?"

"That you've been fired, that you mismanaged your money so you're desperate for a job, and only your ex will take you on."

Kate blinked at him.

Nate winced. "Will!"

Will spread his arms wide and just missed knocking a tray out of Nicole's hands. "Sorry."

The server winked, and kept on going.

"As I was saying, I don't believe it. Anyone who knows you from high school would know you'd never mismanage your money. Get yourself fired? Well, you can be pretty stubborn."

"And ambitious, let's not forget that," Kate said dryly. "Considering you were a few years behind me at school, you think you know me pretty well. Or maybe it's just Tony you know well."

Nate snorted, and she couldn't decide if Will reddened a bit.

"Now, Kate—"

"No, I have not been fired; I'm merely taking a sabbatical after years of working too much. And I'm working here because I'm going stir-crazy. Shopping and reading were getting old fast—and one of the waitresses had to take a few weeks off. You have my permission to tell that to anyone you'd like." She leaned toward the next table. "Mrs. Ericson, you can tell your friends, too."

Doc Ericson looked abashed for both himself and his wife, who diligently began to eat her kale salad, as if she was oblivious.

To Will and Nate, Kate said, "Gentlemen, I'll let you look at the menu now."

When she caught sight of Tony frowning at her, she left the table quickly, but to her surprise, his disapproving gaze remained on the table rather than her. Or maybe it was focused on Will.

She stopped at the bar. "They said you know what beer they like?"

"I'll take it to them," he said, a fixed smile on his face as he looked at Will.

"Uh . . . he was just teasing me. I didn't mind."

"Uh-huh."

Though she would have liked to stick around and watch, the kitchen bell rang and she knew an order was ready. Since she was closest to the kitchen, it was up to her to deliver it. But the whole time, she couldn't help wondering—was Tony upset about the rumors on her behalf? Because there was certainly no reason for him to be jealous she'd spent time chatting with his friends, one of whom happened to be single. But sadly, not her type, if she went by recent history, anyway. She suspected Will owned only one suit, since he was a cowboy by trade. She didn't think she could qualify the men she dated by their number of suits, but it sure looked that way. She felt pretty shallow.

When she came back to take their order, Tony had sat down at the four-top with Will and Nate.

"Are you trying to make me nervous, Boss?" she said.

"No need to be nervous if you do your job well. Describe the Lo Mein Tofu Stir Fry."

Will grimaced. "I'm not ordering that. I need meat. I can't believe Chef makes that."

"He's full of surprises." Tony still looked at her, waiting.

She remembered he wasn't certain she was up to the challenge, then gave him her sweetest smile. "Chef makes it with sweet and sour tofu, bok choy, soy sprouts, lo mein, garlic, and ginger, finished with scallions."

Will whistled while Nate took a sip of his beer and grinned.

"I take it you'll be having that now?" she said to Will.

He shook his head and reluctantly admitted, "Although it does sound good."

"I'll have it," Nate said, closing his menu. "I'll save shepherd's pie for next time."

Will ordered the flatiron steak and Kate went off to place their order. Forty-five minutes later, they were shrugging into their coats.

"Left you a big tip," Will told her.

"For my son's college fund, where Tony's depositing my earnings. Thanks!"

He laughed.

Tony came out of the office, throwing his big hockey bag over his shoulder.

"Maybe you should have left that outside," she said. "Hockey bags smell. Remind me to stay out of your office on Wednesdays."

He only arched a brow to that. "You've met Stephen, the manager. He's in charge. If you need help, ask. I'll be back in a couple hours."

She almost felt like a married couple again, for he didn't tell any other server or bartender that. But she was new, she reminded herself. "Aye aye, Boss."

He rolled his eyes and turned, coming to such an abrupt halt that she ran into his bag and stumbled. He grabbed her arm before she crashed into a luckily unoccupied table. As she righted herself, she came face-to-face with Lyndsay.

Lyndsay stared at her in confusion.

Kate patted Tony's hockey bag. "There, you almost dropped it. Glad to help."

"You here to come to my game, Lynds?" Tony asked.

"Nope, here for dinner. And it looks like I'll get my fondest wish—Kate can serve me."

Will looked disappointed, like he wanted to stay for the show, but Nate dragged him out the front door. Tony gave Kate a last look, as if in silent apology. She waved.

"Hi, Lyndsay, would you like to sit at the bar or at a table?"

"A table, please. Lamar looks far too busy behind the bar."

Ned and Ted were watching them with open fascination when Kate led Lyndsay past.

"You guys catching flies in those mouths?" Lyndsay asked.

Kate covered a laugh as she pointed to a two-top.

"You want me to get this, Kate?" Nicole asked, walking past with dirty dishes.

"No, I can manage. Lyndsay, give me a moment and I'll be back with a menu and some water."

Nicole looked around. "We're getting slower. Why don't you take your break right now? I'll cover your tables."

Nicole looked sympathetic, as if she knew the entire history between Lyndsay and Kate. Did this town know everyone's story?

Kate forced a smile. "Thanks. I'll take care of Lyndsay, though."

She ended up running food to another table first, but that only took a moment. When she returned with the promised items, she said, "Hi, Lyndsay."

Lyndsay nodded, eyeing Kate with interest. "This isn't the uniform of a well-tailored lawyer."

"Nope, I'm on sabbatical right now and needed something to pass the time."

Lyndsay arched a brow, saying pleasantly, "So you asked your ex-husband?"

"Technically, he asked me. It was a challenge—I don't think he thought I'd agree."

"Pretty stupid of him."

"I thought it was nice."

"Yeah, he's too nice."

"Stick around. You can watch people point and stare and whisper. They're not so nice." Kate sighed. "I'll let you look over the menu."

She turned her back, then heard Lyndsay sigh.

"Kate, sit down. I'm not here to make trouble."

Kate turned around. Lyndsay was picking at a corner of the menu, not meeting her gaze.

Kate sat opposite her and said softly, "I'm glad to hear that. It was a long time ago, Lynds. I'm not asking for forgiveness for causing Tony pain, because that's up to you."

"Would you be able to forgive someone who broke your brother's heart?"

Kate gave a twisted smile. "I don't know. I would hope so. Maybe after nine years—"

"You didn't just break *his* heart, did you? You never told me a thing, never confided in me, when I told you everything, *everything!*" Her voice rose a bit at the end, and she flushed and sat back as several customers glanced at her.

Kate sighed. "How could I talk to you about the troubles I was having with your brother? It wouldn't be fair to you."

"Well, Tony took his cue from you—he never confided in me either."

That probably hurt worse than Kate's betrayal, but she didn't point that out. "Tony and I discussed it all those years ago, wondered who we should tell we were having problems. We kept hoping we could work things out so no one would have to know and worry about us. That didn't happen. But can we at least leave it in the past?"

"Because he has." Lyndsay shook her head. "He's pretty amazing."

Kate nodded, but she felt uncomfortable. Was she supposed to agree that her ex was amazing? That could send mixed signals. And she wasn't so sure he thought everything was in the past.

As for herself, she sometimes wondered if she gave up her high school girlfriends after law school because she hadn't deserved them—she'd failed at her marriage after all, and had to devote all her time to her career to prove it had been worth it. For a long time after the divorce, she hadn't done anything for herself, and that included having friends.

Lyndsay sighed. "All right. I'll take the Cobb salad."

Kate went and placed the order, then stood by the wait station, watching Lyndsay. Her head was bent, but she didn't look at her phone, like so many solitary customers would.

Kate went back to her table. "My break isn't up yet. Mind if I sit down?"

Lyndsay shrugged.

"So how's teaching?"

After a long pause, Lyndsay said, "It's okay. More paperwork than it used to be, less freedom to choose what I want to teach. But you're a parent, I'm sure you've heard that before."

Kate nodded. "Dating anybody?"

Lyndsay shrugged again. "A dentist from Carbondale. He's nice. Got an ex-wife and kids, though, so he's not too serious."

"Guess there's a lot of that going around," Kate said with faint sarcasm.

"You date guys with kids?" Lyndsay asked with only a little interest.

"Sometimes. I never meet the kids, though, and I've never introduced Ethan. I don't seem to be able to get that far in a relationship. The older we get, the more anyone single has a lot of complications in his life."

Lyndsay nodded.

Nicole brought out the Cobb salad and set it in front of Lyndsay, eyeing the two women as if they might attack each other.

"We're playing nice," Lyndsay said sweetly.

Nicole backed away, hands upraised.

Lyndsay's gaze met Kate's, and Kate thought Lyndsay gave her a faint smile. But then she cleared her throat and lifted her fork.

"I better get back to work," Kate said, standing up and pushing in her chair. "Have fun watching all my admirers."

"Oh, I will."

Tony sat in the back seat of Will's pickup on the way to Aspen, watching the hypnotic quality of snow coming right at the window in the headlights.

"Are you going to freeze me out all night?" Will teased.

"I'm not freezing you out. I said everything I needed to earlier."

There was another minute-long pause.

"I still can't believe you told her all the rumors about her," Tony said in a disgusted voice.

Will groaned. "Come on! She's a big girl. She should know what people are saying—*I'd* want to know."

"Look, she's going through a tough time."

"She *says* she's just taking a break from work—guess there's more to it."

"It's personal."

"Funny how you know about it," Nate said, twisting on the bench to glance at Tony with interest.

"We share a kid. We still have to talk."

"He said 'have to,'" Nate pointed out to Will. "Did you hear that? As if it's difficult to deal with each other. Told you he wasn't thinking about ex-sex."

Tony choked on the sip of water he'd just taken out of his Nalgene, then spit it out on his hockey bag. "Dammit, guys, look what you made me do."

"I think that bag could use some water," Will said. "Lots of water. And soap."

Nate turned his head and gave Tony a smile. "So you *are* thinking about ex-sex?"

"Of course not! We've been over for nine years. That's for guys who can't get over a breakup."

"Not always," Will said conversationally. "But yeah, the few times I've done it, it's been within a couple months of the breakup."

"That never works out for anybody," Tony said, shaking his head. "Neither of you moves on."

"Well, I'd have to disagree. St. Nate here probably never had ex-sex, so he can't have an opinion."

"Nope," Nate agreed pleasantly.

"If you don't like to think of it as ex-sex, think of it as the other cliché, friends with benefits."

Tony swallowed and looked out the foggy window into the darkness, feeling uneasy. "Look, we have a kid together, one who lives at my house. And Kate's living with her parents."

"So the housing situation is all that's stopping you?" Nate asked with interest.

"My mind just goes to logistics first," Tony insisted. "I have not given one serious thought to sex with her."

"What does that mean?" Will asked, laughing. "So you've had horny thoughts about her, just not ones you took seriously?"

Tony sighed and said nothing.

"I knew it!" Will said to Nate.

"Damn, I always lose our bets," Nate said.

"You bet about my sex life?" Tony demanded.

"Just kidding." Nate gave him a grin from the front bench, then his smile faded. "But, Tony, things are going that well with your ex-wife?"

Tony shrugged. "We seem to be sort of okay as friends. I remember the bad things occasionally—you can't forget that, especially when . . ." He trailed off. *Especially when she was the love of my life, and there doesn't seem to be another.*

Nate just nodded in sympathy.

"Especially when what?" Will demanded.

"He doesn't need to tell us," Nate said.

"Sure he does. We're his best friends."

"There's nothing to tell," Tony insisted. "I'm not looking for a long-term relationship with other women, because I've got a kid who might suffer."

Will met his eyes in the rearview mirror. "Then what's stopping you from ex-sex with your wife?"

"Too complicated. Let's leave it at that."

But now Tony was going to be plagued by memories of the mind-blowing sex he'd shared with Kate so long ago. She'd made him wait through sophomore and junior year of high school, saying they were too young, and part of him had agreed—and part of him had not. Making out had certainly been a lot of fun. But the pleasure had been even sweeter when, on a warm spring day, they'd driven to a remote trail to go hiking and she'd surprised him by saying she'd been on the pill for two months, and they were finally alone. Leave it to Kate to have everything planned, but boy, he'd appreciated it. They'd made love outdoors, and he'd never forget it as long as he lived—the spectacular beauty of Kate, naked on a blanket, the dappled sun through the trees making patterns on her body. They'd both been eager, and things had gone too quickly the first time, but they'd had hours to practice, and the second—and third—time had been amazing.

Tony grimaced and told himself to stop thinking about the past. He wasn't going to have sex with Kate because . . . because of everything that had happened between them.

Damn, he needed a cold shower. An ice rink would have to do.

Chapter 9

Kate finished putting the linens bag near the back door and returned to a deserted bar. Lamar had already gone home, and since Nicole had finished her side work quickly, she'd gone, too, along with manager Stephen. Chef Baranski was overseeing the kitchen cleaning. The radio was still softly playing and taking callers, and an old woman's voice said, "Why did you change the music? In the middle of the night, my donkeys want to hear classical and jazz."

Kate snorted and thought, *Only in Valentine Valley*.

She was just about to start putting the chairs upside down on the tables when someone knocked on the front door. She looked up and saw Tony.

Smiling, she unlocked and let him in. "So how did it go?"

And then she saw the small bandage oozing blood on his right cheek.

She gasped. "Tony!"

He shrugged and dropped his bag near the door. "It looks worse than it is."

"But it's bleeding through the bandage! Weren't you wearing a helmet, a face mask?"

"Of course I was—I don't want to lose my teeth. But we were warming up, and someone on the other team was hitting too hard, and I'd taken off my helmet to adjust . . . never mind the details."

She followed him into his office. "You could have lost an eye!"

"I know, I know."

"And you need a new bandage."

"This was a new bandage after the game, and I ripped off the scab that had formed." He rummaged through his shelves until he found the medicine kit.

"Maybe you need stitches?"

"Naw, I'm fine. I have antiseptic things in here somewhere."

She pushed his big hands out of the way, found the little packet, and opened it. "Sit down on the desk so I can reach you."

"Kate—"

"Shh!"

With a sigh he complied, sitting on the edge of the desk. That put his face a little above hers, and she had to stand between his knees. She bit her lip as she tried to be gentle peeling off the bandage.

"Just rip it away," he said with amusement.

So she did, and she was the only one who winced. The cut wasn't too long, nor was it an open gash or oozing blood too badly. Using the damp antiseptic wipe, she gently cleansed it, then looked for a bigger, square bandage. After applying it, she stood still, admiring her work.

"There," she murmured with satisfaction.

Tony wasn't smiling anymore. Those chocolate brown eyes were staring at her as if out of the past, back when he'd desired her, needed her.

And she realized she was standing between his thighs. The shock of awareness and heat that moved through her body was swift and overwhelming. He put his hands on her waist, as if he knew she was suddenly weak with longing.

"What are we doing?" she whispered.

But she didn't move away.

"I think I'm kissing you," he said, leaning closer.

Their breaths merged, the heat of him seared her.

"Stop me now," he warned in a hoarse voice.

Their lips almost, almost touched.

And she couldn't speak, didn't want to deny him, found herself deep in the past, where Tony had been the only boy, then the only man, who'd drawn her, who'd made her desperate for his touch, who'd made her lose herself.

He kissed her, openmouthed and hungrily, no gentle exploration but inspiring a renewal of a desperation that she'd buried within her for over nine years. He pulled her against him, her hips into the openness of his, her aching breasts flattening against his broad chest, her head turning until it practically rested on his shoulder. She felt greedy with the need of him, desperate for the taste of his tongue. And then his hands slid to cup her backside, pressing her even harder against the erection outlined by his jeans. She let her hands roam him, remembering his biceps and shoulders, the broad planes supporting his collarbones, the lean pillar of his neck. His hair was thick and warm, and so good to touch.

Their mouths explored as if in homecoming, as memories swamped her of laughing kisses, tender kisses, urgent kisses. Tony was still all of that for her, and no one had ever made her feel like this but him.

That made her break off the kiss and stare at him, wide-eyed. His eyes smoldered as they watched her mouth. He didn't look like he could stop, and for a moment, she wondered if she could, if Tony once again could create a passion that made her forget everything but him.

And then they heard a sound. She turned her head and saw the chef pausing in the doorway. He glanced at them and just kept walking.

"Oh, my God," Kate said, backing away.

Tony sighed and leaned his hands back on the desk as if his bones needed support. He dislodged a stack of files, which tumbled to the floor, but he made no move to pick them up.

"He saw us!" she whispered.

"Yeah, he did. We weren't doing anything illegal," he said, his voice still husky, but eminently practical as always.

She touched the back of her hand to her damp mouth, even as she gaped at him. "Tony!" She didn't know where to start, couldn't understand why he didn't see all the problems.

He straightened up, and suddenly he was so tall in the small room, overwhelming, very male. For a moment, he didn't move, and the hesitation had her both hoping he'd touch her and praying he wouldn't. He came toward her, putting his hands flat on the wall on either side of her head. He leaned down and nuzzled the side of her neck into her hair.

"Tony," she said more faintly, even as a wave of desire made her shudder. "We can't do this."

"Why not? We're both single."

"You're—you're acting like we're two people who've never dated, let alone been m-married." She stifled a moan and closed her eyes as he took her earlobe between his teeth and bit gently. She could hear his harsh breathing, felt the heat of his body so close.

"If it helps, pretend we're strangers." He licked her neck long and slow.

She groaned aloud, then ducked away from him, reaching to close the door. "Whatever physical attraction we may still feel, Tony De Luca, we both know that emotionally, this is a disaster in the making. And pretend we're strangers? Like that would work?"

"You're right—we're not strangers. I kinda thought this last week had proven we'd become friends, finally, after all this time."

"Friends! Ohhhh." She put a hand on her forehead and winced. "I get it—you mean friends with benefits."

He folded his arms and continued to stare down at her. "Kate, I'm just as surprised as you that every feeling of desire I ever had for you has still been there all this time, waiting for—I don't know, extended time together, time to heal, whatever. One of my biggest regrets of our marriage was that we didn't talk enough. We just assumed that since we'd been together our entire lives, we knew what the other was thinking."

That made her flinch. He was so right.

"I'm not ever going to stay silent again," he continued, "even if it's about sex. I admit, I haven't given this—us—any thought at all. I know there would be consequences, and I sure as hell don't want to hurt Ethan. It's probably a bad idea. But I can't stop thinking"—his voice dropped to a gravelly whisper—"how good I can make you feel."

She stared at him, unable to speak. His eyes were hot again, and he was looking at her like she was the night's special and he could eat her up.

A firm no was on the tip of her tongue, but she couldn't make it come out. Now she couldn't stop thinking about sex either, imagining pulling off his shirt, running her hands over the ridges of his stomach and up his chest, and remembering, oh, remembering how good he really had made her feel.

Tony studied her, and she knew her expression gave away too much.

She hugged herself. "I . . . I have to go. Ethan—Ethan must be expecting me."

"It's a weeknight. He's on his usual schedule, hanging out with"—he paused in thought—"the widows."

"They can't be babysitting him."

"They told me they miss him, and he gets a kick out of it. Every so often they pick him up, take him out to dinner, and bring him back to the boardinghouse, where they spoil him rotten. He does odd jobs for them while he's there." He looked at her mouth again. "So my house is empty this evening."

To her surprise, she started to laugh. "Oh, Tony, this is . . . this is . . . I never thought—"

"Aha, I can still make you laugh," he said with satisfaction.

He bent to pick up the folders they'd dislodged, and she knelt to help him.

"You don't have to do that," he said, his voice hasty.

She didn't understand his concern. "The mess is my fault, too."

And then she saw something with the words *Valentine Valley* in bold print. She pulled it out even as he tried to grab it from her hands.

It was a wall calendar, with a gorgeous view of their valley and mountains and the title "The Men of Valentine Valley."

She gaped at it, then at him. Was he blushing? Could that mean—? "Tony—are you in this?"

He sank back on his heels with a heavy sigh. "It was for the Valentine Valley Preservation Fund," he said lamely.

"The *widows* made you do this?"

"Well, they didn't *make* me. They asked."

She began to page through it, staring in shock at all the men she knew, posing mostly without shirts. There was Chris Sweet, Emily's brother, reading by a fire in January; Dom Shaw, Monica's brother, posing with flowers and chocolate for February. Page after page of men she knew—and then she reached May, and saw

Tony hip-deep in the Fryingpan River, fly fishing. The sun gleamed off his chest, curved along the muscles of his arms, and highlighted his dark hair.

Glancing up, she found him grimacing as he watched her.

She smiled. "You look really good."

He rolled his eyes.

She kept paging through until she found the July group shot at the hot springs behind the Sweetheart Inn. "Wow," she mouthed, looking at the selection of men in their bathing suits, all grouped in and around the hot springs. "Hey, you're in back. I can hardly see—"

"That's enough." He took it away from her, buried it in the middle of the stack of folders, and shoved it onto his desk.

He pulled her to her feet, and though Kate was tempted to hold onto his hand, she backed away and opened the door. The kitchen was quiet and dark, only the radio making any sound in the restaurant. She went into the main room and started stacking the chairs on the tables.

"So how did you and my sister do?"

With a start, she turned and found Tony leaning against the bar, watching her. And suddenly the quiet and sense of aloneness was almost as intimate as their kiss.

She cleared her throat and continued to stack chairs. "We did fine. I think we've even declared a truce."

"That's good to hear."

"We talked about her job and dating. Polite conversation, not too deep."

"It's a start."

She walked to the back room to continue stacking chairs, and he followed her in, leaning against the doorjamb to watch her.

She glanced at him over her shoulder. "You want me to be on good terms with your sister again? Why?"

He shrugged. "She doesn't seem happy lately. Maybe getting over part of the past can help."

Her hand on a chair, Kate paused. "Has something happened?"

"I don't know, she won't admit to anything. I'm not asking you to get information out of her or anything—"

"Good, because I wouldn't spy."

"—I'm only saying I hope forgiving an old friend will somehow help."

She nodded, finished the last chair, and started for the door. He stepped to one side, but she was still forced to squeeze past him and her breasts just brushed his chest, causing her stomach to flutter.

"Unfair," she scolded, walking backward to face him.

He grinned.

"I'm out of here." She grabbed her jacket from the back and hurried toward the door before he could stop her. He didn't try, and she was almost disappointed. *Uh-oh.*

Tony watched Kate run away, and he wasn't surprised. What had really surprised him was himself. It was as if one conversation about ex-sex had made every horny thought about Kate something that couldn't be ignored. He hadn't meant to suggest anything at all, but then she'd touched his face, stood between his thighs, and suddenly he hadn't been able to think of anything else but her, exploring her body, which he'd once known as well as his own. His logical mind with all its warning bells had faded so far away that he'd only been able to hear the pounding of his heart, feel the desperation in his trembling hands.

To hold Kate again had been . . . mind-blowing.

To know she still felt the same desire had only made everything better. So the attraction hadn't gone away. He couldn't be surprised, and it was a relief to openly acknowledge it.

But as he slowly turned off the last of the lights and his body cooled and his mind reasserted itself, Tony was almost glad Kate had been the sensible one. Not glad, exactly, but . . . maybe relieved.

It was a mistake to think they could just stop thinking and forget about everybody else but themselves.

Ethan was getting dropped off at Tony's next door when Kate arrived home. Sure, Tony had the house to himself, she thought, shaking her head. Kate waved to Mrs. Thalberg as she drove away in her old station wagon. On the icy sidewalk, Kate and Ethan talked a few minutes about his evening with the widows, then he started toward Tony's to finish up some homework.

"If you need help, just let me know!" she called hopefully.

He kept walking but did a slow turn. "Mom, you hate math."

"Doesn't mean I'm bad at it."

"Good night." He waved and closed the door behind him.

Kate sighed. They were raising a self-sufficient young man. Why was it so difficult for a mom to accept that her son might not need her so much?

Inside, her dad was asleep in his big recliner, and her mom was crocheting while watching TV. Barney trotted over to greet her, smelling her legs with interest.

"You smell the French fries, boy?" Kate asked, rubbing his hips as he walked between her legs.

Christina looked up. "Kate, how was your shift?"

"Okay," she said, tucking her legs beneath her on the couch. "Lots of whispers as people wonder what I'm doing there, but that was anticipated. I even saw Lyndsay, and as I told Tony, I think we have a truce."

"Oh, that's good. I know you've missed her."

"I don't think I've talked about her," Kate said in confusion.

"And you haven't really talked about another best friend, so I thought maybe no one had taken her place."

Kate nodded slowly, for that was true.

"I heard something tonight about Ethan," Christina continued. "Mrs. Thalberg called me—the eldest Mrs. Thalberg," she amended, smiling.

"I know the widows had Ethan this evening. I just saw him and he seemed fine."

"Apparently he let slip that the ski club wants him

to be on one of the competitive teams rather than the rec team."

"Well, that's exciting," Kate said in confusion. "I'm surprised he didn't tell me."

"Mrs. Thalberg said he plans to turn them down, which is probably why he didn't call you."

"But why? Did he tell her?"

"Apparently he was reluctant to do so, but at last he admitted he'd have to be in Aspen every weekend to train."

The pain in Kate's stomach surprised her as she thought about her son living in two different households in two different towns, unable to spend enough time with one team.

Christina reached over and touched her hand. "I'm sorry, honey. There are so many times when we want something for our kids, and they just can't have it. Obviously Ethan knows what's important, and that's being with you."

Kate nodded. "He's a good, thoughtful kid. But . . . damn, I feel bad about this."

"Surely there are teams in Vail."

"Same problem—he's not there enough to train with them."

"Maybe he doesn't even want to compete. It might simply be fun for him."

Kate nodded, but her heart ached. Of course he'd stayed in Valentine the occasional weekend for some big event, but on a regular basis, it just wouldn't work out.

She went to her bedroom soon after, but she wasn't really tired. She just didn't want to see her mom's sympathetic glances. Barney had come with her, and as she roamed around the room restlessly, he lay down with his head on his paws and just watched her. The walls still held some childhood pictures, championship teams she and her brothers had been on, marching band competitions. She smiled at a picture of her and Lyndsay, arms around each other, their instruments in their hands. It made her wonder where her trombone was, and to her surprise, it was right there in the closet, tucked behind her mom's summer wardrobe. Kate's own clothes were crammed in there, too, getting wrinkled.

She'd given up the trombone in college, not because she hadn't liked it but because she'd had no time. Ethan's schedule was making him give up something he might love—but it wasn't by his choice.

She sighed, feeling dispirited as she changed into flannel pajamas and crawled into bed. She had to leave the door open so Barney could wander the house when he wanted. Lots of privacy, she thought.

Sleep eluded her, and she found herself thinking of Tony, although she'd deliberately pushed him from her mind when she'd gotten home so her mother wouldn't suspect anything.

God, she was hiding a relationship when there really wasn't one, except as exes and parents to Ethan.

But he was right next door.

The kiss surfaced in her mind like the heat of a volcano, spilling over to make her feel uncomfortably hot, even in the dead of winter. She threw back the blanket and comforter with a groan and stared into the darkness.

How could she feel this way after all these years? She walked around the room, but the cold only invigorated her. As she moved past the window, the curtain still drawn back so she could see the moon, she caught a glimpse of a lit window next door.

Don't look, she told herself, but too late. She stopped and saw Tony, standing backlit in his bedroom window, staring at her. With a groan she ducked to the side. Maybe he hadn't seen her. Unable to control herself, she peered around the edge—and he waved at her.

She closed the curtains and got back in bed, pulling the covers over her head.

She couldn't live next door to him anymore. She needed her own closet, she needed a little space to breathe without anyone asking her questions, needed a place where Ethan could come be with her and not feel that he should just run home to sleep. She needed her own place.

Chapter 10

At nine in the morning, just after she got back from her run through the freshly fallen snow, Kate received a call from her colleague Michelle Grady asking for insight on the GAC Biochemical project. Kate told her as much as she could, but she was finding it difficult to hold back on the exact problem that was a private matter between her and the partners. She almost spilled the "undocumented file" issue, and stopped herself just in time. But it was gnawing at her night and day—she was going to have to do something about it. But what would keep her out of trouble with the senior partners? She'd been paralyzed for the last week, but she couldn't stay that way anymore. They wanted her to rethink her priorities—but wasn't one of her priorities public health?

She arrived at Tony's before it opened to take her turn sweeping and mopping the floors. The first person she saw in the kitchen was Chef Baranski. She held her breath, waiting for him to mention the kiss he'd seen, but all he did was grunt and nod and continue the food prep for the day. Maybe it really wasn't a big deal to anyone but her.

She calmed herself, then leaned her head into Tony's office, where he was working on the computer. He turned his head to look at her, and for a moment, she could have gotten lost in the sexy awareness she saw there. And then he looked away, and she could breathe again.

"How's your battle wound?" she asked.

He pointed to the new bandage on his right cheek. "You did a good job. It's healing."

"Great. Can I talk to you about Ethan?" She pulled in a chair from the hall.

"What's up?"

She explained what her mom had told her about Ethan and the ski club. "So what do we do?"

He lounged back in his chair and regarded her thoughtfully. "Do? I'd say that unless Ethan comes to us, we don't do anything. He's a smart kid. I'm sure he's probably seen this coming."

"But I feel terrible!"

"Did he seem angry when you spoke with him?"

"Well . . . no," she admitted.

"This isn't the first time he's been affected by living in two different places. And it won't be the last. Maybe he doesn't even care about competing."

"If he didn't care, why did he mention it to the widows?"

He shrugged. "I don't know what to tell you, Kate."

She got to her feet restlessly, but there was nowhere to pace except around her chair. "I still feel terrible."

"Because we're divorced? Don't. We've done the best we can, and he's a good kid. We're doing something right."

She nodded, but the ache in her chest made her eyes sting. At times like this, she questioned every decision she'd ever made.

"I'll never forget when he was little," she began in a soft voice, "and I was still in school, and he'd cry when we had to leave Valentine."

"He was a toddler," Tony said patiently. "He understands everything now."

Kate leaned on the back of the chair, squeezing the top of it. "And then there was that time when he was three and we heard him telling his teddy bear in a little stern voice that he had to do homework and couldn't play." She shuddered and squeezed back the tears. "He was sounding just like me. In some ways, I'm glad he doesn't see me working long hours evening after evening. I don't want him to be . . . driven, unable to really relax. You know, like me."

"He's got the best of both of us," Tony said gently.

"Sometimes I think my determination to provide for his future really backfired in his present."

Tony didn't say anything for a moment; he just looked at her. She tried to master her emotions, but lately, they were always so close to the surface.

"I think you're letting your work issues affect your private life too much," he said at last. "Don't second-guess every decision we've ever made. He's a good kid everyone likes, and he's not in trouble. We've done okay so far. And if he brings up the competitive snowboarding, *then* we'll see how he feels and deal with it."

She nodded. "Okay, thanks. I guess I'll go . . . stock the sugar caddies."

She should really try to emulate Tony in this—she was the worrier, always so focused on the future. He didn't angst over a problem until it actually happened and needed to be solved. He very much lived in the present. His attitude used to annoy her, but lately, she'd give anything to just enjoy things as they happened.

She was pleasantly distracted when the widows came to Tony's Tavern for a committee meeting. They were part of the Valentine Valley Preservation Fund committee, the main worker bees, according to Kate's mom. They fund-raised for grant money to redevelop historic buildings, and they also did their best to support local businesses rather than chain stores, all of which helped Valentine attract tourists and be a good family place to live. Kate was all for that.

"Kate, so you *are* workin' here!" Mrs. Palmer cried with her thick Western accent.

Kate blushed as other customers looked around, but she didn't worry that Mrs. Palmer meant to offend. "Yes, ma'am. I needed something to do."

"I do hope things are going well with your law firm," Mrs. Thalberg said, her eyes full of warmth and worry.

"I'm just taking some time off," Kate said, hoping she sounded reassuring rather than defensive.

The ladies bustled into the back room, Mrs. Thalberg carrying a large bag with a notebook sticking out, Mrs. Ludlow moving slowly with her walker, Mrs. Palmer sashaying in a Christmas dress with elves in the pattern. Kate wondered if she wore a different holiday-themed outfit every day of the Christmas season . . .

"Just water's fine for now, Kate," said Mrs. Thalberg. "We're waiting on a few more committee members."

Mrs. Ludlow proceeded to pull a knitting project out of her bag.

"Would you ladies like a menu?"

"I always order the same thing—fish and chips," Mrs. Ludlow said, glancing at Kate through her glasses. "And please keep an eye out for Eileen Sweet, Katherine dear. You know what she looks like?"

"Sure, she owns the Sweetheart Inn. But I have to say—I never thought she'd step foot in a tavern."

Mrs. Palmer frowned. "She's not a member of the Valentine Valley Preservation Fund, but she's helped out with the Christmas market. We may not agree on everythin', but she has the town's best interests at heart. Have you visited the market yet, Kate?"

"Not yet, but I plan to. Thank goodness we still have a few weeks until Christmas."

"You need to come for your Christmas shoppin', your decoratin', or just to people watch," Mrs. Palmer said, her eyes full of delight. "Tony even has a booth where he sells hot spiced wine."

"I didn't know that," Kate said.

"Oh, he hired a few people part-time to man it," Mrs. Thalberg explained.

"And we advertise for him on Facebook," Mrs.

Ludlow said, "which is a good thing, because he never does so for himself."

Kate blinked rapidly, trying to keep from grinning at the thought of the seventy-something widows navigating Facebook. "Wait a minute—he advertises. He has a website, I've seen it."

"Yes, but the new wave of advertising is on Facebook," Mrs. Ludlow explained patiently, as if Kate had been a new student. "Tony says the website is enough, that his customers find him. I keep explaining that he could have more customers, but apparently he doesn't agree."

Kate tried to imagine this conversation between the sweet white-haired lady and Tony. It made her want to giggle.

"Yes, I happen to agree with you, Connie," said another woman from behind Kate.

Kate turned around to see the formidable Mrs. Eileen Sweet, matriarch of the Sweetheart Inn and ranch. She was dressed elegantly in lavender, her black coat over one arm. She held the coat out to Kate, who took it and hung it on the coat hooks along the back wall. When Kate turned around, she saw Mrs. Thalberg frowning at Mrs. Sweet.

"She's our server, not a coat check girl," Mrs. Thalberg said dryly.

Mrs. Sweet stiffened, eyeing the other woman with narrowed eyes from beneath the brim of her equally elegant hat.

Kate didn't want to be the cause of any arguments. "Ladies, please, I don't mind. We're kind of slow right now anyway. I'll hang all your coats. You don't want them falling off onto the floor—although I did mop it this morning."

They tried to protest, but she ignored them, then brought water and menus before escaping once again.

Out near the bar, she saw Tony talking to his dad. Tony caught sight of her, and she overheated with embarrassment about what they'd been doing last night.

"Hi, Mr. De Luca," she said, forcing cheerfulness.

Tony raised an eyebrow at her, and she told herself to take it down a notch.

Mr. De Luca nodded at her. "Kate, nice to see you. Are the widows in the back room?"

"They are. Are you on their committee, too?"

"Yep. And in Rosemary's poker club, too."

"Mrs. Thalberg plays poker." Kate mentally added this new twist to her perception of the little old ladies.

Tony eyed his dad. "And he's been teaching Sunday school with *Rosemary* for years now."

His dad eyed him back. "And that's a bad thing?"

Tony raised both hands. "Not at all, Dad."

Mr. De Luca ambled toward the back room.

"What was that about?" Kate asked, leaning on the bar.

She noticed Tony's gaze dip to her barely visible cleavage, but he looked away before she could elbow him.

"Just teasing him," he said. "I know for certain when I was a kid he never dated anyone after Mom's death."

Kate rolled her eyes. "I don't know how you can know that for certain."

"Well, you have me there. But I'm pretty certain. He dated occasionally in his sixties, but nothing serious."

"You worried he's lonely?"

Tony shrugged. "A bit." He looked toward the back room. "But he certainly knows a lot of women."

Kate eyed him. "*Tsk tsk*. Those ladies made you sound like you're in the dark ages because they advertised your Christmas booth on Facebook *for* you."

Tony rolled his eyes. "Not this again."

"Social media—it's everywhere, Tony."

"Look, I have a website for the tavern, and I even have my personal page on Facebook."

"But only because Ethan dragged you on kicking and screaming. He told me."

Tony chuckled. "Okay, so it's kinda fun to see people's boarding photos and stuff like that. But anyone can see my list of events on the website, or on posters hung in the windows."

"What kind of events?"

"You'll be working one—the Broncos Brunch. We're really busy on Sundays during football season."

She leaned against the bar and eyed him curiously. "What else do you do?"

"We have a pub crawl, where a couple of local bars get together and advertise each other's special drinks for a night. We have a trivia night occasionally, and a live band on weekdays to draw more customers in. It's been working."

"Sure, but you could always do more. Facebook lets you notify your regular customers, who might then remember to tell their friends."

"Uh-huh. What are you, a Facebook salesman?"

"No, just a new employee who thinks you could increase your customer base."

His smile faded a bit as he studied her. "I'll take it under advisement. Maybe you should go back and take the widows' orders."

"I hear Chef ringing the bell."

"I'll run the food. Don't keep those ladies waiting, or they'll dis me on Facebook."

She chuckled and went into the back room. The orders were swiftly taken, and then she got to hear them praise this year's new Christmas market idea, where a percentage of the profits went to the preservation fund. They all were in agreement, however much they seemed to rub each other the wrong way in their personal lives. Or to be honest, how Mrs. Sweet rubbed certain ladies the wrong way.

"So," said Mrs. Thalberg an hour later as Kate began to pick up their dirty dishes, "how do your parents feel about you working for the competition?"

Kate froze with the first plate in her hand. "Well, I never thought of it that way. I guess I don't consider a bar as competing against an Italian restaurant. Each serves a different need, don't you think?"

"True," Mrs. Sweet said. "Just as I don't consider an Italian restaurant as competition for the restaurant at the inn. There's room for many varieties."

Kate wasn't sure that was a compliment—she saw by Mrs. Palmer's expression that the lady was *certain* it wasn't but she let it go.

Mrs. Sweet eyed her with interest. "Your family

must think it strange that not only are you working for a rival but he's also your ex-husband."

"We've always remained on decent terms for our son's sake."

"And does it not make for awkward situations?" Mrs. Sweet asked.

Kate prayed she was not blushing, and she deliberately avoided looking at Mr. De Luca. "Not awkward, no. Although let me set the record straight. Regardless of what you might hear, I did not lose my job, and I am not broke."

The ladies chuckled.

"Tony tells me he challenged her when she had nothing to do," Mr. De Luca said. Then he eyed Kate with approval. "Looks like you proved you could handle yourself."

She hoped her smile wasn't as lame as it felt. "Thanks."

"Nothing to do?" Mrs. Sweet asked sharply. "Aren't you on vacation?"

"A two-month sabbatical."

Mrs. Sweet looked skeptical, but before she could say anything else, Tony stepped into the doorway. "Kate? You have another table."

She took as many dirty dishes as she could handle. "I'll be back in a little while. Hope your meeting is going well."

As she put the dirty dishes in the bus bin behind the bar, she said to Tony, "Thanks for saving me."

"You do have a table—although I could have started it for you. What was going on back there?"

"Lots of personal questions about why I'm working for you."

"You didn't explain that you were hot for me?"

The silverware crashed together as she dropped it in the bin before pulling herself together again. Breezing by him, she said, "You wish." Then she had another thought. "Hey, do me a favor. Write your sister's cell phone number down for me."

"Why?"

"We have a truce, remember? I'm going to take it another step further."

"Okay, I'll give you her home phone, too. You know how bad reception can be around here. And in return for that favor, I want reassurances that my sister is okay."

"No details she doesn't authorize," Kate said, grabbing glasses of ice water for her table.

"Fine."

From behind the bar, Tony watched Kate surreptitiously. She smiled at her new customers, bubbled with friendliness, all things he would never associate with her lawyer persona. She really had remembered all her old people skills.

Then he remembered her suggestions about using social media to market the tavern. For a moment, he flashed into the past and wondered if she was trying to get him more business because she didn't think he was doing well enough on his own, that the tavern wasn't quite good enough for her.

And then he stopped himself; that was an old response to an old attitude. Kate was working for him now, and though she certainly didn't need the money, she was doing a good job and obviously trying to help him with her ideas.

He wasn't surprised that she still felt guilty over all the work she'd had to do in law school, the work that had taken her away from Ethan. She loved their son, and Tony knew it was difficult to be away from him. Maybe that guilt was part of the reason she was here at the tavern.

Chapter 11

"Lyndsay? It's Kate."

There was a momentary silence. Kate winced, hoping the mountain cell phone interference wasn't going to make this more difficult.

"Kate," Lyndsay began slowly. "Is everything okay?"

"Oh, yeah, of course. I didn't mean to startle you or anything. And I waited until I thought you'd be done with school before calling. I was wondering, with our truce and everything, if you'd go to the Christmas market with me tonight."

It was Friday afternoon, Kate had the day off, and she figured she should start to see more people—and not just in a work capacity.

"Oh."

Lyndsay gave another long pause, and Kate found her shoulders sagging.

"Okay, I guess," Lyndsay said. "I'm a couple blocks

over from Grace Street. I could walk to you and then we could go together."

Kate felt an absurd desire to pump a fist in the air. "Great! The widows were at the tavern yesterday discussing the market, and it made me really curious. Have you gone?"

"Nope, I'm a virgin, too."

Kate smiled. "I hear there are food booths, too. I guess I'll skip dinner and see what we find."

"I'll be there around six. That okay?"

"It's a date. See you then." Kate hung up, feeling relieved and happy.

She already had a good start on her day, having had a conversation with Howie Jr., of Deering Family Real Estate. He'd been a few years behind her in high school and seemed genuinely pleased that she was at least temporarily in town. They'd discussed what she wanted, and by midafternoon, he'd e-mailed a half dozen listings for her to look at online. Once she picked the ones she liked, they would set up a time to see them this weekend. She was already giddy about it. Her mother had been a little disappointed, but she'd understood.

When Lyndsay knocked on the door, Kate shrugged into her heavy jacket and answered it. Lyndsay was wearing a winter headband over her ears again. "Did I tell you how good you look in bangs?" Kate said.

Lyndsay blinked. "Thanks. And I like your hair short."

"Thanks back. Now that we're done admiring each other, let's go!" As they stepped onto the porch and walked down the stairs, Kate glanced at Tony's house.

"I did invite Ethan, but he very politely declined. I don't think Christmas crafts are a teenage boy's idea of fun."

"Since I'm with kids his age all day long, I can agree with your assessment."

They smiled at each other. It wasn't a completely relaxed smile, but Kate thought there was progress. As the snow softly fell, they cut across Seventh Street, then walked up Nellie.

"I know Ethan's never had you for a teacher," Kate said, hands deep in her pockets for warmth. "Was that deliberate?"

"School policy."

"So . . . do the other teachers say good things?"

Lyndsay laughed. "You've seen his report cards. He's a dream to teach, and no one has anything bad to say."

"Whew, glad to hear it. His success is mostly due to your brother, who keeps on top of things during the week."

"Well I know that, but it's nice to see you do, too. And now you can stop buttering me up."

They exchanged a more relaxed grin.

When they reached the park that lined Silver Creek, Kate gasped at the beauty of the gazebo outlined in white lights, with a tall evergreen behind it illuminated with even more lights. Streams of people moved past them, and she saw a little village of wooden huts, with open doorways and half walls on three sides. They were hung with pine branches and lights, lit from inside so shoppers could see all their wares. Her mouth watered at the hot dogs and pretzels, the cheese displays, the German waffles, and the Christmas pastries from Sugar and Spice. Emily waved at them, but her little booth was mobbed, so Kate and Lyndsay kept walking. Besides Tony's Tavern's hot spiced wine, they could have specialty coffees and hot chocolate, even a great selection of international beers. Every Christmas tree decoration was available, from home-made knitted crafts to European glass ornaments, along with specialty gifts. There was a booth where kids could make their own Christmas ornaments.

Kate couldn't help shaking her head in wonder as they strolled the aisles. "This is just beautiful! And the aroma . . ."

"I know, my mouth is watering. I need a hot dog."

"I might try the German waffles—they even had pesto-flavored with sour cream."

While they ate and wandered, teenagers either said hi to Lyndsay or went out of their way to avoid her. The college-age kids stopped her to catch up.

"Hazards of the job," Lyndsay said at one point. "You can't take the rejection seriously, because there's a lot of rejection at this age."

"I don't get it. I liked my teachers."

"Oh, believe me, I always like teacher's pets like you."

Kate laughed, even as she licked sour cream off her thumb. "Yeah, I was a good girl—but you weren't much different."

"I might have been good, but I didn't get the grades you did."

Kate frowned. "I was a little obsessed."

"Well, it got you a free ride to college, didn't it?"

Kate shrugged. "I guess you're right. Shall we do some Christmas shopping?"

They passed another hour at the Christmas market, until both were loaded down with bags. The snow had begun to fall a little more steadily, and Kate couldn't feel her nose anymore. Her big furry boots were keeping her feet warm, but Lyndsay admitted her leather boots were falling down on the job.

"Mind if we stop at Espresso Yourself?" Kate asked. "I'd love to just sit and talk."

Lyndsay nodded, although she did look curious. "Surprised you don't want to go to Sugar and Spice. You know everyone who works there."

"And that's the reason I can't go there tonight. I promise I'll explain."

At the coffee shop on Main Street, there was a wall of specialty coffees on display like knickknacks, lots of overstuffed chairs and booths, and a long counter where you could order even as you looked at mouthwatering donuts, pastries, and cookies.

"The owner, Suzie, buys hers from the Sweetheart Inn," Lyndsay whispered as they sat down to wait for their order. "I think Sugar and Spice is better, but they can hardly use the competition's pastries, right?"

When their order came, they held their hot mugs in their cold hands and breathed in the steam. Kate looked hesitantly at her once-best friend, and suddenly the need to talk seemed to spill out of her.

"Lyndsay, I hate to bother you with this, but I could really use some advice."

Lyndsay stared at her a bit apprehensively. "It doesn't have to do with Tony, does it?"

Kate chuckled. "No, and maybe now you see why I didn't ask your advice before."

"Well, maybe. Is it Ethan?"

"No, it's my law firm, and the reason I'm on sabbatical."

Lyndsay straightened up. "I'm certainly interested. I don't know if I can help, but I think I can be objective."

"And that's just what I need. Can you keep this private as well? I shouldn't even be talking to you about it, but I'm feeling pretty frustrated, and I don't know what else to do."

"Of course I'll keep this between us."

Kate let out her breath. "Thanks. I hope you don't mind if I seem to rattle on. It's a complicated situation, and well, ask questions anytime you want."

"Okay, fire away." Lyndsay took another sip of her latte and looked at Kate with a serious expression.

"So . . . I've been representing a biochemical engineering company. They're trying to get a new cattle growth hormone—we'll just call it Hormone X—approved by the FDA. I handle the legal aspects, submitting applications for them, etc. Well, I discovered an undated report that the company obviously hadn't meant to include. It referenced a cattle growth hormone but didn't specifically say it was related to Hormone X. Apparently it's been known in very rare cases to cause humans to have flu symptoms just by eating the beef from the treated cow."

Lyndsay wrinkled her nose. "That sounds bad."

"I know. But again, the important part, according to the senior partners, is that it's not labeled as Hormone X. If it had been, then this side effect would have had to be disclosed to the FDA. It could cost my client a hundred million if denied. Having to go back to the drawing board on research could cost almost as much, and they might still be denied. I have to be so careful here. If something will injure the public, I have an ethical duty to investigate. *But,* and this is the big *but,* the report didn't say it was about Hormone X, so according to the two senior partners I'm working with, I have no duty to ask for additional info, or even to include it in the packet I send to the FDA. We're just supposed to assume it's for another project still in the research phase."

"So you discussed this with the senior partners," Lyndsay said, not even bothering to phrase it as a question.

"You would be right. I really want to ask my client to clarify the report, but the partners don't want to piss off a good client or scare away any others if this got out. So . . . I kept bringing it up."

Lyndsay winced. "And got yourself a nice long sabbatical."

"They want me to 'get my priorities straight,'" she said, using air quotes. "They told my clients I'm on leave for family reasons—they don't want clients thinking the firm is unstable. But I know my priorities. If I broke attorney-client privilege, I'd lose my license. I don't want to do that. I just want to ask our client about the report. This whole mess has really scared me.

Everything I've worked for could go up in smoke. I love the law, Lynds, but part of why I chose a big-city firm was because I knew it would support Ethan no matter what happened, give him the best chance at a great life. I sacrificed so much that I even ended up sacrificing time with my son—only to find out I'm not trusted? I don't even know if it's worth it anymore."

Lyndsay reached across the table and touched her arm. "I'm sorry."

"No, please don't be. I made my choices—including this client. I know they're ambitious and driven—they're good at what they do. In some ways, it's like looking in a mirror," she added with a wince. "And not in a good way."

"No point putting yourself down," Lyndsay said. "You're trying to figure out the right thing to do here."

"And that's my dilemma. Any suggestions?"

Lyndsay took a sip of her latte, brows lowered in concentration. "Well . . . can you do any digging on your own, to put your mind at rest about your client? I don't know how long you've been working for them, but maybe there's some internet research you can do, to see if there's stuff way in their past, something like a pattern, you know?"

"Hmm," Kate said, stirring her coffee absently. "I did a lot of research when I first worked for them, but maybe I should go farther into the deep, dark past. Just because I didn't come across any issues doesn't mean they're not buried somewhere. Lyndsay, thanks for the reminder."

"And then, if you find they made a habit of getting

in trouble, you make a decision about what to do. But at least you'd have history to back you up."

"Okay, I'll do it. Thank you!" Kate took a sip of her coffee, then grinned. "Speaking of something buried in the past, I found my trombone in a closet."

"A blast from the past. I still play the trumpet, you know."

"You're kidding! That's great."

"Yeah, I get together with some people and play sometimes. You should come."

The invitation made Kate's eyes sting, and she blinked rapidly. "Thanks, I'd really like that—even though I'm woefully out of practice." She cleared her throat. "Do you still write? I remember reading your stuff in high school."

Lyndsay actually blushed. "Yeah, but don't tell anyone. I've had some rejections, and I think about self-publishing, but I haven't tried that either."

"Can I read some of it?" Kate asked eagerly.

"No! I would feel ridiculous."

"Oh, come on! Wasn't I your editor in high school?"

Lyndsay laughed. "Yeah, well, I was a lot braver then." She sighed. "Someday, maybe."

And they smiled at each other.

In between work shifts over the weekend, Kate saw a few houses with Howie Deering, then took Ethan through her top two and let him help make the decision. They chose a little Cape Cod on Sixth Street, only a couple blocks from Tony's, which would make it easier for Ethan to go back and forth. The second floor was right beneath the steep roof, and since it had a bathroom, Ethan called the whole second floor his own.

Kate loved that even the linens were provided in the fully equipped house. The kitchen, dining room, and living room were all an open floor plan, with dark wood floors and scattered rugs. The paintings on the wall were all of the Roaring Fork Valley, representing every season. The fireplace had a gas starter, and she anticipated evenings spent on the cream-colored sofa, staring into that fire. Maybe if she tried hard enough, this really could be a relaxing vacation for her—when she wasn't researching GAC Biochemical or working at Tony's. Okay, maybe she was only capable of so much relaxing.

"All you need to do is buy groceries, Mom," Ethan said, looking into the fridge. "They've already got ketchup, mustard, mayo . . ."

Kate laughed. "Is this a hint that you're hungry?"

"No," he said innocently, "just letting you know. When are you moving in?"

"Mr. Deering says I can move in today. I've already packed my luggage. Let's go get it."

It was Sunday evening, and Christina had invited her sons over for dinner, as if Kate had been moving out of their home for the first time. Kate took a lot of ribbing about working at Tony's instead of Carmina's, and she knew Walt was more serious than teasing, but she did her best to take the jokes with good humor. By the time her brothers left, she was really ready to be in her own place and relax.

After helping clean up in the kitchen, Ethan slid on his coat. "Hey, Mom, I have a big project spread all over the basement floor at Dad's. It's due tomorrow. Mind if I miss your first night in the new and temporary house?"

She smiled at his strange wording, then dismissed her curiosity. It *was* a temporary house. "Of course not. But I need a kiss."

He made a big production of rolling his eyes as he kissed her cheek. Then he kissed his grandma and squatted to pet Barney on his dog bed before heading home.

Kate ran upstairs looking for last-minute stuff.

"Wait, you have to take leftovers," Christina insisted as Kate piled her second and last suitcase in the front hall.

But it wasn't just leftovers from that night's ziti. Her mom had also prepared a couple casseroles.

"You can freeze these and defrost as needed," Christina said.

Kate frowned. "Mom, when did you have time to do all this? I know you were at the restaurant, and Joe's team had that foul-shooting fund-raiser while I was working."

"Oh, it was easy."

"But Mom, I don't think you take it easy enough."

Christina arched a brow. "I'm only sixty-one. That's the new forty-one. And who are you to talk? You can't even take a proper vacation."

"Well, not a two-month one, anyway. I guess I know where I get my overworking tendencies from. Maybe you should show me a better example and sit down and read a book."

"You remind me, and we'll do it together."

Kate rolled her eyes. She kissed her mom on the cheek and quietly said, "Thank you. Thank you for everything, especially for not making me feel bad about moving out. I'll stop by all the time."

"You do that. And come to the restaurant more, too."

"I will!"

After loading her suitcase and the food in the car, Kate drove the few blocks to her new—and temporary—home. With a sigh of happiness, she closed the door behind her and leaned against it, looking around at the pretty interior. First thing she did was start a fire.

She put away the food her mom had given her and was just making a grocery list when there was a knock on her back door. Frowning, she moved the curtain aside—and Tony waved at her.

She felt a shock of pleasure but tried to hide it as she opened the door. "What are you doing here?"

"Came to see the new place. I even snuck through your backyard."

"Like I'm a guilty secret?"

"No, a guilty pleasure."

That sent a frisson of delight up her spine, but she held on to a frown—just barely.

"Come on, it's cold out here," he said.

Sighing, she stepped back. "I see you managed to avoid getting here in time to help unload the car."

"You don't want your neighbors to see me, right? I know everybody, and it could get back to . . . somebody." After slipping off his boots and leaving them on a mat near the door, he put his coat on a hook.

She gave him a wry grin. "We'd be gossip for a week. You know this town. And there's Ethan."

"I know. We don't want the kid to come to the wrong conclusions." He looked around. "Nice place."

"Yeah, I'm amazed I was able to rent it for such a long period during the winter season. But it's a new vacation rental, so I lucked out. Want a tour?"

"Thought you'd never ask," he said. "And then I'll go, I promise."

His voice was lower than normal, as if she'd asked him to bed. Swallowing, she turned away. As she walked through the two bedrooms downstairs and the one upstairs, he was always just behind her, a little too close. The hairs on the back of her neck were raised, and she was having a hard time talking about the house, when she was having fantasies about him touching her.

"You—you don't have to follow me so closely," she said, sounding breathless, though she tried not to.

He put both hands on the door frame and leaned indolently toward her. "I was just taking the tour."

"Now you're trying too hard to sound innocent." She crossed her arms beneath her breasts when she realized her hands were trembling. It had been a long time since a man had made her feel so desired.

"I didn't say I was innocent. I'm amazed I didn't run right into you, since I was mostly looking at your ass."

She should have laughed, but her mouth was dry and blood was pounding in her ears, and she thought her skin would burn if he touched her.

Then the front doorbell rang.

She sprang away from him. "You've gotta hide. I can't explain why you're here without Ethan."

"Yeah, all right, I get that. Whoever it is will want a tour. I'll be in the basement."

She flung his coat and boots at him as he opened the basement door, even as the doorbell rang again. Closing the door on his smiling face, she took a deep breath and walked calmly to the front door. Through the peephole, she saw Lyndsay, then winced.

Pasting a smile on her face, she opened the door. "Hi, Lynds! This is a late night for a schoolteacher."

Lyndsay laughed and stepped onto the tiled square that marked the front entrance, handing over a bottle of wine. "That's why I can't stay too long." She looked around. "Nice place!"

"Thanks. And thanks so much for the wine." For politeness' sake, Kate had to ask, "Want me to take your coat and break out some wineglasses?" when all she really wanted was to have Lyndsay leave before she saw something Kate didn't want her to see. Yeah, they were friends once more, but if Lyndsay knew who was in the basement, she'd think Kate was going to hurt him all over again.

"Naw, no time tonight. The wine is a housewarming gift for you. I'll just kick my boots off and walk around."

Kate repeated the tour she'd just given, glancing hurriedly away from one particular door. "That's the basement. Dank and unfinished."

"Too bad. Thought there'd be a Ping-Pong table down there or something."

Kate laughed. "We used to play for hours in your parents' basement."

Lyndsay put her back to the fire and shivered. "Until Tony butted in and insisted on playing."

"He did love to bug us." Kate wanted to get off the subject.

"Or he loved to bug *you*. But apparently he doesn't bug you too much now, since you seem to have no problem working with him."

"We're sort of friends, I guess," Kate said, not quite able to meet Lyndsay's eyes. "He treats me like any of the servers. Nine years is a long time apart. Emotions settle down." *Some of them.*

"I'm glad. I'm glad for all of us." Lyndsay's smile turned softer. "I kind of feel like a weight has been lifted off me."

Kate hugged her. "Me, too."

They squeezed each other a moment, then let go.

"Well, I'll say good night," Lyndsay said, stepping back into her boots and zipping up the sides. "Got a little more prep to do before school tomorrow."

"Say hi to Ethan for me."

"Oh, he'd love that."

They both laughed.

"Did you start researching your client?" Lyndsay asked.

"Not yet. I wanted to settle into the house first. But I'll definitely have time now."

When Lyndsay had left, Kate looked out the front window, waving as her friend drove away. She gave a satisfied sigh, glad to be able to say "her friend" about Lyndsay again.

"You know, there *is* a Ping-Pong table down here," Tony said.

She gasped, almost having forgotten he was there in her happiness at making up with his sister. "You were listening."

"Of course I was. I had to be ready with a story in case she insisted on seeing the basement."

Watching him walk closer, Kate put her hands on her hips to keep from touching him. "And what was the story?"

"I was checking the furnace for you. Ethan was concerned."

He stood there, lanky and broad-shouldered, looking utterly irresistible as the crackle of logs in the fireplace filled the silence.

"I should make you go home," she finally whispered.

He whispered back, "I know you're right. Do you want me to?"

She bit her lip, unable to say anything, and just looked at his mouth.

He took her upper arms in his hands and drew her against him. She moaned at the hard warmth of his body against her thighs, her belly, her breasts. One hand he kept flat against her lower back, the other he used to cup her face.

"Kate," he whispered. "I can't stop thinking about you."

She leaned her cheek deeper into his hand. "Maybe it's sex you can't stop thinking about."

His fingers moved through her hair, caressing her. "You and sex seem to be all wrapped together in my mind." He pressed his hips into hers. "See?"

She couldn't mistake his erection. He leaned down and kissed her far more gently this time, running his tongue along her lips and dipping between to explore her mouth. She clung to him, standing on tiptoe to mold herself against him.

Then his hand slipped down over her butt, cupping her, bringing her even closer. She rubbed against him as if she couldn't wait to be touched. He kissed her cheek, her forehead, the other cheek, and she dropped her head back as he made his way down her neck. She was lost in sensation, in need, and was dangerously close to no turning back.

Chapter 12

Tony was on fire, like his skin was aflame and only the coolness of Kate would ease his desperation. She tasted like the sweetest peach; he could have licked every inch of her skin. He nibbled on her neck, bit gently where it met her shoulder, felt her shudder in his arms.

And then he let his hand cup her breast from below, felt the thin bra, the hard point of her nipple, and imagined what she'd look like without the oversize shirt.

Would she look the same naked? He wanted to know. He wanted it too much.

He groaned and broke the kiss.

She looked up at him with those plaintive lavender eyes, tender and moist, those eyes he'd once looked into and known he could deny her nothing. Desire made her lips part, made her moan—

He realized he was still holding her breast, and for just a moment, he let himself feel the hardness of her nipple against his palm. He wanted to bury his face between those breasts and give them both pleasure.

But he let her go. "God help me, I'm regretting stopping already."

"Me, too," she admitted reluctantly, then reached up to run her fingers through her tangled hair as if she didn't know what to do with herself.

He watched the sight as if in a daze. Her shirt caught on her breasts, emphasizing them by firelight. Her blond hair practically glowed, reflecting the flickering light.

And then she smiled at him. "Let me get your coat," she said, going into the kitchen.

He followed her. "I'm going out the back door anyway." He shrugged into his coat and pulled on his boots. "Sweet dreams."

He went out into the snow, thinking he could use a little cooling down.

But as he walked, hands in his pockets, cowboy hat keeping the worst of the snow from his face, he realized that he felt . . . lighter, more content, ever since Kate had shown up in Valentine Valley. It was as if without her, his life had been more routine, quiet, sad. Not that he'd ever shown that to Ethan. Tony had known that the failure of his marriage had left a deep hole in his heart, but he hadn't imagined how just being with Kate again on a regular basis would change him. It was dangerous, he knew. He should back off right now—but could he?

For several days, all Kate did was work at Tony's, conduct internet research on her client, decorate her house and a Christmas tree with some of her childhood ornaments with Ethan, squeeze in some walks with Barney, and attend Joe's basketball game. The research filled up her time, and she was glad to have it. She felt . . . better, more like herself, more in control of her career. It kept her from the yawning precipice of wondering if she was failing after all she'd put into her law career, wondering about everything it had cost her.

And then there was Tony, always watching her when no one was looking. The fact that he desired her after everything they'd been through made her feel wanted and important. But it was scary, too, because she knew that with one wrong move, one or both of them could be terribly hurt again. And she'd vowed never to risk another divorce. And if she didn't find a man she could trust that way? Then she wouldn't marry.

While she was at work, she thought often about the widows' suggestion that Tony's Tavern needed to be on Facebook. Tony didn't want to hear this again, she knew, but she wanted to be of help besides serving. There had to be some big, extravagant event he'd want to advertise, a way to convince him he needed to use social media. But what?

Through all this, Ethan spent a few extra nights at her new place, and she almost felt like a regular mom. But this left Tony alone more than he was used to, and she wanted to ask what he did with himself. She couldn't be so personal, though; not after the intimacy they'd shared. But she hoped he didn't feel bad about

Ethan seeming to choose her for a while. The only unusual thing was Ethan declaring that he liked having
two different homes. It countered the ski club dilemma,
which he still hadn't brought up to her. And although
she was glad he was so easily accommodated, something about Ethan's assertion nagged at her, though she
couldn't think what.

On Friday afternoon, she was finishing up her side
work as Nicole and Erika took over for the evening
shift. Lyndsay came by and sat at the bar. Kate put her
apron in the linen bag in the kitchen, grabbed the beer
she'd left under the counter, and joined Lyndsay at the
bar.

"Drinking on the job?" Lyndsay said, smiling.

"It's my shift drink. We're allowed to have it as we
finish up the shift. Right, Tony?" Kate included him in
the conversation because he was obviously listening.
She sipped her beer and watched him, keeping a smile
hidden.

"Sure." The phone rang, and he rolled his eyes. "Has
to be the tenth call in the last ten minutes."

"It's Friday during the holidays," she said.

He cradled the phone against his shoulder and
walked away.

"Speaking of holidays, you doing anything tonight?"
Lyndsay asked.

"Nope, although I'm not sure what Ethan has going
on."

"All the stores are having a Christmas open house.
Special sales, goodies—anything to make us shop. Do
you want to stroll around?"

Kate nodded. "That sounds wonderful. Let me change, grab something to eat, and I'll be ready."

"Food you cook?" Tony said, from where he stood at the POS. "Is that wise?"

"Hey, I've gotten pretty good over the years," she said, slightly lying.

He glanced at her, smiling. "You and Ethan seem to go out to eat a lot on the weekends."

"Just a boy's exaggeration." But she briefly turned her head away from him so her eyes wouldn't give her away. "Hey, Tony, does Ethan have plans tonight?"

"He's spending the night at Brad's." His brows lowered. "He didn't let you know? It is your time with him."

"Don't get all frowning-dad on me. It's no problem. It actually frees me for a girls' night out."

She and Lyndsay smiled at each other.

Kate stir-fried chicken and vegetables when she got home, then dressed in warm jeans and tall furry boots. Her parka was well lined and would keep her warm between stores. She met up with Lyndsay outside, and they walked toward Main Street.

"Oh, have you been to Leather and Lace yet?" Lyndsay asked. "Whitney owns it. Really beautiful lingerie."

"I haven't. Let's go!"

The store was in an old Victorian on Fourth Street just off Main. There were golden balls hung from varied-length ribbons in the large plate glass windows that bracketed the front door, and solitary candles in the upper story. Inside, Kate fell in love with the old-fashioned displays—the antique dressers and buffets, the way the lingerie was draped across hat boxes and large, old-fashioned jewelry boxes. The Christmas decorations were old fashioned, too, like little ceramic elves set up amidst pine boughs and, of course, plenty of lights strung everywhere. There was a tray of tiny little European chocolates for the open house.

The lingerie itself was elegant and sexy, and just for a moment, Kate thought of wearing it for Tony.

Damn, he was on her mind too much in Valentine Valley.

"What do you think of the leather necklaces?" Lyndsay asked, pointing to the jewelry section. "Josh Thalberg makes those each individually."

"Wow, I've heard about his work, but I've never seen it. I think I remember something from last year—didn't he get famous for a while?"

"His picture did. Women drooled over it, and some even came to town looking for him."

"I remember him as being a private guy. That must have been difficult. Well, with all that notoriety, I just have to own one."

As Kate was making her choice, Whitney spotted them and came over. "Hi, ladies!"

"No baby on your hip," Kate said, smiling.

"Not today, but believe me, sometimes Livvie comes to work with Mommy."

"What about Daddy's work?" Lyndsay asked.

"Oh, he's already had our precious baby up on a horse—while I covered my eyes and tried not to look."

They all chuckled.

"Josh's leather work is incredible," Kate said. "I'm having a hard time choosing just one."

"Thanks. You should see the beautiful Baby's First Christmas ornament he carved for Livvie. I'm such a wuss—I cried when I saw it."

They chatted a few more minutes, then let Whitney get back to work. Kate and Lyndsay each made a few purchases before heading to the next store, La Belle Femme. There, they were offered ribbon candy as they browsed through the uniquely designed women's clothing. At the Vista Gallery of Art, they sipped punch and strolled through four seasons' worth of landscapes from the Roaring Fork Valley and Glenwood Springs, all the way down to Independence Pass.

Out on Main Street, shoppers were out in force, along with carolers and Dickens characters. When Scrooge was led past them by the Ghost of Christmas Future, several little kids hid behind their parents. In the distance, they could hear the sleigh bells from the horse and wagon giving people free rides through town.

At Monica's Flowers and Gifts, Monica offered a selection of Christmas cookies, which she confessed were from Sugar and Spice next door.

"Don't tell Em I told you," Monica whispered, smiling toward another couple as they browsed through her consignment crafts made by local artists. "She thought it was unfair to give her bakery more than one store's promotion." She waved a hand. "Oh, please."

"How's Travis's new business?" Lyndsay asked. "Oh, sorry, Kate, but did you meet Monica's boyfriend, Travis, last week?"

"I don't think so."

"He's ex-Secret Service, and discovered Valentine

when he helped prep the presidential wedding last May. Now he's starting his own executive protection firm in Aspen."

"Almost ready to open officially," Monica said with obvious pride. "Of course, he's done some work *unofficially* in the last couple months. He'd protected the children of a Saudi prince a few years ago, and the man insisted on hiring him again, even though he wasn't Secret Service anymore. Apparently Travis is very good at computer games with little princes."

Kate was rather astonished. "And a man with such a worldwide past wanted to move to Valentine Valley?"

Monica grinned. "I am rather hard to resist." As they all laughed, she added, "Are you going to Sugar and Spice?"

"Sure, it was going to be part of our rounds tonight," Lyndsay said.

"Come at nine after closing. We'll all be hanging out."

"Thanks for the invite," Kate said. It still surprised her that Tony's friends wanted to include her. Monica was another person a few years behind her in school, so she'd never known her all that well. But Tony had forged a deep circle of friends in Valentine the last nine years, and she found she envied it. The fact that he didn't mind sharing it with her was more touching than she wanted to admit.

Kate and Lyndsay wandered through the other stores, finishing up their Christmas shopping, to Kate's satisfaction. They showed up at Sugar and Spice about fifteen minutes before closing, only to find many of their friends already milling around, buying snacks and hot drinks, talking about their purchases.

Mrs. Thalberg, who was behind the cash register, called, "Kate!"

Kate approached with a smile. "Hi, Mrs. Thalberg. Hope you guys had a successful open house."

"We did. But I hear tell you rented a house for the next few weeks."

"I did, though it was hard to leave my mom," Kate admitted. "But it's kind of nice to spread out, you know?"

"Of course. Fish and family each start to stink after three days."

Kate snorted a laugh.

"Benjamin Franklin," said Mrs. Ludlow.

Mrs. Palmer shot her a wide-eyed stare. "Don't tell me you're goin' batty already."

"Benjamin Franklin originated that phrase," Mrs. Ludlow said patiently. "Well, the correct version is actually 'Guests, like fish, begin to smell after three days.'"

Mrs. Palmer rolled her eyes. "Schoolteachers."

"Hey, Kate, get to the end of the line," Will teased from his place midway back.

She stepped away from the display counter, both hands upraised. "God forbid I get between a man and his pastries."

"Cheesecake, thank you," he said. "But I'll cut you some slack and treat you ladies. What will you have?"

Kate could have sworn Lyndsay actually blushed.

"I'll have peach cobbler and a latte," Lyndsay said.

"Chocolate mousse cake and hot chocolate for me," Kate added. "Thanks, Will."

"A chocolate lover," Will said. "I like that."

"Are you blushing?" Kate whispered to Lyndsay as they walked away.

"No! I'm just feeling hot after being outside."

Lyndsay looked at her like she was nuts, so Kate let it go.

Will joined them at a table with their goodies just as the last of the regular customers left. Emily turned the CLOSED sign facing out.

While Kate ate and chatted with Lyndsay and Will, she saw Tony come through the front door, then hold it open for Josh Thalberg. This was the first time she'd seen Josh with the baby, who looked adorable in a pink jacket with a hood that gave her bunny ears. There was just something about big strong men holding a baby that got to a woman.

She noticed Tony glance her way, then do a subtle double take. She wasn't sure what it was about until Will flashed his smile at her, the dimple in his chin emphasizing his strong, handsome jaw. The man was a born flirt.

Was Tony surprised to see her with an eligible man after they'd both forgotten themselves over a kiss? She felt a little self-conscious, then told herself to get over it. She could talk with Will. But she kept feeling Tony's gaze on her occasionally, and much as he was his smiling, genial self, she wondered what he was thinking.

To her surprise, he sat right down at her table.

Will grinned at him. "Hey, Tony, left the tavern early?"

"Stephen's got it under control."

Will nodded, then slyly glanced at Kate. "I hear you couldn't stand living next door to my boy here."

She swallowed a piece of cake and eyed Will. "Are you suggesting something?" she teased back. "I do work for the man, so it's obvious we have no problems."

Will turned to Tony. "No problems at all?"

Tony shook his head, giving Kate a glance that skimmed over her and kept moving. She gave a little internal sigh of relief. She didn't want to be a topic of conversation that could get back to Ethan. Lyndsay looked between them, gave the smallest frown that made Kate hold her breath, then went back to eating, seemingly unconcerned.

Emily came out from behind the counter to take Olivia, beating out the widows who clustered around her. They took off the baby's coat, then oohed and aahed over Rudolph the Red-Nosed Reindeer on her tummy. Eventually, the older women departed for the evening, and Emily did the dance women do when holding babies, sashaying around the floor before showing Olivia the little collection of Santas on the coffee counter. Olivia, not quite seven months old, blinked drowsily.

Will saw where Kate was looking. "Em wants a baby bad."

"Hopefully the adoption happens soon," she answered.

"Do you want more kids some day?" Will suddenly asked.

Kate blinked at him in surprise, and to her regret,

she glanced at Tony. "Well, I guess I haven't thought about it. You need a guy for that."

"So you don't know if you want to get married again?"

She wondered if Will was going to continue the personal questions. It wasn't that she minded—if only Tony hadn't been there.

"I'd have to meet the right guy to get married again," she said. "And then . . . yeah, I'd probably want another baby." To her surprise, she blushed.

Lyndsay laughed and elbowed her. "Look at you."

Kate elbowed her back.

"You two might as well be in school again," Tony said, although he looked pleased about it.

Brooke came in with Monica, and Matt Sweet called, "Let's talk wedding plans!"

Adam pulled Brooke into his lap.

"I've got no wedding plans," Monica said, going to sit near Travis.

"She can't even make up her mind about living together," Travis said dryly.

"Hey, we've only been dating seven months. And you were gone for four of those."

"Guilty as charged," Travis said. "Hey, it takes a while to retire from the Secret Service."

There were good-natured groans, and Travis, whose auburn hair was still cut in a military fashion, nodded his head almost regally.

"When the time is right, I'll think about letting you move in," Monica teased, her eyes sly as she leaned into Travis.

"Good thing I'm patient," he said gruffly.

"Well, I'm not," Adam said, slamming a hand down on the table and making everyone jump. "Which is why we're getting married Christmas Eve."

There were gasps of excitement and questions overlapping each other, leading Kate to realize that this was the first official announcement. Enjoying the merriment, she found herself noticing that Lyndsay was smiling, but there was a faint aura of sadness that disappeared so quickly that Kate questioned seeing it. But she remembered Tony saying that Kate wasn't happy. Did it hurt her to see others happy? Kate remembered feeling that way for a time after the divorce, when her pain had seemed magnified in the face of others' contentment. She hoped Lyndsay could eventually talk to her about it, but it could be a long time before their old trust was totally rebuilt.

"Christmas Eve," Nate said, shaking his head. "Sorry you can't use the gazebo like Em and I did, but smart people get married in the summer."

"Hey, we're more original than that, big brother," Brooke said, smiling superiorly. "We're getting married in the riding arena."

Josh was distracted enough from making faces at his baby to say to his sister, "I know you love your new place, but in the winter? Don't you want your guests to enjoy themselves?"

"We're going to rent those giant portable heaters," Brooke said, "and put in one of those temporary dance floors. You dance enough, you'll stay warm."

Kate watched the happy contentment of Brooke and Adam, who answered questions patiently and kept looking at each other with all the love and promise of the future shining in their eyes. And Kate felt . . . old. It had been a long time since she'd felt that excited about the future—or anything else that didn't involve Ethan. But she was only thirty-three years old. Did she want to live through her son for the rest of her life?

Tony was watching her again, his eyes inscrutable. *He* excited her. It had been a long time since a guy had been bold enough to pursue her, and . . . she liked it.

Not that she thought it was a good idea, of course.

The wedding conversation at last turned to Chris Sweet, Will's and Emily's quieter brother, and his fiancée, Heather Armstrong. Heather had come to town from San Francisco to be one of Emily's bridesmaids. Kate had heard that whole story from her mom last year, how Emily's wedding had been livened up with the revelation of a secret romance.

Chris and Heather simply looked at each other with amusement, and shook their heads.

"We may be engaged," Heather said, blushing a redhead's bright blush, "but I'm still growing my business. No time to plan yet."

"What does she do again?" Kate whispered to Lyndsay.

"She owns As You Like It Catering. She's in one of the old Victorians on Second Street. Her food's really good."

For a while Brooke and the girls continued to talk

color schemes and Western wedding decorations, while, as they had in middle school, the guys gravitated to the other side of the bakery, talking football, ranching, or hockey. Gradually the discussion merged again. Kate heard about Brooke's riding school, Adam helping to build houses for military vets, Monica's passion for the environment, even Tony's woodworking, which Ethan had occasionally mentioned to her. They all had hobbies or volunteer work to be excited about, and she realized that even now, researching a law case was all she was doing with her spare time.

"You have a weird look on your face," Lyndsay said quietly.

Kate hesitated before saying, "I don't know. I'm not the oldest person here—"

"You're close."

Kate grinned. "True. But I *feel* like the oldest person here, like my best years are behind me and but for the odd date here and there, all I do is work."

"We have too much in common," Lyndsay said with a sigh.

"But at least you do stuff to keep yourself refreshed, like your band. Even on sabbatical, the only things I'm focusing on are Ethan and my old client."

"And your new job at Tony's," Lyndsay pointed out, beginning to smile.

Kate shrugged and glanced at him, only to realize he'd been watching her. She and Lyndsay hadn't been whispering or hiding their conversation, but Kate still felt awkward.

"Oh, yes, the tavern is keeping me occupied," she

said, feeling herself blush. "And though technically that's work, I actually like talking to people. I feel more connected, and it's wonderful to catch up with people I haven't seen in years."

Tony arched a brow and folded his arms over his chest, still watching her. She felt a flush of embarrassed warmth, remembering how she hadn't understood how he could enjoy a job that wasn't what she'd consider "a career." But that wasn't what her dismay was really about.

"Maybe you're too serious," Will said.

She jumped, having forgotten he was on her other side. "So we're *all* going to discuss my deficiencies?"

"Being serious isn't a deficiency," Will said, "but you take it to extremes."

"And you know me so well, Will Sweet?" she said, trying to be lighthearted.

"You did get awfully serious in college," Lyndsay said reluctantly.

"Well, I *had* to be serious." She could hear the defensiveness in her tone, and she wanted to wince. She kept waiting for Tony to say something, but he remained silent. "I had to have the best grades to get into law school."

"Of course you did," Lyndsay said quickly, "but maybe it got to be a habit. And you can unlearn habits."

A habit? Working wasn't a habit, it was . . . all she would allow herself. She'd spent her childhood learning the importance of it. But . . . had she somehow begun to think she didn't deserve more?

"You should come out to the ranch," Will said. "Get back on a horse, do some riding in the mountains."

"Well, that's a nice invitation, but—"

"Just a suggestion, no pressure. Not a date or anything," he said, chuckling as he looked at Tony.

There was an awkward pause.

Will groaned. "You guys are all so sensitive, tiptoeing around each other."

"I don't think you can call offering my ex-wife a job 'tiptoeing' around her," Tony said dryly. "And Kate can do anything she'd like to do on her sabbatical."

She couldn't look at him, because she knew what he wanted her to do. And it probably wasn't dating Will. She didn't want to date Will, but did she really want her next extracurricular activity to be sleeping with her ex-husband?

The evening was winding down when someone suggested a walk to work off all the dessert they'd eaten. The sky was pure black, stars scattered across like sequins on a dark Christmas ornament. The air was crisp and mountain fresh, her breath a fog in the lamplight on Main Street.

Kate told herself she was with friends again and should enjoy herself.

But she felt Tony behind her, and though he was a quiet guy, he was even quieter than normal. She felt his focus as if she'd had a target on her back. It was almost as if she could feel his gaze on her legs, her butt. When she'd been without her coat in the bakery, he'd glanced at her breasts more than once, until she'd felt that even the sweater had been restrictive.

And now, under the starry night, one by one the members of the group separated, heading toward their respective homes, calling cheerful good nights. She waved and smiled, but it was feeling more and more difficult to ignore Tony behind her, ignore what he wanted.

Chapter 13

Tony found himself eventually walking with just his sister and Kate. When Lyndsay turned down Mabel Street, waving good-bye, he continued to walk at Kate's side.

She eyed him. "This is Valentine Valley. You do know that I can walk home safely. And I didn't see you escorting your sister home."

"That's because this isn't about protecting your delicate self. I'm alone tonight, you're alone tonight." He kept walking beside her, hands in his pockets.

She inhaled swiftly but didn't say anything. He wondered if she was trying to think of all the reasons sleeping together was such a bad idea, like he was. And then, like the little devil on his shoulder, he reminded himself that they were adults, they both knew what they were getting into, no one had any notions that sex would lead to anything more. They'd slept together hundreds and hundreds of times.

Yet it was so risky, especially when their lives would be entwined forever regardless. But all he could think about was how long it had been since he'd touched her. Had her body changed? Had *she* changed? He thought she had, in many ways.

By unspoken agreement, they walked down her shadowy driveway, staying away from the lighted front porch. At the back door, she swung her purse off her shoulder, dug clumsily for the keys, then accidentally dumped them on the snowy stoop. He grabbed them first, unlocked her door, and swung it wide.

"I'm safely home," she whispered, as if a crowd might overhear her. "Thanks for the escort."

He leaned one arm against the doorway, knowing he should leave but unable to move.

"Are you waiting for a kiss good night?" she murmured. "Like we're at the end of a date?"

Moonlight flickered through the bare branches of trees, etching her face. "I know we're not dating."

He dipped his head toward her, and she didn't back away. Her lips were chilly on the outside, so moist and warm on the inside. He tilted his head and took her deeper, heard a low sound from her, but it wasn't a protest.

She suddenly arched her head away. "Inside."

They practically fell over the threshold in their eagerness. After shutting the door, he leaned her against a wall and laughed against her mouth. She wasn't laughing, she was throwing her gloves aside, unzipping his ski jacket, and putting her hands on his chest.

"You're so warm," she murmured between kisses.

"Let's get you warm."

"You mean you don't want my freezing hands on your naked flesh?"

"Something like that."

They peeled clothes off, leaving them in a line from the back door to the master bedroom. He took her hand and hauled her toward the bathroom.

"Into the shower you go," he ordered. "That'll warm us up."

She kept stripping until the tantalizing lingerie was the only thing covering what he wanted, what he needed. Too slowly, she slithered out of them until she was completely naked, and he found he couldn't breathe. She pulled his shirt up over his head, and he suddenly remembered the tattoo.

She paused, and he winced as she took in the heart with the stake through it.

"It's not what you think. It was a joke about working nights and being a vampire. Will dared me to—"

To his relief, she kissed it, then she pulled his head down and kissed him. "Take off your jeans."

When she bent over to start the water in the tub, he didn't think he was going to be capable of removing his jeans. He only wanted to unzip them so he could put his cold hands on her warm hips and guide himself deep inside her.

"Kate." Her name came out as a croak.

She looked over her shoulder, and she knew him too well to misunderstand anything he was thinking. Her grin was wicked, and as she straightened up, her breasts jiggled, and his attention was directed there.

She rolled her eyes. "So easily distracted." Stepping

into the shower, she let the water sluice down her body, tumbling over her breasts, to meet at the center of her thighs. "I'm waiting."

He'd never removed jeans so fast in his life. And then he was inside, closing the glass door, looking at the steam that had already begun to rise around her like mist at the shrine of a goddess. Her damp hair had turned dark and curly with the heat, and her eyes laughed at him.

He stood close enough so that he could feel her breasts brush his chest, while he put his hands on the water over her head and rubbed them together. The temperature was almost painful to his freezing hands, but he didn't care.

"Touch me," she finally said.

When he cupped her breasts, it was like coming home. He lifted them each to his mouth and took turns pleasuring them, suckling, nibbling, drawing as much into his mouth as he could. He still remembered everything she liked. How could he ever forget, since they'd been each other's firsts, and done all their practicing and learning and exploring with each other?

When she took his penis in her hand, he inhaled on a groan. He had a last brain cell left to think. "Wait, wait, I don't have a condom. You shouldn't—"

"I'm on the pill."

There was no sweeter sentence in the world. "But I wouldn't blame you if—"

"I know you, Tony."

She stroked and teased and cupped him, and he kissed her with growing desperation, as the water rained down around them and splashed against their closed eyes. When he cupped between her thighs, she cried out. She was moist regardless of the water, moist with the need he shared. He stroked the way she liked best, until she was whimpering against his wet chest and clutching his arm as if she'd fall without him. He slid his fingers inside her and she came apart, shuddering in his arms with the force of her orgasm.

It was still the sweet feeling of fulfillment it had always been, knowing that this strong woman could be so vulnerable with him.

He turned her back against the shower wall and lifted her leg, pressing his hips to hers.

She moaned. "In here?"

"In here." He had to bend to slide between her thighs, and with a curse, he simply picked her up so that her legs slid around his hips. She was lighter than he remembered—or he was too far gone to care about anything beyond being inside her.

And then he sank deep into her, the force of his thrust pinning her to the wall. The water splashed down his back, beaded across her upturned face. He could see the triumph there, the fulfillment, and he wanted to feel that way, too. He started to move then, and the moist heat of her was almost too much.

"God, this feels so good," he said hoarsely against her cheek.

And then he kissed her, slanting his lips across hers, mating with her mouth like he mated with her body. He tried to draw it out, but the heat of the shower, the whimpers of pleasure she was making, the bliss of being inside her, all combined. He was trembling and desperate when at last he felt her convulse around him with another orgasm. At last he could release all the passion he'd once and forever feel for her. He groaned and gave her body everything.

Kate couldn't remember the last time she'd felt so at peace, so lazy with satisfaction. Being held in Tony's strong arms was something she'd never imagined happening again, and it was difficult at first to not flash back on everything they'd shared, every emotion, from incredible joy to the depths of sorrow.

But she wasn't going to think of that, not now, not when she had him inside her, still pulsing with the echoes of his climax. He rubbed against her one more time and she gasped.

With a giggle, she whispered, "I think we're losing the hot water."

He lifted his head, so dazed-looking that she wondered if he'd even noticed the drop in temperature. He didn't speak as she shut off the water, but he did manage to find the towels on a little shelf on the wall. And then he patted her dry with a tenderness that brought a lump to her throat, aroused an emotion she didn't want to name. She took the towel from him without meeting his eyes and wrapped it around herself.

"Thanks," she said, stepping past him and out onto the bathroom floor.

He'd sensed the change in her mood, but her smile seemed to reassure him.

And then she saw that tattoo on his chest again.

He touched it self-consciously with his hand. "Yeah, I know. Some women like it, some don't."

She felt a pang of *How many women have there been?* but she didn't dwell on it. It had been nine long years. She might have been his first, but she wouldn't be his last.

He stood there dripping on her bathroom rug, looking good enough that she could lick him like a giant piece of candy. He seemed more . . . rugged than he'd been as a young man, with leaner planes and harder angles.

But he was watching her now, looking a bit wary. "Should I get dressed?"

"When I have a comfortable bed, and it's not even eleven o'clock?"

His grin was the same, rakish and adorable all at the same time. He didn't bother wrapping a towel around himself, only dried off and hung it back up.

"That's a change," she commented. "Towels where they should be."

"I do have a son who needs to be guided."

She knew he was teasing, but it was difficult not to counter, We *have a son.* Oh, she was overthinking everything now.

She let the towel drop, enjoying the way his gaze roamed her hungrily until she didn't think about anything but feeling him inside her again. She curled a finger to lure him, walking backward into her bedroom so she could watch him stalk toward her. He was still more than ready for her, so after she pulled the covers down, she forced him to sit when he would have tumbled her onto the sheets. She straddled his lap, then rubbed herself along his penis until he was gasping. Only then did she take him inside and sink down.

This time she controlled their pace, watching his face for the clues that hadn't changed for all these years. The way his eyes seemed hooded, the tightening of his mouth, the occasional grimace that was almost a smile of pleasure and pain mixed together. She waited for him to beg for an end, but she ended up being the one who reveled in his mouth at her breasts, and at last increased her rhythm and put an end to it.

With a groan, she slid off his lap and they both sank back on the bed. She meant to stretch out on her back, but she found herself on her side, watching him. Both of them had flushed, warm skin from the shower, and she didn't think she'd ever feel cold again. His chest rose and fell rapidly, his expression was peaceful and relaxed, but his erection still looked ready for action.

She laughed softly.

He opened his eyes and glanced to the side at her. "What?"

She gestured with her chin down his body. "You're still ready for another go-around?"

"It's been a long time," he said with a deep sigh.

"How long?"

He glanced again, sharper this time. "How personal are we getting?"

"I don't think it's any more personal than what we just did. And I'm not about to be utterly silent."

"Really?" he said, affecting sadness.

She hit his arm and he laughed.

"No, really," she insisted, coming up on her elbow. "If I tell you how long it's been, you'll have to tell me."

His gaze dropped to her breasts. "Fair enough. Let's hear it."

"Okay, it's been two years."

He grimaced. "That's a long time."

"Yeah, tell me about it."

"I'm surprised you didn't come with just a kiss." And he pulled her against his side.

She laughed, but she was almost serious as she said, "So this cuddling isn't exactly sex. Is it allowed?"

"We're in your bedroom, post-sex, and we're alone. Anything counts."

"I think we need some ground rules."

He chuckled. "You're such a lawyer."

"I just want us each to know what to expect. But go ahead, first tell me how long it's been for you."

"Seven months."

"Well, in guy time that's at least five years."

Against her cheek, she felt the chuckle reverberate through his chest, and she appreciated when he reached to pull the blankets up to their waists.

"Maybe not five years, but it's been a long time," he said. "Good thing you came almost as fast as me."

She smiled. "Ground rules now?"

He reached to settle his hand on her breast. "I didn't come into this with a plan. And this feels too good to overthink it."

"I don't want to overthink it either, trust me. But we

should know what to expect. This is just sex between us, right?"

He studied her. "Yeah. Are you okay with that?"

She looked down where his hand rested on her breast, then cupped it there. "Yes. I wouldn't have done this otherwise. But we're not dating or making plans, right? We're not expecting anything of each other. We'll take each day as it comes."

He rolled onto his side, taking her into his arms and speaking between kisses. "And comes . . . and comes . . . and comes."

At last he got up to get dressed, and she watched him with pleasure she didn't second-guess. He wouldn't let her get out of bed, so she simply enjoyed the show. At last he stood above her in his zippered coat and jeans, winter hat dangling from his fingertips.

He bent down to kiss her again. "Good night. I don't think you work tomorrow, so whenever I see you, I'll see you."

"Oh, you'll see me tomorrow. I'm picking up Ethan for a day in Glenwood Springs. It's been years since I've been to the hot springs. He doesn't have a lot of his stuff here, so it will just be easier for him to go home."

"Then tomorrow it is."

As she watched him walk out of her bedroom and heard the back door open and close, she stared at the ceiling and wondered what the hell had gotten into her.

Tony had gotten into her, and the thought of sex after two years and . . . it had been worth it.

Chapter 14

At nine the next morning, Tony opened his door to find Kate standing there, dressed in a fashionably puffy vest that would have fit in in Aspen—or Vail, where she lived. Her jeans were tight the length of her legs, all the way into her tall leather boots. He leaned against the door frame and just looked her up and down, silently remembering those long legs wrapped around his waist, the hot water running over their bodies.

"Are you going to invite me in," she asked, then whispered, "before I read every desire on your face?"

There was a blush on her cheeks he knew didn't come from the cold. "I don't know. You sure you're taking my son to the hot springs, not horseback riding with Will?"

Her purple eyes sparkled with merriment. "Did that casual invitation bother you, ex-husband of mine? You did a pretty good job of hiding it from everyone else, though not from me. Is that why you—"

He covered her mouth with his hand.

"I don't care who you date," he said idly, wondering if it would be difficult to get those tight jeans off her without her help.

"Sleep with," she said in a lower voice. "You care about that."

"Only because I know you'll be sleeping with me for a while." He leaned closer, heard her breath hitch. "And I didn't see you looking this flustered when Will asked you out."

"Because he didn't really ask me out," she insisted, not meeting his eyes. "Honestly, do you think he'd ask a woman out in front of her ex-husband?"

"Will? Sure he would."

Her eyes widened. "Oh. I didn't take it that way."

"Well . . . I don't think he exactly meant it that way either."

Shaking her head, she rubbed her gloved hands together.

"Come on in, Ethan's not quite ready yet."

After unzipping and removing her boots and leaving her vest on a chair, she followed Tony down the hall to his kitchen. Over his shoulder, he saw her peer into the living room with interest, but he hadn't really changed anything since the last time she'd been there. Just comfortable furniture and a big TV for sports and Ethan's video games.

In the kitchen, he had the newspaper spread over the table, a few dishes in the sink, and a full pot of coffee.

"Want some?" he gestured to the pot. "Help yourself."

Smiling, she took a mug off the top of the toaster—handy, close to the pot—and poured herself a cup.

"Want part of the paper?" he asked. Maybe if they read the paper, he wouldn't stare at her and drool, remembering what they'd done less than twelve hours ago.

She shook her head. "I have something I want to talk about. It's why I came early."

He was automatically wary and vaguely surprised to feel that way.

She knew him too well. "Tony, it's nothing major. I just couldn't sleep last night, and I lay in bed *thinking*."

She emphasized the last word because the thought of her in bed without him had made him look at her breasts, encased in a tight purple sweater.

He grinned. "Thinking of what?" He let his foot touch hers under the table, the age-old game.

She gave him a mock frown, glanced toward the doorway, and whispered, "Stop that!" then spoke in a normal voice. "It all started when the widows pointed out that you don't advertise Tony's on social media."

He rolled his eyes and slouched back in the chair. "Not this again."

"No, listen. I kept thinking there might be a way for me to prove to you the advantages, but you'd need something new and interesting to promote. And with all the talk last night of people's hobbies and interests, it made me realize I could be a part of some event at Tony's, too."

He kept a frown off his face, but he was feeling it. Whenever she started talking about changing things at the tavern, he got defensive. He kept telling himself there was no reason for it, that she was just trying to help, that she truly had changed. But it was hard to forget that once upon a time, she hadn't thought tending bar was enough of a career for him.

"So, the guitarist from the band playing Wednesday night hit on me, and we got talking."

That distracted him. "Why didn't you tell me? I'd have kicked him out for harassing my servers."

She took a sip of coffee, eyeing him from beneath her brows. "That's why I didn't tell you. He was a funny kid and I didn't mind."

"Kid, huh?"

"I don't know, twenty-one, twenty-two? He had the long hair in a ponytail."

"Yeah, I remember him. And I'll keep watch next time."

She cocked her head. "You'll keep watch on me?"

"No, on him. Nicole or any of the others don't need that either."

"You think *Nicole* would mind?"

They paused, then shared a chuckle.

"But he gave me an idea," Kate continued, leaning toward him. "Perhaps we need something bigger to promote, some way to celebrate the season, get people excited."

"The season's already here, Kate. And I already told you the events I hold."

"I know, I know, but I'm thinking something bigger than a pub crawl, held between Christmas and New Year's. There's always a lull, and it's not like we could do something so last minute on New Year's Eve. Every band is booked, according to Patrick."

"Band? You want to hire Patrick's band again? Holly and the Cowboys?"

"Not just Patrick's. I think Tony's needs a *festival* of bands, one long evening or part of the day, where a handful of bands play."

He gaped at her. "A festival—do you know how much work you're talking? And where would we put all these bands? A band already takes up too much room in the back and—"

"Wait, wait, you didn't let me finish. We'll hold it outside in the parking lot! We rent one of those out-door stages on wheels, blast some portable heaters at the bands—hearing they were going to use those at Brooke's wedding reminded me about them and sparked the final idea. We set up a tent for beer sales, tents for food—Chef's food, of course. While bands are changing over, people might come inside to get warm and order even more. You make this a big event by promoting it through social media and the tradi-tional methods, of course, posters, your website, etc. What do you think?"

Kate was bright with an excitement he hadn't seen in her in a long time—if you didn't count last night. It made her eyes luminous, her skin flushed, and much as he thought she looked gorgeous, her looks couldn't sway him in anything but sex. There was a resistance deep in his gut to changing something about the tavern he was so proud of.

"Kate, I don't think so."

Her happy smile faded. "But why? I know there are a lot of details to be worked out, but I'm willing to do the work."

"Did you ever think that maybe you should be relaxing over the holidays like regular people would if they had some free time? Now you want to add another job to server—event coordinator?"

"But Tony, you know me, I like to keep busy."

"I do know you—and you like to keep *too* busy. I know what you're trying so hard not to think about."

She frowned. "And what am I trying hard not to think about?"

"Your job, of course—your real one. It's sticking in your craw that your bosses don't agree with you."

"Well, of course it bothers me that they won't at least compromise. It means they don't trust that I know what I'm doing."

"And now you see why I'm resistant to this festival idea."

Her mouth dropped open. "You think I don't trust that you know how to run your own business?"

"I don't know, Kate. You never exactly trusted me before."

She inhaled sharply—and then they both heard a floorboard creak. Ethan was standing in the doorway, looking both sheepish and embarrassed.

"Sorry. Not used to knocking on the kitchen door," he said, backing out.

"No, Ethan, don't go," Kate said, giving Tony a glare that their son couldn't see. "We're just having a disagreement about work. It's nothing."

Ethan sighed with more drama than normal. "So you're moving back to Vail."

Her eyes widened. "Not right now. Why would you think that?"

"No reason." Ethan went to the cupboard and reached for a box of cereal.

Kate met Tony's gaze, and the anger of their argument had turned to bewilderment. Tony shrugged. The kid was just confused by finding them arguing. Hell, maybe it brought up an echo of a memory from when Ethan was a little boy. But they'd always been very careful not to argue in front of him.

So while Ethan ate his cereal, Kate listed off the things they were going to do in Glenwood Springs.

At last she turned her gaze back to Tony. "I know I've made this trip sound so exciting. You're welcome to join us."

"No, thanks. I've got to work later today."

At last they were out the door, and Tony was left alone to mull over what he'd said to her. Only the truth—that she'd never trusted him. A wife who loved her husband trusted that he could provide for them. And it had been damn obvious, by how focused she'd been on her law degree toward the end of their marriage, that she hadn't. Not that she shouldn't have wanted to be a lawyer, but to sacrifice their family life? To work herself so hard that he sometimes had to remind her to eat? Watching her get thin and stressed had been terrible. He'd loved her so much.

It had always seemed like she'd wanted respect from everyone else—law professors, fellow students, and now his customers—more than she'd wanted love from her family, from him.

But that was unfair. He knew living apart from her family, her son, had taught her the importance of love in her life. Maybe it was he who couldn't let go of the past.

Kate floated in the giant outdoor pool at Glenwood Springs, the heat rising in a mist that hung over her, making her feel languorous and relaxed, although her mind still resisted by churning away. The Flat Top Mountains rose above her, and she planned to take Ethan into the Glenwood Caverns high above the valley later that afternoon. He was swimming laps in the heat, racing a friend he'd run into. She shuddered. It was too hot for exercise.

So she floated and let the heat work on her muscles, but it wouldn't work on her brain.

Tony thought she hadn't trusted him.

During the arguments that had led to their divorce, it had been about wanting different things in life: her, Denver and the successful big-city law career she'd worked so hard for; him, the small-town life of Valentine Valley. Neither of them had seen their future the same way, and neither of them had been able to persuade the other to change. Their arguments had been more about confusion and desperation rather than hatred. But always, deep inside, she'd felt that *someone* had had to provide for Ethan and their future. She'd thought he'd had no ambition, and as someone with probably *too* much ambition, she just hadn't been able to accept that. And she hadn't wanted to be the one with the salary, and therefore all the power, in their relationship.

But was Tony right—had it really been about trust?

Maybe it had; maybe Tony was right about the fact that she'd thought him untrustworthy, which had somehow sabotaged them both, sabotaged their marriage. She groaned and closed her eyes. The disintegration of a marriage was never just one person's fault, but it hurt to think she could be so shortsighted as to affect a man's confidence.

Failure weighed heavily on her. She'd failed her marriage, but she had worked hard not to fail at being a mom. Now she was failing as a lawyer. The lump that welled up in her throat caught her by surprise, and she looked around to make sure Ethan wasn't nearby. He was rising up out of the water, shooting a ball at someone, playing dodgeball in the pool.

With all of her worries about failure, her son was proof that she'd done something right.

On the twenty-five-minute drive home from Glenwood Springs, Ethan got a text from Kate's mom, inviting them both to dinner. Kate told him to say they happily accepted.

"Mom, I wouldn't say 'happily' in a text."

"Just write it! It's polite and Grandma will appreciate it."

He groaned.

At the Fenellis', she was not at all surprised to see Tony there—he did live next door. But what did surprise Kate was that Tony and her dad were building a bookcase in the living room. She well remembered the woodworking Tony had learned from his dad, but he'd never done much of it early in their marriage—no room for a workshop in their tiny apartment, and certainly no time. But now, a tool belt around his waist, he looked all rugged and manly, guiding her dad through the process with the same patience he showed every customer at the tavern.

He glanced up at her when she came in, gave a nod, then a smile to Ethan, and went back to work. She tried to pretend it was nothing, but inside, she was wracked with guilt mixed with desire mixed with confusion and even determination.

"Just one more shelf, Christina," her dad called.

He used a hammer on something, and Barney barked with excitement.

"Tom, if you make me overcook the chicken parm, I will not be happy!" Christina called from the kitchen. "Oh, hi, Kate!" She bustled into the living room to give Kate a kiss. "Tony, you are staying for dinner."

"Maybe you want time with Kate," he replied. "You see me all the time."

"No, it's okay," Kate said. "You certainly deserve a meal after this hard work." She walked over to the bookcase. "Really nice work, guys. Dad, did you actually put on this scroll trim?"

"It was mostly Tony," Tom said, his face shining with perspiration.

"Not true," Tony said. "I showed him how, and he did a few himself."

Tony wasn't quite looking at her, and she wondered if he thought she was still angry with him. She was still upset, but more about the past and her failures than him.

But he might still be angry with her . . .

And then her brothers started trooping in, distracting her. Walt handed the baby to Kate while he and Diana undressed the other two. Jim brought a bottle of wine he wanted his parents to try.

"You need to stock this at Carmina's. My customers love it."

Dave brought a date and introduced her to Kate as Jessica Fitzjames, a reporter at the *Valentine Gazette*. She was a young woman in her twenties, with long, wavy blond hair and curious, intelligent eyes.

"Nice to meet you, Kate. Haven't I seen you serving at Tony's Tavern?"

"She's really a lawyer," Dave said. "It's a long story. That's her ex-husband, Tony."

Tony nodded as he washed and dried off his hands.

"Of course I know Tony," Jessica said, then she looked between the two of them. "Wow, I've heard of amicable divorces, but I've never met anyone like you two."

"This is their kid," Dave said, elbowing Ethan, and Kate noticed in surprise that her brother and her son were about the same height.

"Oh, that makes sense," Jessica said.

"Did you guys see the Christmas story in the *Ga-*

zette," Dave began, "the one for kids, and they have to finish it to win prizes? Jessica wrote that."

Christina smiled at Jessica in surprised astonishment. "That's wonderful, Jessica! I thought that was the most adorable story about a lost reindeer."

"And we've gotten some incredible endings, at all grade levels. We'll be posting them Christmas Day."

When they all sat down at the big table, Kate told what she'd learned about the Glenwood Caverns and how they'd been used in the nineteenth century.

"Picnics where they dressed up in their best clothes!" Ethan proclaimed, still chewing a slice of buttered bread. "It sounds so crazy."

"But we know why they went," Kate said. "You're above the whole Roaring Fork Valley, with the mountains lining both sides. I almost felt like I could see clear to Aspen."

Ethan said to his dad, "You got a lot farther with the bookcase."

"Sorry you missed it," Tony said. "You'll have more chances to practice."

Ethan grinned. "Remember when you tried to have me help make my own toy box?"

"You were six, and so convinced you could wield a hammer like I did."

Kate winced. "Oh, wait—that was the time you broke your toe!"

Everyone laughed as Ethan grew a little red. "Well, yeah, I didn't say I had great aim."

She remembered Tony's remorse when he had called to tell her what had happened. He took it as badly as if he'd personally caused the accident. He was such a good dad—a good man. And she was determined to help grow his business, whether he thought it was a trust issue or not. She just . . . owed him.

That night, along with her law research, Kate started looking up regulations for holding an event, the special permit required, and how it was mostly about the decibel level of an outdoor concert. She stayed up too late, writing down estimates of what the stage would cost, notes about contacting sound equipment specialists, and what kind of food they might serve outside.

When Tony didn't come over, she told herself it was because of Ethan. Was that just an excuse, though? Now that they'd brought up such a painful part of their marriage, could they forget it had been said? Should they?

But their lovemaking seemed to have turned on a switch inside her, making her restless. She was achy with need in all the places he'd touched, even though she was still upset with herself. They'd vowed not to let the past interfere with the present, but they'd gotten it wrong almost immediately.

Maybe last night had been the final intimate moment she'd have with him.

Chapter 15

Tony had a difficult time falling asleep that night, thinking about sex and Kate and how he'd made a mess of things by bringing up what couldn't be changed. He'd thought for sure she'd stay furious with him, and inwardly he'd grimaced when he'd heard that her parents had invited her to dinner. To his surprise, she'd acted as if nothing had happened, had even snuck a glance or two at him that he hadn't been able to interpret. She hadn't seemed angry, though. They'd spent years acting like friends for their son's benefit; she could probably assume the guise of friendship without even thinking about it anymore.

But it was a little more difficult for him.

He'd almost felt like he'd been back in high school again, when he'd been around her parents all the time, even working for them so that he could sleep with their daughter. He might have been thirty-three now, but it almost felt the same way, a guilty feeling of excitement.

He wasn't sure when he finally fell asleep, but it was surprising to be awakened by a text from his son early on Sunday morning.

Going to mass early. Will is taking us boarding.
I'm teaching Mom. Bet he won't mind if U come.
U working?

Will was taking Kate snowboarding? Tony felt a surge of annoyance that he hadn't seen this coming. Will was the one who'd said she was too serious, that she should have more fun. So now Will was putting his words into practice.

Damn straight Tony was going. He might be fine with Kate dating whomever she wanted—back in Vail. But if she was going to sleep with him, he didn't want her dating his best friend.

But maybe she didn't plan to sleep with him any-more . . .

He showed up at Kate's just as Will arrived. They both got out of their pickup trucks and glanced at each other.

Will smiled even as his eyebrows lowered. "You coming with us?"

"Ethan invited me," Tony said cheerfully. "Haven't gone in a while."

"Great."

"Should I put my board in your pickup?"

"Sure." Will moved ahead of him to reach Kate's front door first.

Tony let him have that minor triumph, then just hung

out on the walkway, waiting. Ethan spilled out the door soon enough, carrying his board, going on about the wax he'd applied. Then he saw Tony.

"Hey, Dad, glad you're going. Might need both of you to pick Mom up when she falls."

"I heard that," Kate said.

She emerged from the house wearing a teal blue ski jacket and mint-colored ski pants. She looked pretty damned cute, her short blond hair as messy as when he'd had her in bed.

She saw Tony, and though her eyes briefly widened, she smiled. "I didn't know you were coming."

"Ethan invited me. Hope you don't mind."

She looked between Will and Tony, bit her lip as she always did when she was amused, and headed for Will's pickup.

More and more Tony was thinking she'd gotten over their argument.

On the half-hour drive to Snowmass Village, Will regaled them all with stories of ranch life in the winter, how that morning he'd had to break the ice on the water troughs. Tony, who sat in the back with Ethan, just listened with contentment. Will was a good-natured blowhard, and Tony'd just let his friend talk Kate to death.

Once they'd rented Kate a snowboard and helmet in the village, Tony and Will stayed in the background and let Ethan teach his mom on the hill. It gave Tony a great feeling of pride to watch how patient his son was, how good he was at boarding. He saw Kate's occasional sad looks when Ethan wasn't looking, and he knew she was still concerned that he couldn't be on a team because of their custody arrangement.

Kate had skied in her youth, and that helped a bit. After an hour, they left the easier green circle runs. Once they made it to Bull Run, it was obvious that Kate was beginning to enjoy herself. She fell quite a bit, but sometimes she had a good, long run, and watching her and Ethan celebrate just made Tony's day.

When Tony and Will were waiting for Kate to finish a short run, Will eyed him through his goggles. "You look pretty happy for a man spending the day with his ex-wife—and one who's forced to ski groomed trails on a powder day."

"Yeah, I can't help myself. I'm just so impressed with my kid—not that I'm patting myself on the back for being a good parent or anything."

"Of course not," Will said with faint sarcasm.

They grinned at each other.

"It's still always crazy to me that you're not that much older than me, and you have a teenage son already."

"Tell me about it," Tony said. "I'm the youngest parent at any school event."

"To me, that makes you pretty damned old. Do you even have any interest in dating, old man?"

Tony chuckled. "We'll see who's old," he said, then bent and headed downhill, feeling the wind whip past his face as he carved through the soft groom underfoot. He beat Will to the next knoll, where Kate was catching her breath. He slid hard to a stop, spraying her with snow.

"Nice job!" Tony called, seeing her beam at him through his goggles.

Her cheeks were red with the cold, and the goggles couldn't hide the sparkle in her eyes. "Thanks! I think I'm getting the hang of it."

"Ethan's a pretty good teacher. Speaking of Ethan . . ." Tony looked around.

She pointed farther downhill just as Will caught up with them. "He met up with a girl from his class. See the one in pink and yellow?"

"Is he deserting us already?" Will asked.

"Not yet," Kate said, "but I may let him go soon."

They all rode up on the lift together and took another run.

Next time up, they all saw Ethan's friend waving at him. Ethan looked a little redder than he had a moment ago and awkwardly waved.

"You guys go ahead," Kate said. "I want to take my time. I'll meet you at the Alpine Springs lift. Ethan, go join your friend. Really."

He waved and took off.

Kate looked at Tony and Will. "Go ahead, I'm tired of holding you all up. Happy trails!"

Tony nodded and headed down the first hill, then rode to the side.

Will stopped beside him. "What's up?"

"I don't like leaving her alone this early in her training. I want to make sure she makes it down all right. You can go on ahead."

"Naw, that's okay. But I gotta tell you—I'm shocked you're sticking with her. You know the rule: There are no friends on a powder day —let alone ex-wives."

Tony shrugged good-naturedly. They looked uphill

just as Kate came over the roller too fast. She tried to keep her balance over the board, but her arms windmilled as she lost control.

Tony said, "Come on, baby, you got it—you got it—damn."

Will lifted his goggles and briefly stared at him, but Tony wasn't paying attention.

Flying off trail, Kate headed right into the trees. His gut clenched, and he saw Will lower his goggles, frowning his worry.

"I got her," Tony said.

He didn't know what was in his voice, but Will's look grew piercing. "So it's like that?" he called as Tony began to take off.

"Yeah, it's like that," Tony said, then called over his shoulder, "Keep your mouth shut about it, okay?"

Will yelled, "Okay, but I'll pull out my cell, waiting for your call if she needs real help."

Tony traversed across the hill as fast as he could and followed her path through the powder. Thankfully, the trees were widely spaced, and several skiers had come through in a few places, leaving tracks. He saw Kate's bright coat in a pillow of snow. She was on her back, trying to brace herself upright. Tony felt the weight of relief in a rush of shaky emotion. Thank God she was all right and hadn't fallen headfirst into a tree well. But she couldn't get out of her bindings, leaving her stuck where she'd fallen.

He pulled up next to her. "Kate?"

She turned her head swiftly, then collapsed back on her elbows. "Tony! I feel like an idiot. I'm stuck!"

He braced himself on a tree, leaning over her to grin, even as he lifted his goggles onto his helmet.

"Stop laughing at me!" But she returned his grin.

"I saw the whole thing—it must have been scary when you flew off into the trees."

"I didn't even have time to think about it, I was so busy trying to stay upright."

She was covered in patches of snow, including her face. She'd be getting cold pretty soon if he didn't get her out of the deep drift. He reached out a hand and they took each other's wrists. She pulled him over into the powder, and he tumbled beside her.

"How do you like it now?"

She started laughing and he joined in, before coming up on his elbow to remove his glove and wipe the snow off her cold face.

Their smiles died.

"I'm sorry," Tony said quietly. "I didn't mean to argue yesterday."

"Me neither," she whispered.

She looked up at him, her eyes all soft as they lingered on his mouth. He leaned down to kiss her, their cold lips soon warm against each other. He pressed his mouth to each spot where the snow had chilled her face, then came back to her mouth.

"Hmm, you taste like lip balm," he murmured.

She chuckled. "I don't think there's much more you can do with all these clothes separating us."

"You'd be surprised." He'd gone husky saying that, but then he had to sigh. "Okay, let's get you up."

"And get you up," she reminded him.

"Now that sounds dirty."

They laughed again. He helped her get out of her bindings, then popped his back foot out. He stood up and pulled her with him, grumbling that she could have picked a better place to fall.

"Anything hurt? I was so busy kissing you I never thought to ask."

"No, no, I'm fine. But do you think there's an easy way back onto the trail?"

"Let me go first and you follow in my track. In fact, why don't you walk out and I'll carry your board."

Slowly he moved through the trees, looking behind to watch her trudge through waist-deep snow. At last they emerged onto a lower section of the run.

Will was waiting for them. When he saw them, he got up from his perch on the slope. "Kate, glad to see you're all right."

"Me, too." She took her board from Tony.

"Yeah, she had to swim out of there," Tony said as she stepped back into her bindings.

Will gave Tony a searching glance, and Tony tried to look impassive, rather than too innocent and obvious. Will rolled his eyes.

Looking downhill, Kate didn't see their exchange. "Ethan doesn't know about this, does he? I don't want my son to know quite how bad I am."

"No, he's long gone," Will said. "He's probably at the base of the mountain, still chasing that girl."

And Will glanced at Tony as if thinking the same thing about him.

Tony shrugged, but he wasn't too worried about Will keeping his secret. Will might be a flirt and the center of every party, but he was a loyal friend.

After an afternoon of more successful runs, Kate wanted to celebrate her accomplishment by taking them all to dinner at Jim's upscale Italian restaurant, Mirabella's. The décor was clean and modern, but with a mountain flair—exposed woodwork and antique light fixtures. Candles sparkled on the crystal wineglasses and shone on Kate's animated face as they talked.

Tony couldn't stop watching her, and he hoped that it seemed natural for the conversation. The ride home was quieter. Ethan and Kate dozed in the back, and Tony sat in the front seat to keep Will company as he drove. When Will insisted on dropping off Kate and Ethan first, Tony said he could walk, but Will oh so graciously insisted on personally driving him home.

"Okay, spill," Will said as he backed out of Kate's driveway.

"Spill what?"

"You could barely keep your eyes off her. Are you falling in love again?"

"No," Tony said firmly.

"Then what the hell were you doing for so long in the trees when she fell?"

"None of your business."

"Seriously, dude? Did you take me up on the idea of ex-sex?"

"In the trees? Like we had that much time." Tony hesitated to say more, knowing he was a bad liar.

"No shit! You've already done it. Ex-sex. I was kidding with you when I first brought it up—I never thought you had it in you."

Tony shot him a look. "What does that mean?"

"You're usually pretty straightlaced for a guy who owns a bar, has a tattoo, and rides a Harley."

"Like you said, it's just sex."

Will pulled into Tony's driveway, put the pickup into park, then gaped at him. "And she went along with that?"

Tony finally smiled as he shook his head. "Surprisingly, yeah."

"Damn," Will said. "No more date invitations from me."

"Nope, at least not until after she moves back to Vail."

"And you'd let me date her."

Though Tony got a strange feeling in his chest, he nodded. "Sure. It's up to her."

"Huh. Well, good luck keeping it from everyone—including Ethan. It would suck if he thought you were getting back together."

Tony inwardly winced. "I don't remember you bringing that up when you were urging me to sleep with her."

Will gave a crooked grin. "That's because I never thought you'd go through with it. How long's it been?"

"Just a couple days. And don't ask any more details. I don't share."

Will raised both hands. "Okay, okay. I'm done. Take it easy."

"Thanks for the ride."

"Thanks for the entertainment."

Monday afternoon, Kate arrived early for her shift at Tony's Tavern. She had a leather portfolio full of facts and figures, all neatly printed, for Tony's consideration. He was in his office on the computer when he looked up and saw her. His mouth fell open a little, and she felt a surge of satisfaction.

"Where's your regular shirt?" he asked in a strained voice.

She looked down at the tank top with the generous neckline. "Nicole seems to get better tips than I do. Ethan needs his college fund, so I thought—what the hell. Do you like my skirt?"

"I can see a lot of your legs."

"And you hate that," she teased.

She leaned over to put her portfolio on the desk and watched with pleasure when his gaze dipped to her cleavage and stayed there.

"You're trying to soften me up for something," he said. "Just tell me what it is while I can still think straight."

Laughing softly, she straightened. "My proposal for the band festival."

Tony eyed her. "Didn't this cause us to have an argument the other day?"

"It did, but I thought we were moving past that. Just look it over. I know there's some money up front, but I've given you some projections of the revenue I think it can bring in. Be open-minded, and we'll talk after the shift."

She felt his gaze on her until she turned the corner into the hallway.

Throughout the evening, she kept glancing at him, wondering if he'd read it. But keeping him in her line of sight also let her see everything else he did—the way he oversaw his employees without being a tyrant, his easy relationship with Chef Baranski. But mostly, she watched him with people. There was a sad drunk at the farthest end of the bar, close to the wall—as if the man was trying to hide. She'd seen him before, and he usually sat alone, watching a college basketball game or talking to the bartender. Tonight, it was Tony bending his head to listen, leaning his elbows on the bar to have a serious discussion about whatever long speech the man gave. The drunk wasn't belligerent; he concentrated on Tony's face, swaying slightly, as if Tony was his lifeline.

Kate felt a glow of warmth that stayed with her. As the evening started winding down, she found herself leaning against the bar as she waited for her last two tables to need her. Tony was mixing a few drinks beside her.

"So did you have fun snowboarding?" he asked.

She winced. "Sure, but I'm paying for it today. There are bruises in places I don't want to think about."

"Gee, I hope that doesn't interfere with certain other activities."

She shook her head. "Always thinking about yourself, De Luca, always thinking about yourself."

He handed her the tray of drinks. "Only thinking about you, Fenelli."

When she returned and entered her order in the POS, he said, "You know, Ethan's only concerned that you're having fun."

She sighed. "Everyone seems worried about that. I know I keep busy and work hard, but sometimes that's fun for me."

"Well, I know that. But you used to have other things, too, before college and work."

When she didn't say anything, he said quietly, "You can let yourself have fun, even back in Vail. Don't punish yourself."

His gentle tone made her throat tighten. She took a deep breath and smiled brightly. "Did you look at my portfolio?"

"Stop! We're having a discussion about fun. Remember in our first year of college, I used to come to your dorm and drag you out of there, pretending we were going to the library?"

"Yeah, I learned that was your tagline for anything *but* the library."

"Hey, I had to be creative. We didn't go to the same school, so I had to find some way to be with you and get your nose out of your books."

"I kept telling you you were going the wrong way, and you led me right off campus to a park, where you pulled the most amazing picnic out of your backpack."

"Hardly an original idea, but I was desperate. You were looking hollow-eyed and pale."

"I was feeling pretty overwhelmed at first. I thought I'd worked hard in high school and was so prepared for college. But the classes required much more work. There just weren't enough hours in the day." She glanced at him and smiled. "And although I might have protested, I did enjoy it when you took me away from all that."

"And I don't think you've changed. Besides this job, you've been working on this portfolio—"

"Did you read it?" she interrupted eagerly.

"Not yet. I bet you've been working on something else besides the portfolio."

"Oh, my table needs me. I'll be back!"

But she couldn't avoid him for long.

"I know you," he said. "You haven't been 'getting your priorities straight,' you've been working on that law case."

"Well, I have to do something! The public health might be at stake. I talked it over with your sister, and since I can't deal with the company myself, I'm researching them to find a way to put my mind at ease. They're a reputable company, and I'm honestly not finding anything in their history to lead me to believe they might mislead us and the FDA."

"Then that should make you feel better."

"Not yet. I'll let you know."

They had a quiet moment beside each other as Tony polished glasses.

"You know," she said, "you might be shocked that I'm willing to admit this, but though I resisted moving to Vail—it felt like a demotion, even though I was a junior partner—"

"You were the managing partner of the office. They put you in charge."

"I know, I know, but you know how focused I was on Denver."

"I know."

His voice had lost that teasing edge, and she knew she skated close to the edge of their past problems.

"But I found I actually liked the slower volume of work in a smaller office. I liked living in Vail, leaving behind the stress of traffic and the bigger office. In Denver, I was starting to have trouble sleeping." She hesitated. "Not sure I should be admitting this to you."

"I think better of you for admitting the truth. I bet you got too skinny in Denver, too. I always used to have to remind you to eat."

"I didn't really like being pressured to eat," she grumbled. "Sometimes it felt like you were going to pretend the fork was an airplane."

They glanced at each other and smiled. She looked into those warm chocolate eyes, and something in her breathing gave a hitch. Their smiles died, and then as if by unspoken agreement, they quickly moved apart and went back to work.

After closing, when Kate was bringing the linens into the kitchen, Chef Baranski stood alone, looking at his phone.

"Excuse me, Chef," she said, trying to get by him in the narrow aisle.

He harrumphed but stepped aside. When she returned, he gave her a look. "Tony's happier than he's been in a while," he said with no preamble.

She swallowed almost nervously. "Oh. I didn't realize he was acting any differently."

"That's because you're not usually here. He's a quiet,

steady guy, no great highs or lows. And then you show up."

"Is that bad?" she asked hesitantly.

"I don't know. Guess we'll see when you leave."

He stepped aside and she escaped, but as she put chairs upside down on tables, she couldn't help wondering—was Chef trying to warn her that Tony was going to get hurt?

But Tony was the one who'd begun this sexual dance. He was a grown man and would have to accept the consequences of his choices. And she *had* to leave; she had to prove her integrity to Clements, Lebowitz, and Yang. If he was sad when she left, it would probably be because he missed the sex. Whatever else had happened, they'd always done that really well.

Except . . . except the last year of their marriage, when she'd been in law school and so stressed and exhausted, even their sex life had taken a hit. It hadn't been right of her, she knew that now, but at the time, she'd barely been able to focus on anything but the overwhelming number of cases she'd had to study. And Ethan. She'd missed important things in his life—Tony had seen his first steps, Ethan had said "Dada" first, and instead of a cling-to-Mommy phase, he'd wanted Tony. All those things had been hard enough to deal with, and she'd almost begun to resent that Tony had wanted even more from her.

She'd been so wrong.

She finished her work in the back room, and when she came out, there were few lights near the bar. The kitchen was dark, and she realized Chef had gone home. Just Tony's office light was on, and he was reading her portfolio.

She stood silently in the doorway and simply watched him, the way his dark head was bent as he read, the curve of his neck beneath his hair, which hung a little too long. Those broad shoulders had borne the load of father, husband, and business owner.

He looked up and saw her. "So do you want to discuss . . ."

She pulled off her tank top. Her bra was black and lacy, and his mouth sagged as he looked at it. And then she removed it, hanging it off a box on the nearest shelf. She crawled onto the office chair, straddling his lap, her skirt inching higher on her thighs, then put her hands in his hair to tilt his head back and kiss him.

The kisses were mindless and wild, deep and exciting. With a groan, he worked his way down her neck, sucking, tasting, then arched her back until he could take her nipple into his mouth. Kate shuddered, pressing her hips into his. His jeans might have gotten in his way, but it was an interesting sensation against her delicate underwear. His tongue worked magic as she rubbed against him. He moved between her breasts, as if he couldn't bear to leave one alone for long.

To her shock, he suddenly swore, swiveled the chair, picked her up, and deposited her on his desk. She only vaguely heard things tumble out of the way behind her, because all she could focus on was how he shoved her skirt higher and spread her legs, holding her thighs wide as he bent his head. The first touch of his mouth on her silky underwear made her cry out. He licked her through it, then ran his tongue along the edge and underneath. She shuddered and dropped back on her elbows, bumping her head into the wall behind. But nothing distracted her, nothing stopped her focus on the rising tide of passion that hurdled her higher and higher.

And then Tony was over her and inside her, his body thrusting, holding her hips to guide her just as he wanted. She caressed his chest, his nipples. More stuff fell onto the floor, but she was mindless by this point, nothing but Tony and their need and their desperation.

She climaxed almost violently, shuddering hard, and with a groan he followed her into bliss, his thrusts slowing. Now she felt the awkwardness of her head bent against the wall, his body pinning her to the desk, his shoulders almost touching both the side wall and bookshelf on the other side.

She started to laugh, unable to help herself.

He straightened and looked down at her, still breathing hard. "Am I funny?"

"No, but my neck will develop a crick in it if I don't move soon."

Without breaking their connection, he pulled her off the desk and collapsed back on the chair, with her still straddling him. Slouching, his head resting on the seat back, he watched her between half-closed eyelids. She smiled and gyrated languorously, still feeling him hard inside her.

"Jesus, I missed this," he murmured hoarsely.

"So I'm the best lay you've had."

"Well, I'm not saying that . . ."

"Hey!"

She went to get off him and he caught her hips and held her firmly to him. She hesitated for a moment, then slowly lay onto him, pillowing her head on his shoulder, her face against his neck. He smelled so good, and she felt more relaxed and at peace than she had in a long time. Her bare breasts against his cotton shirt felt erotic and daring. His arms came up around her, and he held her to him. She felt a momentary unease; if they were just about sex, then maybe they shouldn't linger afterward. But . . . she couldn't make herself move.

"Oh, I was supposed to give you a message from the widows," Tony said, caressing her bare back. "We're all invited to the boardinghouse Tuesday for dinner."

" 'We're all'?"

"You, me, and Ethan."

"Uh-oh, why does this make me nervous?" She kissed his neck idly.

"Don't know. I've given up trying to anticipate their moves ages ago."

"They used to scare me when I was little."

"You never told me that."

"Well, I was really little, four or five. BT, Before Tony."

He gave a snort of amusement. "Why did they scare you?"

She felt his big hand begin to slowly comb through her hair, and it was heavenly. "They were friends of my grandma, of course, and before she moved to Arizona, she occasionally took me with her when they got together to play cards. They were really competitive, I understood that eventually. But then—they were shrieking and slapping down cards and shouting with laughter and occasionally swearing. I was a pretty serious, quiet kid, and they just . . . scared me."

He gave a soft laugh. "But you got over it."

They were quiet for long minutes, and at last Tony sighed. "Looks like I'm not exactly ready for round two anymore. Guess we should call it a night."

She straightened up, and while he studied her breasts again, she looked around until she spotted the portfolio.

"Did you finish it?"

"I want to mull it over some more."

"Don't take too long, okay? We don't have much time."

"I know you put a lot of thought into it. I appreciate it."

"And is that a grudging undertone I hear?"

"Not really, I . . . I don't know."

"Okay, okay, no pressure. I think it'll be a fun thing for all our friends and customers to look forward to, but I certainly won't insist. You're the boss."

"Right now I think your breasts are in charge, because I can't seem to do anything but focus on them." He leaned in and gave the gentlest kiss to first one tip and then the other.

She shivered. Trying not to think of the warmth such a tender kiss inspired, she at last slid from his lap. While he zipped up, she tugged down her skirt, and found her bra and shirt. He'd actually torn her underwear, but she didn't mention it. It gave her a little thrill.

"I think we're presentable," she said. "Say hi to Ethan for me."

"Say hi to your bed for me."

She laughed and went to find her jacket. As she zipped it up, she ducked her head back in the office. "Wonder what the widows have in store for us . . ."

"I'm almost afraid to find out."

Chapter 16

As Tony and Ethan got into his pickup truck early Tuesday evening, Tony looked at his son, the keys still in his hand.

Ethan glanced at him. "You have to start the car to drive it, Dad."

"Gee, thanks, I wasn't sure. But if I drive it, we'll be at your mom's in three minutes, and we won't have time to talk."

"What do you want to talk about?" Ethan asked, wearing a frown of curiosity.

"I don't know. I guess I just wondered how you've been with your mom living here and working for me and everything." Tony wasn't really sure what he wanted to hear, but his secret relationship with Kate was making him wonder if Ethan could sense a change.

Ethan's eyes widened. "Well, of course it's okay for Mom to be here. I don't have to drive two hours to Vail and back on the weekends. Don't worry, I'm not one of those stupid kids who thinks his parents will get back together. Now if one of you would suffer from parental guilt and buy me a new phone, I'd be even happier."

"Yeah, I don't think so. When you have some regular money coming in, we'll talk."

"Dad—"

"But you really don't have any problems with the changes around here?"

"Gotta admit, I wonder if it's hard to work together. You fought the other morning."

"That was a disagreement, not a fight."

"Mom said the same thing. What did you two do, write a script?"

Tony sighed. "I just want you to remember you can talk to me about anything."

"Just not a phone."

Tony gave up and started the car. At Kate's house, without being told, Ethan hopped out and let his mom sit in front. Tony figured it was so he could text without being noticed, but maybe not. Kate was wearing a long wool coat over nice pants, with leather boots peeking out underneath. Her hair was casually disheveled, and her eyes gleamed as she smiled at him above the big scarf that wrapped around her neck.

And for just a moment, he wondered how his life would have been different if they'd never divorced, if this had been just another family outing for the three of them—if there would have been a fourth.

And he stopped that thought right in its tracks. He

wasn't having a relationship with her, they weren't married—they were having ex-sex. That was it.

But people were starting to associate them together, and that probably wasn't wise. But part of that was his fault—he'd hired her. And now she was having ideas about his business she had no . . . business having.

But that wasn't true. Throughout this festival idea, she'd never once brought up the fact that she was technically an investor. He had to admire that.

They crossed the bridge over Silver Creek, then turned down the snow-covered road on Silver Creek Ranch land. The Widows' Boardinghouse had a big sign outside advertising it as such, as if they really took in boarders. But anyone who knew them knew they were widows and best friends who'd decided to live together after their husbands had died. Nate had renovated the old Victorian himself, fixing plumbing and walls and painting. As Tony drove down the driveway to park near the back door, he couldn't help but admire the wraparound porch, strung now with Christmas lights, and the lit candy canes lining the drive.

"I helped them with the decorating a couple weeks ago," Ethan said.

Kate smiled over the back of the seat. "That was nice of you."

"Yeah, their grandkids are all grown up, and their great-grandkids are too little. I'm like their in-between grandchild, they said. Whatever that means."

"Isn't that your dad's car?" Kate suddenly asked Tony.

He pulled in next to an old jeep. "Yep. Isn't that peculiar."

"Well, he's on their preservation fund committee," Kate pointed out. "They're all friends."

"Uh-huh."

Ethan hopped out, and Kate whispered to Tony, "Don't show too much curiosity, or they might show too much about us."

"You're worried they're on to us?" Tony asked in surprise.

She opened the door and glanced at him. "I don't know. Besides being afraid of them when I was a kid, I thought they had mystical powers."

He laughed, got out of the pickup, and walked around the front. "Mystical powers?"

"Mind readers. You know Mrs. Palmer reads tarot cards, right? She once sat me down to 'practice' on me, and I swear she knew I was going to be a lawyer before I did."

"Now I know who to blame," he said under his breath.

She looked back at him as she walked up the steps to the porch. "What was that?"

"Nothing."

Ethan already had his coat off in the cow-themed kitchen. Tony swore that every time he came by, they had some new knickknack. As he hung his coat on the bull horns near the door, he saw cows on the kitchen towels and black-and-white-spotted bowls holding fruit on the table in the kitchen nook.

And then he saw his dad coming through the door from the dining room, and he was wearing an apron that said MOO! on the front. Tony gaped.

Mario reddened.

"He was frying the chicken," Mrs. Thalberg said matter-of-factly. "It spatters."

So his dad wasn't only a guest; he'd helped prepare the meal. Now wasn't that interesting. "Dad, you should have worn your work overalls."

"Probably," Mario said impassively.

"No point settling down in here," Mrs. Ludlow said in her no-nonsense voice. "Dinner's hot and ready to be served."

"Thanks for bein' on time," Mrs. Palmer said, linking her arm with Tony's.

Her dress had candy canes on it today in diagonal stripes, matching the driveway decorations. He felt festive every time he saw her.

The dining room table overflowed with fried chicken and salad, corn bread and asparagus. In the corner of the room was a desk that still had a big square computer monitor, which had seen better days. Nate had lamented more than once that he'd offered to buy them a new one, but they liked their old computer and didn't want to learn anything else.

As they ate dinner, the widows never ran out of things to say, discussing the success of their first Christmas market and plans to improve it for the next year. Tony's dad was a part of each discussion, and Tony thought he noticed him speaking more often than not to Mrs. Thalberg.

And then, as if on cue, they turned as one to look at Kate.

Mrs. Ludlow's graceful hands moved gently through the air as she talked, and she peered at Kate pointedly through her glasses. "So you've been away from your law firm for several weeks now, Katherine."

Kate swallowed her food the wrong way and started to cough.

Ethan pounded her back. "You okay, Mom?"

Kate nodded, eyes watering, and took a sip of her wine. "Sorry . . . just startled at the sudden change of topic. Yes, Mrs. Ludlow, I've been in Valentine Valley for three weeks now."

"Do you miss your work?"

"I do, but I'm filling my time with other projects. And getting ready for Christmas, of course."

"We know you're working for Tony," Mrs. Thalberg said, sending him a brief smile, "but what else are you doing?"

"She went snowboarding for the first time last Sunday," Ethan said, in between bites of his buttered roll. "I taught her."

"I'm so impressed," Mrs. Palmer said, her hand pressed to her chest. "I always wanted to give that a try."

The guests gaped at her, while the other two widows just shook their heads.

"I cross-country skied all my life," she insisted. "But when I broke my hip, my grandson Adam said he'd tie me up like a calf if I risked my health again. Did you like it, Kate?"

"I did, ma'am," she said, smiling. "Ethan's a good teacher."

"I didn't teach her to lose control and run into the woods," Ethan pointed out.

Tony looked down at his plate and took another bite of fried chicken.

"Oh, dear," Mrs. Ludlow said with concern. "You weren't hurt?"

"Dad rescued her," Ethan volunteered. "He told me all about it."

Tony hid a wince as the three widows eyed him curiously. "I was closest," he said. "Love the asparagus."

Mrs. Thalberg passed him the bowl then said to Kate, "You should be having more fun like snowboarding. I swear, child, you've spent your life working toward a goal."

And she couldn't stop, Tony thought, but he wasn't about to bring up her festival idea.

"You should remind yourself of the fun things you've done and not focus on work," Mrs. Ludlow said. "It's rare for adults to have this kind of time off, Katherine. You can reevaluate your life and your choices."

Tony shot his dad a quick frown. What the hell were they all about?

"That's sound advice," Kate said noncommittally.

"For instance," said Mrs. Ludlow, turning to Tony, "you see Katherine regularly. Perhaps you can encourage her by asking what fun things she's done recently."

Kate didn't bother to hide her eye roll. "Mrs. Ludlow, I'm fine. I exercise—"

"For your health," Ethan interrupted. "Good thing I taught you boarding for fun."

"Thank you, E.," she said, then continued, "I have dinners out—"

"It's always about work," Ethan said.

"Ethan." Tony said his name in a warning tone.

"And I like to read," Kate said firmly, daring their son with her pointed gaze to say something else.

Ethan mumbled, "Work briefs," and took a big bite of his drumstick.

The widows laughed, and Tony saw Kate force a smile.

"What my son doesn't mention is how often I crush him at Xbox—video games," she said sweetly.

He hunched his shoulders.

"And I know something fun we can do together," she added in a bright tone.

Tony almost felt sorry for the kid.

"Did you ladies read the reindeer story in the *Valentine Gazette*?"

"Oh, that lovely story by Jessica Fitzjames," Mrs. Palmer said, clapping her hands together.

"Well, they're choosing which kids in elementary, middle, and high schools wrote the best ending." Kate gave Ethan's hand a squeeze. "I'd love to help you write your own ending."

"Aw, Mom," Ethan mumbled.

It was a while before she released his hand.

They spent another hour with the widows having Christmas cookies in the parlor, which the widows had decorated with their various crafts, from crocheted afghans to a painted screen near the fireplace. But for the holidays, there were dozens of little Christmas figurines everywhere, so much so that Tony was afraid to move too much for fear of knocking one over.

Being together at the widows', it was almost as if

he and Kate were a married couple again rather than divorced. It made him uneasy. Instead, he rattled on about how good the Christmas cookies were, and that they could win a competition.

After dropping off Kate and seeing Ethan ensconced with his homework an hour later, Tony stood in the screened-in porch in his backyard, shivering in his jacket, and called her. "What the hell was that about?" he asked.

"I have no idea. If I didn't know better, I'd think they were matchmaking!"

"They don't have any idea about us—they can't."

"Well, we spend a lot of time together, mostly because of Ethan."

"'Mostly'?" he teased. "Please. We spend a lot of time together because I stupidly gave you a job."

There was a moment of silence. He grimaced and closed his eyes.

"Stupidly?" she asked in a quiet voice.

"Sorry. Meant that as a joke, and it came out badly. I obviously don't have a problem with you at work. Hell, I'll never think of my office the same way again."

"Maybe you regret it because of my band festival idea."

He sighed. "No, I don't regret it."

"Then tell me the truth, Tony. What do you think?"

"Okay." He rubbed his free hand on his arm to warm it and stomped his feet. "For someone new to the 'event coordinator' position, you gave the proposal a lot of thought, and estimated the details well."

"Thanks," she said.

Her voice sounded a little breathless with pleasure, and that's when he knew he was going to give in.

"It's more money than I'm used to spending, but maybe you're right, that it's time to take a chance. You have the green light."

"Great!" she said warmly.

"*But*—and this is a big but—I can pull the plug if it seems like it's not working out. You have to check with me every step of the way. Agreed?"

"Agreed."

She'd answered so quickly that he knew she didn't think it was possible he'd need to cancel. But then she'd always been confident in everything.

Which was probably why the setback with her law firm really seemed to have knocked her for a loop.

He'd once liked her ambition, but he felt like it had ruined their marriage. To see it again up close made him feel uneasy.

Kate came in for the day shift on Wednesday feeling energized and excited. She tracked Tony down in his office, and for a moment, they looked at each other, remembering what they'd recently been doing in this small room.

Kate cleared her throat. "You wanted an update on the festival."

He lounged back in his chair, hands folded on his stomach. "And I just gave you the okay last night."

"Well, I don't have much time. I researched the special permit and got the rules—mostly it's all about decibels. We'll have to be careful about that. I started a Facebook page for the tavern—I made you an admin—and a Twitter account, too. I'll be getting sponsors, too, and banners advertising them. I hope potential sponsors don't balk because I'm your ex-wife!"

Tony held up both hands. "Whoa, there! What about all this talk of knowing how to have fun?"

"But this *is* fun for me. I wouldn't be doing it otherwise."

His brow furrowed as if with skepticism, but he didn't contradict her.

"I'm aiming for the Saturday between Christmas and New Year's, so I have to settle on the bands quickly. I read an article that Jessica Fitzjames wrote on local bands. I've asked her for help, so she's coming today to talk—at the end of my shift, don't worry."

He stood up and took her face in his hands, startling her.

"Kate, I don't worry. You'll handle everything. You always do." He kissed the tip of her nose and walked out the door.

She stared at the empty doorway, not sure if that was a compliment. Then she shrugged and decided to take it that way. No point in thinking the worst. That only gave her a stomachache.

Her first table during the lunch rush was a middle-aged guy in a suit, constantly on his cell phone. He barely put it aside to place his order, and while he was eating, he was texting. She passed by once as he was grumbling.

She paused and asked, "Did you need something, sir?"

"No, just work stuff," he said impatiently. "You're lucky you don't have a high-stress job."

She hid a smile. "Well, when we get swamped, it can be very stressful. Some customers don't appreciate that we have several tables to juggle."

He looked around. "Oh, yeah, right."

And then his phone rang. While he answered it, she quietly placed his check on the table and kept going.

When she came back to pick up his credit card, she asked, "Do you have a favorite band?"

He blinked at her. "Band?"

"You know, singing, playing instruments? We're having a band festival in a few weeks, and I'd love to contact groups popular with our customers."

He actually paused to think. "Double Cyn. They're a folk group. But they're national, not local. You might not be able to get them."

"Thanks, I'll give it a shot."

She asked other patrons about their favorite bands that afternoon, and by the time she got to Ned and Ted, the identical twin plumbers, they grumbled that she wasn't paying attention to them.

"I saved the best for last," she insisted. "So who's your favorite local band?"

"Toke Lobo and the Pack," they said in unison.

"They're from Colorado," Ned said.

"They sing country," Ted added.

"Sounds good," she said. "They're on my list."

Kate's shift ended and Erika took over. Kate headed to Tony's office to tell him about the bands customers had mentioned, and he looked up the contact info for the couple who'd already played at the tavern.

"You have another hockey game tonight, right?" Kate asked.

"If it's Wednesday and winter, it's hockey," he said, swiveling his chair to look at her.

"I'd like to come if you don't mind."

He studied her, and she couldn't quite read his expression.

"I'm not sure that's a good idea. We already work together, have the same friends . . ."

"And I want to see you play. But I don't want to make you uncomfortable. Ethan wants to go—how about if I use him as an excuse? I'll pick him up so you guys can go out afterward. I'll come 'too early' "—she air-quoted the words—"and catch some of the second half."

"Third period?"

She laughed. "Whatever."

"I guess that works."

She turned to go when he called her name.

"Why are you doing this?" he asked. "I thought being secret was enough for you."

"It is, but . . . I just want to see you in action." She gave him a cocky grin. "Maybe Valentine Valley just makes me feel young again."

Chapter 17

There were lots of pickups in the parking lot of the Aspen Ice Garden that evening, which made Kate smile. She passed through the warm lobby, where a couple dozen guys were putting on their skates and pads for the next game. Several watched her walk by, and one even whistled. She should probably have been offended—but she wasn't. Sometimes it was nice to be noticed.

She opened the door and stepped into the rink itself, where the cool air had the brisk smell she always associated with rinks. And then right in front of her, two guys slammed into the boards, making her jump. One of the guys waved at her, and though she wasn't sure who it was beneath the helmet, she waved back.

There was cheering from the small group in the stands, and she saw people she knew, including her son, of course, who was sitting with several teenagers. And then she winced, because Tony's dad was there as well and could have given Ethan a ride. Oh well, Tony obviously hadn't remembered that.

And to her surprise, there was Mrs. Thalberg sitting at Mr. De Luca's side. Now *that* was interesting. Kate had been seeing them together a lot. She climbed up into the bleachers, and although Ethan had known she was coming, he gave her an almost . . . disinterested glance that stung a little bit. Maybe he thought she'd sit outside in the car. But she understood his age, so she sat down by the older couple.

"Hi, Mr. De Luca, Mrs. Thalberg," she said.

Mrs. Thalberg gave her a much more interested look than Ethan had. "Kate, good to see you."

"I'm here to pick up Ethan," Kate quickly explained. "Guess I'm too early."

Mrs. Thalberg's smile deepened, but she didn't say anything.

Mr. De Luca gave a sudden, "Yes!"

Kate focused on the game. "Who's winning?" she asked when she saw that the scoreboard only listed the teams as Home and Visitor.

"The Valentine Massacre," Mr. De Luca said, not taking his eyes off the ice. "Tony just scored."

Number eleven had just scored, so at least now she knew which one he was without having to ask. She watched the game, enjoying the thrill of well-padded men trying to outplay each other for fun. Tony might have aged a few years since the last time she'd watched him play—and that had been in high school—but he hadn't lost his intensity.

When they were young, she'd never understood why

winning and losing hadn't mattered much to him. He'd been just as competitive as she'd been, but when the game had been over, it hadn't mattered who had won. He'd reverted to laid-back Tony, who'd enjoyed playing more than he'd needed to win. Kate had made a career out of winning, though she'd had to lower her obsessive focus for fear she'd develop an ulcer over time.

During a time-out, Mr. De Luca went to buy popcorn, and Kate slid close to Mrs. Thalberg.

"I'm surprised to see you here," she said to the widow.

"Surprised? You shouldn't be. My grandson Nate is number three."

"Oh," Kate said, glancing to where the team huddled together. "I thought you were here as Mr. De Luca's date."

"Well, I do admit that a man with low blood pressure turns me on."

Kate choked on the water bottle she'd started to swig, and Mrs. Thalberg just gave her an innocent smile.

"Kate, there's going to be a wedding shower for Brooke at Josh and Whitney's loft at the ranch this Sunday. Would you like to come?"

"Oh, I don't know if Brooke would want me there. She doesn't know me all that well."

"She's close to Lyndsay, and you seem well on your way to becoming Lyndsay's best friend again. You'll know almost everyone."

Kate felt her cheeks heat with a blush. "Why . . . thank you, Mrs. Thalberg. I'd love to come. I'd like to return the favor by inviting you to the band festival that will be at Tony's Tavern between Christmas and New Year's—I haven't settled on the exact date yet. I'm in negotiations with a few bands, and I'd like to go see a few in person, the ones whose YouTube videos aren't that helpful."

"A festival! What a lovely idea."

"The outdoor stage will be in Tony's parking lot, and Chef will be barbecuing. Hopefully the weather will cooperate."

"You know, Renee reads tarot. She's quite popular. If you'd like her to set up a booth, I'm sure she'd love it."

Kate imagined Mrs. Palmer chatting up band revelers between musical acts. "I think it's a great idea. I'll give her a call. And I'll make sure she has a heater in her booth."

Mr. De Luca returned and sat back down near Mrs. Thalberg. He gave a bag of popcorn to Ethan, who at least thanked his grandfather politely before going back to his friends. Mr. De Luca had even bought a bag for Kate. It was so nice that he could see past the divorce and treat her with kindness. To her surprise, she felt a lump grow in her throat, and she forced herself to look back at the game, blinking rapidly.

Though she was fighting back tears, Kate realized that she was happy—truly happy. Happier than she'd been in a long, long time. She got to see her son almost every day, reacquaint herself with old friends, and hang out with her family. And mostly, she and Tony were friends again.

And then she told herself to snap out of it. She had the ability to make herself happy wherever she lived.

These last few weeks, she'd learned some valuable lessons about being more balanced in her life and doing things for herself as well as for her son.

And the other thing she'd learned was that she needed to have a man in her life again, someone she trusted and had fun with—someone like Tony.

When the game was over, Ethan went to play in the game room with some friends. After his shower, Tony joined them, and Kate told him about Mrs. Palmer's tarot readings. He looked mildly skeptical, and Mrs. Thalberg chuckled.

After Mr. De Luca and Mrs. Thalberg left, Kate touched Tony's arm when he started for the game room to get Ethan.

"Wait. I'm so excited. I have to tell you something. You know I talked to your sister about my law firm problem, right?"

"No, I didn't realize you guys had gotten so close so quickly."

"I know. Crazy, isn't it? In some ways it's like we never were apart. But anyway, she reminded me that I could do more in-depth research on my client than I'd done when I first took them on. At least I'd feel better about having to let it go if the firm forces the issue. Well, I've spent hours and hours looking, and I couldn't find anything bad about the company."

"That's good, right?" he said, leaning against the wall.

"Right. But . . . it doesn't mean they're not doing wrong for the first time, you know. And people could get sick. But I got lucky."

"With someone other than me?" he asked, smiling at her.

She looked around nervously. "Enough with the teasing. I got lucky finding an article about one of the cattle growth hormones my client produces. They named the chemist who'd worked on the project. He's retired now, so maybe I can get him to talk to me."

His smile faded. "Is that wise, Kate? What if he tells tales to his old bosses, who complain to your senior partners?"

"I'll be very careful," she said, sighing. "But . . . I just need to know the truth, Tony."

They were standing close together, talking earnestly, when Ethan came out of the game room. He stopped in his tracks as he saw them, then frowned and turned away.

"What's wrong?" Tony asked, looking over his shoulder at where she was staring.

"Ethan saw us talking—and he didn't look happy about it."

"Maybe he thinks we're talking about him."

"Maybe." But that answer didn't feel right.

"You're not perfect at figuring out a guy's every emotion just from his face," Tony said. "Remember our first dinner party with the high-powered partners you interned with the summer before your graduation?"

She couldn't help smiling, even as she groaned at the memory. "You had that baby food stain on your shirt, and I thought you were miserable about it. I certainly didn't read your expression correctly that night."

"I'm just as guilty. I thought you were embarrassed by me."

"Sadly, it took us a while to figure out what each of us was really thinking," she said quietly.

"Too bad we couldn't figure other things out." Tony's smile faded.

They looked at each other for what seemed like a long time, and regret and sadness washed through her.

Then he gave a crooked grin. "Don't look like that. We're good, right?"

"We're good with Ethan, and we're good with sex," she pointed out. His gaze dipped immediately to her breasts, and she was tempted to tip his chin back up herself. But no touching in public. "As for how we treat each other, you gave me a job as a challenge, as a way to shut me up."

"Yeah, well, I might have been mistaken in my motives. It's worked out okay. I don't mind having you around."

She sighed. "I'd give you a flip remark about that, but if I'm being serious, I can agree with you."

"You're being serious—what a revelation."

She punched him lightly in the arm—and again noticed Ethan watching them with a scowl.

"Okay, either our son is having a bad gaming night, or he doesn't like seeing us together."

"That doesn't make sense."

"Maybe not, but it's all I can deduce."

"Maybe he thinks we should be discussing a new phone for him."

"He's not close enough to know one way or the other." To change the subject, she said, "So you and the team going out tonight?"

"Yeah, we're heading back to Valentine and going to Outlaws."

"Ooh, the enemy."

"It's a country western bar and dance club. Maybe I'm spying."

"Maybe you just don't want to be the boss."

"Maybe that, too."

"Hey, Boss, just so you know, I'm being careful with the bands. Jessica and I are going to hear Red Dye 7 tomorrow night. They're a New York band hanging out in Colorado for the season."

"Sounds good."

But he didn't seem all that interested as his gaze roamed down her body again.

He said softly, "I don't suppose you want to drop Ethan at my place and wait up for me."

Her heart picked up speed at the mere suggestion, and once again she looked around before lowering her voice. "While that's an interesting invitation, I think the point of me picking up Ethan is to spend time with him. And it's a school night."

"When he's usually at my house anyway."

"Now don't go talking custody to me, Mr. De Luca. I like how relaxed we've been about it while I'm in Valentine. It's just not suiting *you* tonight."

"Tony, are you coming?" Nate called from the front of the lobby, where several of the guys had gathered near the door.

Kate turned her head, and she saw sudden surprise widen Nate's eyes, as if he hadn't seen her before. She noticed that Will just smirked, and she wondered what he knew. Come to think of it, since they'd skied last weekend, she hadn't seen much of him at the tavern.

"Hi, guys," she called. "I'll be taking Ethan home with me so you guys can go be manly."

"Thanks," Nate said, but he looked back and forth between them with interest.

"Okay, I'm out of here," she said. "Have fun." As Tony slung his equipment bag over his shoulder and picked up his hockey stick, she hurried toward the game room and leaned inside. "You ready to go, E.?"

He was standing at a pinball machine, finishing a game. He barely glanced over his shoulder. "In a minute, Mom."

She felt a surge of displeasure at his attitude, but now wasn't the time to talk about it. Ethan took his sweet time finishing up, then sauntered to her side. They both headed for the Range Rover.

"So what's going on?" she asked as they drove slowly down Main Street in Aspen before picking up speed after the airport.

He was looking at his phone. "Huh?"

"You can put that down, please."

He sighed melodramatically and lowered the phone to his lap.

"You seemed upset when I was talking to your dad about the festival. Why?"

He shrugged and looked out the window, but the darkness only reflected the frown on his face.

"I asked your opinion about me working for your dad, and you said you had no problem with it. Has that changed?"

"Not really."

He didn't look at her.

"We've been sharing time with you a little differently, too. Has it bothered you?"

"No."

"Then what's going on, Ethan?"

"Nothing."

She inhaled deeply and let it out. "Okay, then. I won't push it. But if you want me to leave you alone, then don't act all upset, like something's wrong."

He didn't answer, just turned his phone over and over in his lap.

She didn't give him permission to use it, and when he didn't seem inclined to talk, she turned on the radio. She'd always liked their long talks—they used to be able to discuss anything. But something else was going on, and she didn't think it was the typical "I'm too cool for my parents" behavior. She'd just have to give him time, and hope that he eventually talked to her.

Kate had the next day off, and Tony told himself that they should spend a day apart occasionally. But he couldn't stop thinking about how she'd told him she was going to see a band with Jessica, and it had taken everything in him not to ask to go along, too.

It was getting too easy to tease her when they were together, and sooner or later someone was going to notice. But he couldn't seem to help himself.

And now that she was planning the festival, she came to talk to him regularly during her shift, telling him about the window posters she was designing that ended with "Like us on Facebook." He couldn't believe the list of sponsors she'd gotten for a festival that would mostly benefit him. True, she was trying to make it a great hangout event between the stress of Christmas and the party of New Year's Eve, so maybe people were just in the holiday spirit.

But consequently, he got to see her excited, watch her face animate until it glowed and those eyes sparkle with delight. He'd forgotten how satisfied it made him just to make her happy. And that was a little unnerving.

He told himself the happier she was, the better the sex would be, and that was certainly true.

He wanted to find other ways to get her alone, so without thinking too much about what it all meant, he showed up at her door before lunch with a plan.

She stared at him in surprise. "If you need me to come into work, you could have called. And you showed up at my *front* door—what a shock. This isn't about sex at lunch?"

"Nope. I think you've been working too hard and need a break."

"I'm home, taking a break," she said with amusement, leaning against the door frame.

"If I know you—and I know you well—you're still working, whether it's on the festival or your law dilemma."

Her eyes lit with merriment, though she didn't speak.

"And you need to get away from it. Come on, I have stuff in the truck."

"Stuff? You have something *planned*? We said no dates."

"This isn't a date—I'm your boss insisting that you take an employee break."

She smiled. "Well, that explains everything."

"Are you coming? Or are we going to stand here letting all the cold air into your house?"

She hesitated for what seemed like a long time, though it could only have been seconds. Her hesitation made him realize that he desperately wanted her to go with him, and he wasn't so sure it was just about sex anymore. But he told himself what did it matter, when she'd be leaving next month anyway? And everything seemed a little dimmer at the thought.

"I'll get my coat," she finally said, shaking her head.

"And scarf and mittens and warm hat. Boots, too."

When she returned, all adorably bundled up, she said, "This is more and more mysterious."

"It won't be. I've fallen back on the old standby I once used to get you away from your studies when we were first in college. A picnic."

As she shut the door, she lifted her face to the cloudy sky. The snow had begun to fall softly, and now it sparkled where it touched her eyelashes.

"A picnic? I hope you mean indoors."

"You'll see."

He drove her up behind the Sweetheart Inn and parked near the plowed path marked HOT SPRINGS.

As he shut off the truck, she gave him a look. "You're kidding."

"Nope, let's go."

He grabbed his backpack and small cooler from the backseat and met her on the path. They walked side by side along the trail that wound along the bank of a stream. The trail steepened as they left the valley floor, then opened up to reveal the rock-edged hot springs pool. Steam from the water rose up into the trees surrounding it. The pool itself overflowed into the stream. A snow-covered wooden bench rested nearby.

"What, no picnic table?" she teased.

He opened up his backpack and removed a waterproof tarp, which he unfolded on the ground next to the heated pool. Then he covered that with a blanket.

"Remove your boots and sit down," he said. "You'll warm right up."

She stepped out of her boots near the edge, then walked into the center of the blanket and sat down, ditching her mittens to rub her hands together near the steam.

"Oh, this is nice. What a great place for a winter picnic!"

"I thought you'd approve. It's not exactly warm, but what the hell."

He laid out the sandwiches Chef had made for him. The man hadn't asked who they were for, but he'd given Tony a raised eyebrow and a smirk, which Tony had good-naturedly ignored. He'd also packed some vegetables and dip, and a couple of bottles of Coke.

She watched him lay out the picnic with an eagerness that reminded him of the girl he'd fallen in love with, the one so impatient for her life to begin, the one so full of confidence and certainty. Life had pummeled her a bit, but he had no doubt her confidence was already rebounding.

Chapter 18

Kate stared at the mini feast Tony had provided and didn't know what to think. She couldn't be surprised at his thoughtfulness—this was the Tony of old, who'd taken care of her, fed her when she forgot to eat, amused her when she'd studied too long. She found herself both aching for and enjoying the memories this picnic brought up. While they ate, the trees sheltered them from any breeze, the snow fell softly all around them, and a haze of mist shimmered over the hot spring.

Had Tony himself been what she'd missed all along? After their divorce, she'd never let a long-term relationship happen; had she been sabotaging her dating life because of memories of Tony? And here she was, letting their relationship start all over again. They'd both sworn it would be just sex, but that kept changing, since they worked together and had a son in common. She'd been seeing Tony more these last few weeks than she'd seen any other man. She was starting to wonder if just . . . being with him was one of the reasons she'd accepted his challenge to serve at the tavern, as if her subconscious had been calling the shots.

The memory of him as a boy had changed into her perception of the man he was, stronger, more confident, no longer the dreamer who didn't know what he wanted in life. He'd *found* himself, maybe at a slower pace than she had, but she felt sad and ashamed that they hadn't been able to give each other time during their marriage, that life—her life, her ambitions—had rushed them forward. She wanted to tell him all these things, but they were too intimate, too much reliving of a past that was gone and couldn't be changed.

But she could change the present.

And suddenly that was the scariest thing imaginable for someone like her, who'd always looked to the future. She turned to a safe subject.

"So, Ethan got an interesting offer."

He put down his sandwich and cocked his head.

"Walt asked him if he wanted to babysit once or twice a week for them."

Tony swallowed his food. "He wanted to bus tables at Carmina's, but I thought he was too young for a real job. Studies are more important."

"What about babysitting? It'd let him earn the money he wants."

"You mean the money for a smartphone."

They smiled at each other, the snow falling softly all around them like a Christmas postcard.

And suddenly, it was too intimate, too tender, and she was worried that sharing their love for Ethan was giving them other ideas.

She removed her scarf and hat, unzipped her coat.

"I didn't think the steam made you that warm," he said, smiling.

His smile died as she continued to remove clothing, beginning to shiver when she was down to her underwear and bra. But even those went, and she enjoyed the way Tony's mouth sagged open as she stood up and climbed down the rock stairs into the pool.

She groaned her delight at the wet heat and sank clear up to her chin, turning to face him as she perched on a rock ledge deep underneath.

Tony was already taking off his clothes. "This is crazy," he said.

"Maybe, but it's Colorado. Have you ever been near a hot springs where there *wasn't* someone naked?"

He laughed, then hopped quickly into the pool and sank right under the water. He emerged, sputtering, his hair plastered to his head. And then he moved toward her, eyes narrowed, face intent in a way that gave her a thrill at being the focus of his desire.

But she held up a hand. "Stop right there. Don't get any ideas. We may be having ex-sex, but not in this pool, not with a chance of infection."

"So you don't care that someone might come upon us in broad daylight having sex?"

"I didn't say that, but since it won't be happening, I don't have to worry about it. Now you may sit beside me if you're a good boy."

He laughed and groaned at the same time, then bodied up against her on the ledge and slipped his arm around her neck. She sighed with contentment and leaned against him. Through half-closed eyes, she watched the steam rise and meet the falling snow. They didn't speak, just breathed and enjoyed the glimpse of the snow-covered mountains through the trees.

And it was a perfect moment, one that made her ache with wonder and joy and the sadness of knowing that it had to end.

He leaned in and kissed her cheek, and she turned and kissed him back, opening her mouth, taking in his tongue, holding him tight.

When their deep kisses became softer, gentler, she murmured, "And this is making out, not foreplay."

He chuckled.

And then someone cleared her throat.

For a moment, every scenario flashed through her mind—it was someone they knew, someone who'd spread the gossip, and then Ethan would hear and become all excited that his parents might be back together.

But no, an old woman, a stranger, smiled at them. She peeled off her long, quilted coat that covered a bathrobe from the Sweetheart Inn. Then that came off to reveal a one-piece bathing suit with a skirt that almost came to her knees. With her feet, Kate was already dislodging dirt in the bottom of the spring to mix with the cascade of bubbles, hoping to obscure their nudity. Tony reached up a hand, and the old woman gladly took it to step down into the rocky pool.

"Ah, no wonder you two were enjoying yourselves," she said as the steam dampened her short salt-and-pepper curls. "This is lovely."

Kate stopped herself from protesting that they weren't *totally* enjoying themselves. No point sounding defensive.

"Are you two staying at the inn?" the old woman asked.

"We're locals," Tony said.

"Ah, and by all the preparation I can see here, young man, I will commend you for your romantic nature."

"Thank you, ma'am."

Kate barely resisted a giggle as she saw that Tony was blushing. When they had to leave, he'd really blush.

They chatted for about ten minutes as the tourist asked questions about things to do in Valentine Valley. She didn't seem to have any interest in leaving, and Kate gradually began to feel uncomfortably warm.

She glanced at Tony. "I think it's about time to get out."

The old lady smiled. "Don't mind me. It's nothing I haven't seen before. I've been married three times."

Chuckling, Kate managed to turn around as she stood, and Tony did the same, giving the poor woman two moons over the hot spring. They kept their backs to her as they took turns using the damp blanket to dry off. The heat of the springs faded and the shivering kicked in. Kate almost fell trying to step into her underwear, but at last she was fully dressed. Tony'd been much quicker than her, and he helped her on with her coat.

As he quickly packed up the last of their picnic, the old woman called, "Have a lovely day!"

Kate waved to her, and by the time they took the first bend in the path and were out of sight of the springs, her laughter erupted deeply and uncontrollably, with a few snorts thrown in.

Tony was grinning at her. "I don't think I've heard you laugh like that in . . . years."

She was weak from it, and held his arm as if she might tumble into a snowbank. "I . . . I can't decide if you were red from the heat or red from flashing that poor old lady!"

"I wouldn't say 'poor,' " he said dryly. "She seemed to be having a great time."

And that set off her laughter all over again. When he put an arm around her to keep her upright, it was the most natural thing in the world to slide her arm around his waist. They walked that way until the inn came into sight. With mutual understanding, they separated for the last solitary steps to the truck.

"I have some snowshoes in the back. Just think—you can tell Ethan you learned to do another fun exercise."

She didn't want to think anymore or question why it was so easy to be with Tony again, as if a sad divorce and nine years of estrangement didn't matter at all.

He'd thought of everything; he'd even brought a pair of snowpants for her. They spent an hour in the foothills behind the inn, hiking up high enough to see Valentine Valley spread out beneath them, blurred by beautiful snow. It was a peaceful time, and if it was hard exercise, she barely noticed, because she was enjoying the crunch of snow under her snowshoes, the gorgeous view, the easy company. They even tried jogging on the return, and he let her win.

Back inside the pickup, they warmed their hands in front of the heat vents as the windshield defrosted.

"Did Ethan tell you about the Christmas choir concert tomorrow during school?"

She stared at him and frowned. "No. I'm surprised you didn't send me the schedule."

He grimaced. "I got it at the beginning of the school year, and since you're not usually here weekdays, it didn't occur to me then. I should have checked my calendar sooner, but . . . anyway, I was about to send you the schedule when Ethan said he'd tell you."

"And he didn't." Kate crossed her arms over her chest. "That brat. I'm starting to take this personally."

"It's so strange to me, his behavior at the rink, and now this. He's always the first who remembers to tell you things. And he knows I can't come because I have to finish inventory."

"It's like he wants to piss me off enough to send me packing. Like I'd leave because of his behavior." And though she was angry, inside she couldn't help the little kernel of hurt that was now lodged next to her heart. "I've taken days off from work and made his big school events before, but most of those are during the evening. I'm going to enjoy looking around his school while it's in session. Maybe your sister will give me a tour."

"Maybe you should have Ethan do that," he suggested as he started the pickup.

From the moment Ethan appeared on the stage shared by Valentine Valley Middle and Elementary schools, Kate had to keep surreptitiously wiping away tears with her fingers. She hadn't bothered to tell him she was coming in advance—she knew when to choose her battles, and an argument might have spoiled her enjoyment of her son's performance. He was one of the taller boys, and he suddenly looked so grown up, his sandy hair almost neat. He'd be in high school next fall. How had that happened?

She hummed quietly along with the Christmas carols, clapped loudly after one girl performed a song she'd written. She looked at the expressions on all their faces, some into the music, others maybe not so much, but the sound of their voices raised in song for the season—oh, damn, she was crying again.

And in that moment, she knew she wanted another child. Maybe two. It hit her hard, because she hadn't even given it any thought in years, had been telling herself she had plenty of time to make a decision. She'd been such a young mom, the youngest at any school event—she still was. But she was thirty-three, with no long-term guy in sight except for her ex, whom she was only supposed to be sleeping with. She would like for Ethan to be home at least a year or two to get to know a little brother or sister before going off to college.

And then she felt selfish, looking at Lyndsay, standing to the side with the other teachers, smiling as she watched the concert. Kate at least had a child, whereas Lyndsay hadn't even met the right man yet.

After the concert, the kids came out to mill around

with their parents. Ethan saw her, to her relief—because she would have tracked him down.

"Hey, Mom, I didn't know you were coming," he said, his hands in his pockets.

"Your dad had inventory and couldn't make it. He was pretty surprised you'd forgotten to tell me about this."

Ethan didn't meet her eyes.

She let it go.

He nodded to his friend Brad, who was approaching, a woman following behind. The woman had the same black hair as her son, although his hung to his shoulders, unlike the woman's. Kate had heard good things about Brad, so she smiled at him.

"You must be Mrs. De Luca," the woman said, holding out her hand.

"Please call me Kate," she said, skirting the last-name issue. "Your son's a good kid."

Brad gave a little snort, and Ethan elbowed him.

"Thanks. I'm Beverly Zeigler. So nice to finally meet you. I hear you live in Vail?"

"Yes, I do. I'd love to have Brad visit us there one of these days. Maybe after the holidays?"

"What a nice invitation. Thank you." She turned to Ethan and gave him a fond look. "How nice for you that your mom finally came to one of your concerts."

Kate blinked in surprise—Beverly's tone was just lovely, but the words, not so much. She was surprised to feel their sting, but she knew it was all about guilt.

Ethan frowned. "Mrs. Zeigler, my mom's come to

lots of my events, mostly the evening ones, but I don't mind."

Well, the kid who wouldn't talk to her last night was now defending her. It was worth getting the rude comment.

Beverly reddened. "I'm so sorry, Kate. I didn't mean that the way it sounded. I was simply happy for Ethan that you could come."

"Thanks," Kate said.

Beverly and Brad moved away soon after.

Ethan watched them go, then shook his head. "Sorry. Maybe I should have warned you. Dad dated her a couple times."

"Oh." Kate looked after the woman in surprise. She seemed a little more uptight than she'd thought Tony would go for, but maybe that's why there'd only been a few dates. "When was this?"

"A couple years ago. No big deal."

Kate glanced at her one last time. Maybe it had been a bigger deal to Beverly.

"Hey, Kate!" Lyndsay called as she threaded her way through the crowd. She started to sling her arm around Ethan's shoulders, then realized he was too tall and went for his waist. "What did you think of our boy, here?"

Ethan reddened, his smile crooked. "Ms. De Luca, come on, we're in school—you know the rules. You invented them."

Lyndsay rolled her eyes. "Well, you thought it would be weird to call me Aunt Lyndsay in front of your friends. 'People might think you're playing favorites, Ms. De Luca.'"

"They all still think I can ask you for favors. Then I showed them that test of yours that I flunked."

"Flunked?" Kate echoed, eyeing her son.

"I still think you did that deliberately." Lyndsay turned to Kate. "Got a couple invitations for you. You doing anything tonight?"

"Can I catch up with Brad?" Ethan said, disentangling himself from his aunt and backing away. "We're, uh, doing homework together after school."

"Homework," Kate said. "How interesting."

"Bye, Mom." Ethan took off.

"It's Friday, isn't it?" Kate said dryly to Lyndsay.

"He's your kid; don't ask me to explain him. Anyway, you work tonight, right?"

"Right."

"I've got two events we can attend together tomorrow night, and both are so exciting, you won't be able to handle it."

Kate chuckled.

"First is the annual gingerbread house contest at the community center. Emily and her little sister Steph are judging."

"Ooh, when it's done, do we get to sample?"

"Uh, no." Lyndsay grinned. "And then afterward, my band is performing at a little jazz club down in Carbondale. You want to watch me make a fool of myself?"

"Do I? Yes!"

Saturday night, the gingerbread house competition was more fascinating than Kate had imagined. There were several dozen entries, some from schools, others from talented artists. There was a youth prize, an amateur prize, and a professional one. She thought the Sweetheart Inn re-creation should have won in the professional category, but someone had made the Valentine Valley town hall to perfection. The amateur prize went to a woman who'd re-created part of Main Street, and the youth prize went to a log cabin that any nineteenth-century silver miner would have been proud to live in.

It was a relief to go to the jazz club for food, since the untouchable gingerbread had made Kate hungry. She had some appetizers while she watched Lyndsay's band perform. It was a small group of six, with some brass and rhythm instruments, all people with regular jobs who loved keeping music in their lives. Kate watched the happiness suffuse their faces, and she remembered how much she'd enjoyed playing the trombone back in high school. She'd given up music—hell, she'd given up so much pursuing her career.

When Lyndsay finally joined her, Kate gave her a big hug.

"That was just wonderful!"

Lyndsay blushed. "Well, I don't know about that. I missed a few notes, and the audiences here are really forgiving."

"Have you played at Tony's?"

"Yeah, once or twice. I feel a lot more nervous then, like everybody knows I only got the gig because of my brother."

"Bull You guys sounded great—*that's* why you got the gig."

They ordered dinner and chatted about the band, then the dentist Lyndsay was casually dating.

"Lynds, do you mind if I ask you something that's maybe too personal? You just tell me if it is."

"Go ahead, but remember I might take my revenge," she said, pointing at Kate with her fork full of steak.

"What ever happened to the guy you dated for a lot of years in college and then afterward? I never asked Tony, because I didn't think it was my business after the divorce."

Lyndsay smiled even as she sighed. "Yeah, Bryan was as close as I ever got to marriage and having it all."

"I'm sorry if I'm bringing up painful memories. Just ignore me."

"No, no, it's okay. I really thought we'd get married. Hell, I was positive he was going to propose when he took me to the French restaurant at the Sweetheart Inn."

"He didn't?"

"Nope. He broke up with me. Wanted it to be in a nice place, you know, as a thank-you or something."

Kate winced, swallowing her pasta. "Oh, that's awful."

"Yeah. I think he just hoped I wouldn't make a scene. Like I would. That should have been my clue that he didn't know me all that well, but at the time . . . well, it hurt. And then he made things worse—further proving I was lucky to be rid of him—by saying he'd begun to feel like I was his sister. His sister!"

"Ugh!"

"I know! What, he slept with his sister? It gives me the creeps remembering it. Whatever. I got some minor revenge quite by accident. Turns out he was dating a zumba instructor, who ended up being a prostitute."

Kate's mouth fell open.

"Yeah. He even got his name in the paper as a john."

Kate giggled, then covered her mouth in shock. "I'm so sorry," she said around her fingers.

Lyndsay laughed. "Don't be. It's funny, now that a lot of time has passed. Maybe not to him." Her smile faded. "But ever since, I feel like I've been floating. Lately, I'm questioning every decision I make, even my teaching career."

"No! Lynds, all you ever wanted to be was a teacher."

Lyndsay shrugged, idly moving her fork through her mashed potatoes and making rivers with the gravy. "I know, and on a good day, I still love it. But . . . it's not quite what I thought it would be, and the paperwork and testing are getting out of control. I . . . I even found myself wondering if you made the choice I should have, leaving town to follow your dreams."

Kate's eyes widened. "Lynds—"

"So if I came across a little hostile a couple weeks ago, it was also about me, not just you and Tony and the divorce."

"I don't exactly feel successful right about now. I know everyone goes through their ups and downs, and my job is pretty down lately. Although I did find a re- tired chemist who worked with my client—oh, never mind, this isn't about me. I don't even know if I made all the right choices. I'm not perfectly happy. I don't have a guy either." She thought about Tony and bit back any words about him.

"But you've got a great kid, Kate."

"I'm glad you think so, but we're heading into a rough patch. He's . . . not happy with me, and I don't know why. I thought it would be great to be here for him through Thanksgiving and Christmas—the one bright spot on this stupid sabbatical."

"He's a teenager, Kate, you know that. Don't let it hurt you."

"I'm trying not to." A tear slipped down Kate's cheek, and she wiped it off quickly. "I've been sort of worried about him since I arrived. He seemed so surprised I could take any time off, even worried about *me*—kind of like I'm worried about my mom overdoing it. Yeah, my parents had a business they needed to focus on as I was growing up, but I took their drive so much to heart, and that's what I've been showing my son. Maybe he resents me. He doesn't even want to watch *It's a Wonderful Life*."

And then they both chuckled, and Kate wiped more tears away. She was glad for the dark, high-backed booths that muted conversations around them.

"And the Christmas train layout at the Hotel Colorado?" Lyndsay asked with gentle humor.

Kate just shook her head, and their chuckles faded. She sighed. "He's growing up, I know. But . . . I don't feel like a lawyer right now, and sometimes I don't even feel like a mom." She sniffed and reached for a tissue in her purse. "If it weren't for Tony . . ." She trailed off and sighed, blowing her nose.

Lyndsay frowned. "Tony?"

Kate stared at her friend, remembering how betrayed

Lyndsay had felt when Kate hadn't confided her marital problems in her. She didn't want to make that mistake again. "Yeah, we're . . . sleeping together."

The word *gape* wasn't strong enough for the way Lyndsay's mouth dropped open and her eyes bugged out.

"You're kidding me."

Kate winced. "Are you angry? Tony said it's called ex-sex and—"

"Ex-sex?" Lyndsay gasped, then covered her mouth and looked around to see if anyone had noticed her outburst. She stared at Kate for a full minute. "I—I—" Then she started to laugh. "Oh, how did I not see this happening?"

"Well, we have kept it pretty secret," Kate insisted.

"I bet it was Tony's idea."

"How did you know?"

"He's a guy. I didn't think you'd be the one to risk everything by trying to seduce him. But hell—this is such a big risk, Kate."

"I know," she said, shoulders bowed.

"Do you regret it?" Lyndsay asked hesitantly.

"No. I can't. We're adults, and though we resisted for a while, I'm not upset about it. We're having fun, and we never had any problem in bed. Wait, that's not true," she suddenly remembered. "But all those problems were mine, my exhaustion, how focused I was on trying to find a way to be a good mom while studying all hours of the day and night. Poor Tony sometimes got left out. I was an idiot."

Lyndsay eyed her thoughtfully. "You sound like you might be regretting the divorce."

Kate stiffened. "I didn't mean it that way—I think. I can't look back on the past, something I can't change. Whatever decisions I made, I can only learn from them."

"What about the present? You can change that."

Kate stared at Lyndsay, feeling her stomach tighten with distress. "I—I don't know what you mean," she said lamely.

"You and my brother are obviously having a great time. Maybe that should tell you something. And I'm not saying that just because I'm his sister. Hell, if I was acting as his sister more than your friend, I'd tell you to stop playing around with my brother's heart again."

"Lynds, it's just sex, I promise. No hearts involved."

"Really? Is it that easy to forget you loved him, that you've loved him since childhood?"

Kate could only stare at her.

"God, you've gone white," Lyndsay said, reaching to touch her hand. "I'm sorry if you haven't thought about this, but you should. Maybe your body is trying to tell your heart something."

Chapter 19

Late Sunday morning, Tony was working in his basement workshop, setting up for the Christmas gift Ethan had asked him to help make for Kate. All around him on the workbench and on metal shelves, he was surrounded by the tools his dad and grandpa had given him over the years, as well as the ones he'd saved up to buy. He was humming to himself, feeling pretty satisfied with the world—some regular sex could do that for a guy.

He heard the door open at the top of the stairs. "Ethan?"

"No, it's Lyndsay. Can I come invade your male sanctuary?"

He laughed. "Get down here."

She came down slowly, then sneezed. "Sawdust always does that to me. Whatchya making?"

"I'm helping Ethan with some Christmas gifts. It's a secret."

"Nothing but some piles of wood, as far as I can see."

"We're behind." He leaned back against the work-bench, crossed his arms over his chest, and studied her. "Don't you have a wedding shower to attend?"

"Yeah, I'm on my way." She swiped a hand across a dusty stool and sat down to face him. "So . . . I had dinner with Kate last night. I hear you two are doing the nasty again."

Tony sighed. He couldn't be surprised that Kate had spilled their secret to Lyndsay. "It's a good thing my son can't overhear this."

"I made sure he was at Kate's."

"So your point is . . . ?"

"Kate didn't want to lie to me again, but I see you had no such problem."

"Lynds, I'm not talking to you about my sex life. That must cross some kind of sibling boundary."

She smiled. "Yeah, I guess it does." Her smile faded. "And maybe another boundary is keeping silent when you think your sibling is making a mistake, but I just can't do it."

He arched a brow. "No one would ever accuse you of keeping your opinions to yourself."

"Nope, I don't want to have any regrets. Tony, if you keep this up, one or both of you will get hurt. I told Kate you both need to think about why you're doing this."

"Because it's fun," he said dryly.

"That's all it is—fun? I remember you as a little kid—you followed her around before you even under-stood why. And by the time you were a teenager, you didn't want anyone else. You couldn't *see* anyone else. And you think those feelings disappeared just because you got divorced?"

She was making him feel uncomfortable, and he wasn't sure why. "Look, Lynds, I appreciate the worry. Really. But nine years—"

"Don't bother with the numbers. I don't think the years matter when you love someone like you loved Kate. She hurt you—hell, you hurt each other—and maybe by pretending it's all about sex, you think you're exorcising the ghost of your marriage or something."

"No," he said patiently, "I think I'm enjoying no-strings-attached sex."

She heaved a sigh and stood up. "You keep telling yourself that. But she's leaving here, Tony, leaving you behind again. I only hope the breakup is on better terms this time."

To his surprise, she kissed his cheek before jogging up the basement stairs.

He realized he was grinding his teeth together, and he made himself stop. His sister was well-meaning, but she was wrong. He'd learned his lesson. He was never going to let any feelings for Kate obscure his good judgment.

It had been many years since Kate had been to the Silver Creek Ranch. She drove up the snow-covered road that wound its way through barren fields, where cows huddled together against the wind. The house and outbuildings all had red roofs, but it was to the barn she was headed. Josh Thalberg had converted the second story into an apartment, where he lived with Whitney and their baby girl.

There were lots of cars parked in the yard, and Kate regretted her high-heeled boots as she was forced to pick her way across frozen ruts in the ground. To her surprise, Lyndsay was waiting for her just inside the big barn doors.

"We should have planned this better," Lyndsay said, pulling her inside and up the stairs, both of their packages bumping walls as they went. "I could have picked you up. Even one less car in the yard would have helped."

Kate paused appreciatively in the doorway of the apartment. It was one big open room, with the furniture designating each section, from kitchen, to great room, to bedroom. Tall windows looked out on the snow-topped mountains, and beautiful landscapes dominated the walls. Fifteen or twenty people already milled about, eating appetizers and drinking Bellinis.

When Kate took her first sip of the Bellini, she hummed her approval. "Lynds, you know what I did after your band concert? Got out my trombone. My lip is gone, but it was fun trying to blast some notes."

"Think you'll pick it up again?"

"Maybe. Or maybe something else musical, like guitar or keyboard. That might be quieter in my condo."

"You mean when you go back to Vail."

"Yep." But Kate didn't meet Lyndsay's curious gaze. She didn't want to talk about Tony, or if things had changed between them. Her decisions were still churning around in her mind and in her heart. And then she saw Whitney, holding Olivia on her hip as she tried to pour another Bellini.

"Let me." Kate swooped up the baby before anyone else could.

"Thanks," Whitney said. "Believe me, at these kinds of events, I barely get to hold her, and the one time I'm hostessing, she wants her mom. But she seems to be doing pretty good with you."

Kate grinned down into the little upturned face with the big eyes and the trembling lips that began to ease into a smile. "I always loved babies. True, it's been a long time since my own was one, and I didn't get to enjoy him nearly as much as I wanted to. Remember to appreciate every moment." She kissed the warm little head with its soft dark hair. The ache to have another of her own rose up inside her, maybe a little girl she could dress in the cutest clothes . . .

She was rewarded with a sigh and a snuggle, as Olivia brought her fist to her mouth and chewed. Kate hummed and swayed.

Lyndsay eyed her. "She looks comfortable—so do you."

Kate just shrugged and sighed with happiness.

"Hello again, Kate."

Kate turned at the mildly familiar voice and saw Beverly Zeigler, Brad's mom—who'd once dated Tony. For just a moment, Kate wondered if they'd slept together, and she felt a shot of jealousy she had no business feeling.

"Hi, Beverly. I didn't know you knew Brooke."

"My son takes riding lessons from her."

"Oh, right, I completely forgot about her riding school."

"How do you know Brooke?" Beverly asked.

"I went to school with her brother, Nate."

"Who's good friends with your ex-husband." Beverly glanced at Lyndsay. "And you seem good friends with Tony's sister, too."

"We've known each other our whole lives." Kate smiled at Lyndsay.

"It's nice to have a sister's support," Beverly said before eventually moving on to the next chatting group.

"What was that about?" Kate whispered.

"She once told me she thought I could have done more to 'help' her when she was dating Tony."

"Like Tony doesn't have a mind of his own?"

"Hmm, yeah. And I'm only helping you by giving you my advice. Did you think about it?"

"Let's not get into it here."

Wearing an amused expression, Lyndsay shook her head.

Brooke approached and gave them both a hug. "So glad you could make it, Kate."

"It was nice of you to include me. I can't believe how much everyone has made me feel welcome."

Brooke laughed. "Well, it's your own hometown, isn't it? Now that you've spent so much time here, think you'll move back someday?"

Kate blinked in surprise. "Well . . . I don't know. I really haven't given it much thought. My job's in Vail right now."

"Which is why I was surprised about you taking a temporary job here instead of relaxing. I think you're crazy."

"Thanks, but it's been fun. For instance, I was going to talk to you and some of the other girls about the band festival I have planned for the Saturday between Christmas and New Year's. Would you be interested in becoming a sponsor? We'd line the parking lot fence with banners promoting you."

"That sounds great. I'm sure the other girls would love to join in. Let's get them together."

"Oh, wait, no," Kate insisted, resetting Olivia on her chest. "This is your shower, I didn't mean to—"

"Nonsense. We're just standing around talking now. And we'd all do anything for Tony."

Yes, everyone loved Tony, and Kate couldn't blame them. Soon enough, all her friends' businesses were "signed up" to be sponsors: Monica's Flowers and Gifts, Sugar and Spice, As You Like It Catering, Leather and Lace, and Thalberg Riding School. She told them about the bands she'd already lined up, and the last one she was going to see.

"The Dead Can Sing is a band?" Brooke's mom asked doubtfully.

Kate smiled at Mrs. Sandy Thalberg, a cheerful, dark-haired woman who leaned on a cane to accommodate her MS. "My son recommended them, so I've got to go hear them perform live. Their videos are . . . confusing," Kate confessed.

"To say the least," Lyndsay added. "Yeah, the kids are obsessed with them. That'll be a whole new generation at your festival—if you like the band."

"I hope I do . . ."

After brunch, Brooke opened gifts, saving the widows' gift for last. Everyone seemed to be holding their breaths as Brooke started to pick up the box and it sagged in her hands.

"It's so heavy," she said warily.

Mrs. Palmer, the groom's grandmother, and Mrs. Thalberg grinned at each other, while Mrs. Ludlow just sighed.

Brooke took off the wrapping, opened the box, and spread wide the tissue paper. "It's . . . plumbing fixtures?"

"It's a chrome-plated dual shower head," Mrs. Palmer said proudly. "One of them comes right off the wall so you can enjoy—"

"Grandma!" Brooke interrupted. "I'm sure we get the point."

"I knew we'd make her blush," Mrs. Thalberg said proudly.

Mrs. Ludlow gave her roommates a long-suffering look. "I barely stopped them from ordering edible body paint online."

There were shouts of laughter, even as Whitney hastily announced dessert. The guests munched on tarts and Christmas cookies provided by Sugar and Spice.

Kate was standing beside the elder Mrs. Thalberg, and they were having a cheerful debate about which cookie was better.

"I don't know, Mrs. Thalberg, those cookies you served when we had dinner at your house—Tony thought they could win a competition. You could give Emily a run for her money."

"Then we *should* have a competition—maybe at your band festival?"

Kate eyed her. "What do you have in mind?"

"Well, we could benefit some kind of charity—oh, wait, maybe our school! That way we could get the young people involved. There could be a Christmas cookie bake-off, and maybe a bake sale at the same time. It would be wonderful if the children did some of the baking as a way to contribute toward their school."

"That's a great idea!" Kate said enthusiastically. "But do we have enough time to pull it off? There's only a week left."

"You leave it to me."

"And me," Lyndsay said. "If you want the kids to bake, middle school kids might be the ones to work with. I'll talk to the principal. They can always use a fund-raiser, and we like teaching kids the responsibility of being involved. Plus, it'll give us something to talk about with them other than Christmas, Christmas, Christmas."

"It is almost that time," Jessica Fitzjames said as she joined their conversation. "I can't believe how many kids have entered my Christmas writing contest at the *Gazette*."

Kate sighed. "I've tried to get Ethan to write something, but he's resisting."

Jessica chuckled. "Yeah, I haven't gotten all that many entries from middle school. But thanks for trying. Any way we can encourage kids to write is good."

She and Jessica clinked punch glasses, but Kate couldn't help thinking that Ethan probably wouldn't do anything she suggested lately . . .

Kate enjoyed another half hour at the shower before she had to go home and get ready for work. She wrote down all the ideas for a bake sale and cookie bake-off, and came up with some templates of posters and announcements, before e-mailing them to Lyndsay to show her principal. Everything was coming together with the festival—though she couldn't say the same for the retired chemist she was trying to track down, who didn't want to answer e-mails. It was Christmas, after all, but she wasn't about to give up.

She got to Tony's Tavern early and helped Erika finish up her tables. It was a Sunday night, and slow, and to her surprise, the grumpy guy she'd had as a customer before came back in, cell phone still pressed to his ear, wearing a rumpled suit, as if he had to work on Sunday.

She left a menu and water while he was talking, and when she returned, she smiled at him, hoping to get one in return. No dice.

"Hey, I remember you," she said cheerfully. "I asked you what band you'd like to see at our band festival, and you said Double Cyn."

"Oh, right," he said absently.

"Well, they agreed to come."

His eyes focused on her for the first time. "Really? To a small place like Valentine Valley? They've had some famous songs. I remember they played with the Boston Pops on the Fourth of July."

"I know, I was shocked, too. My favorite song of theirs is 'Who Can Tell in the Dark.' "

He nodded.

"Their manager said they were going to relax for the holidays in Aspen—what a freak coincidence, huh? You going to come see them?"

"Uh, I don't know, I might be busy."

"What would keep you so busy on the Saturday between Christmas and New Year's? Oh, probably plans with your family."

"No family," he said, scanning the menu as if it didn't matter.

"I'm sorry."

He looked at her like she was nuts. "Why? It's not your problem."

"I know, it's just . . . I bet holidays can be hard without family."

He shrugged. "I'm used to it. I'll take the striped bass."

As she wrote down the rest of his order, he volunteered, "Did you know striped bass were originally brought to Colorado to feed the alligators on a farm?"

"No! How interesting." She couldn't believe she was getting this guy to actually talk to her.

"Yep. And the bass multiplied like crazy, and became more popular to eat than the alligators."

"Thanks for the info. You never know when a customer would like to hear that story. Can I share?"

"Sure."

She went to enter her order in the POS.

Tony came and leaned a hip on the counter next to her. "What was Vince so talkative about?"

"A Colorado striped bass farm. You must know about it."

"Yeah. But I have to tell you, you're the first person in here to get him to stay off his phone, let alone talk."

She grinned. "I'm irresistible."

He looked at her mouth. "I can agree."

She felt herself blush and glanced around. "Sorry, I didn't mean to make that seem like I was flirting."

"I know."

They looked at each other for a long moment, and she remembered Lyndsay's warnings. *Was* she letting herself fall back in love with him? Was she making a terrible mistake? Was it even a mistake? Oh, that was too much to contemplate right now.

"Vince has no family," she said, quickly looking back at the POS.

"I know. His wife and kid died in a car accident about five years ago."

She gasped. "Oh, how terrible!"

"Don't tell him you know—he doesn't like to talk about it."

"How do *you* know?"

"He used to be a regular, had a good time every Saturday night drinking. That changed after his family's death. All he does is work—he's in insurance—and he only recently started coming here again for a meal."

"Maybe he thought he lost time with them by coming here regularly."

"Yeah, I think so."

Poor guy had lost all his family—and she'd practically given hers away without doing everything possible to save it. Almost immediately, her throat closed with the threat of tears.

"Are you okay?" Tony asked with concern.

"Yeah, sure, Vince's story just got to me. Thanks for letting me know."

When she eventually delivered Vince's striped bass, she spent a few minutes talking about Double Cyn, and felt . . . content.

An hour later, she was running food to a table near the front door when it opened.

"Kate!"

It took her a moment to recognize Cal Carpenter, an Aspen lawyer who'd semi-retired to open a small law firm in Valentine Valley. She'd spent a couple of summers interning for him in high school and college, and she used to sit in on his trials, which had fascinated her. He'd shown her the competitiveness of their career, had made her see that every day on the job could be different and exciting. He was a little grayer than she remembered, but he was still handsome and fit, with a great early-season goggle tan.

"Hi, Cal," she said. "Give me a sec."

When she'd delivered her food, she came to him and was surprised by a big bear hug.

"Look at the famous lawyer," Cal said, holding her upper arms and smiling at her. "To think I knew you when." And then he squinted and looked around. "But you're working here . . . ?"

"I'm on a family sabbatical for a couple months," she said, trying to suppress a mortified blush. "Tony's my ex-husband, and what started out as a joke challenge between us sort of turned into a way to pass the time while our son is in school."

"Oh, I get it," he said.

Though he looked like he might not really get it—or maybe he did. Kate was starting to think the heat was on too high, and she wanted to fan herself. It had been a while since people had pointed and whispered while she'd worked, but Cal's scrutiny almost felt the same.

"Can I sit at one of your tables?" Cal asked.

"Sure, right this way. You have your pick. It's a slow night. I think people are relaxing at home after a crazy weekend shopping." Oh, God, now she was babbling.

Cal just smiled at her as he sat down.

"Are you waiting for someone else?" Kate asked.

"Nope, I'm here alone tonight. The wife is off in Aspen—you guessed it—shopping."

"When we have such great stores here?" she teased.

He eyed her. "Since when did you have such a crush on Valentine Valley? I seem to remember you couldn't wait to escape."

"I didn't want to escape the town so much as I wanted the powerful big-city law firm," she said ruefully.

"And did that work out for you?"

She opened her mouth, hesitated, then said, "For a long while it has. I'll be right back with a menu."

She left a menu and water but kept on moving, though she wasn't all that busy. Tony occasionally eyed her with amusement, which only made her feel more flustered.

At last she couldn't delay anymore and went to take Cal's order.

He put down his menu. "I'll have the fried chicken sandwich and coleslaw. And whatever you have on tap."

"Well, we have—"

"Just pick me out something dark. Then come back and talk to me."

She took her time inputting his order and kept clicking the wrong button. She was relieved Tony was suddenly busy at the bar.

She put Cal's beer on the table in front of him.

"Kate, don't be offended, but I have to say this. I've always held a place for you in my tiny firm."

Her eyes widened. "Oh, Cal—"

"Your talents go way beyond our little town, I know, but you'd be surprised how much work there really is in a town like Valentine. And I still have a lot of connections in Aspen, and I steer business this way. I've called myself semi-retired for a long time, but there's always been too much work for that to be true. I'd like it to start being true, but the only person I'd trust to do the job right is you."

"Cal, I'm still working for Clements, Lebowitz, and Yang."

"Okay, but you're taking a lot of time off, which means something's going on. Is someone in your family sick?"

"No, but—"

"Sorry, you don't owe me any explanations or excuses. It's none of my business, as long as everyone is healthy. But I can't hold out forever."

"Thanks for the generous offer, Cal."

She escaped, only to see Tony watching her curiously. She hadn't out and out refused Cal. She really should have; just because she believed her senior partners should have trusted her more didn't mean she should throw away her career with one of Denver's most prestigious law firms. She had something to prove, after all.

But hadn't she spent her twenties proving herself, and what had it gotten her? Her son only on the weekends, and her weekdays crammed with work. And alone—she was alone. So what if she commanded the respect of fellow lawyers? She'd thought it would mean so much more than a pat on the back, but sometimes that's all it felt like.

But not these last couple of weeks. She'd been back with family and friends, rediscovered some things about herself that she'd given up, music and hobbies and just having fun, all because she thought she hadn't deserved them—not when she'd given up on her marriage.

"Yoo hoo," Ted Ferguson said from his customary place at the bar.

Ned waved his hand in front of her eyes. "Control to Kate Fenelli."

She shook her head and smiled. "Sorry, guys, I thought Tony was taking care of you. Is he shirking his duties?"

"Naw, just getting ready for Desantis's bachelor party tomorrow night," Ted said. "He's closing the back room and everything. Since you seem to be doin' so many jobs around here, maybe you're gonna be the dancin' girl."

She laughed aloud. "Now that would be a terrible bachelor party."

Ned whistled. "I don't think so."

She leaned toward him. "You are very sweet."

"I don't mean to be sweet," he grumbled to his brother.

"These guys giving you a tough time?" Tony asked as he entered the room and walked the length of the bar.

"Not at all. Seems I've disappointed them by not being the main attraction at the bachelor party. Sorry, guys, but I'm heading off to see a band perform, the last one to firm up for the festival."

"Where are they performing?" Tony asked.

"Aspen."

"Who's going with you?"

"Nobody. I'm on my own. It's hard for people to get away at Christmas."

"That doesn't seem smart."

"You think I'm in danger in that tough town?" She glanced at the twin plumbers. "Or maybe he wants me to serve the men at the bachelor party."

The twins chuckled as Tony said, "Uh, no."

"I think he won't enjoy having his ex around while he ogles a stripper," Kate said as an aside.

"Who says there's a stripper?" Tony asked.

"You'll have to let me know."

Teasing Tony was fun, but it didn't distract her from Cal Carpenter and his surprising offer. As she went back to Cal's table to bring his food or get him another beer, he never mentioned it again. She told herself he was being polite, but she couldn't stop wondering if everything that had happened to her the last few weeks was leading to something inevitable.

And it was scary and exhilarating all at once.

Chapter 20

Tony didn't go over to Kate's Sunday night. It had been three days since they'd been alone together, but he reminded himself it was just for fun, and it wasn't like he was desperate. Hell, he'd gone a year without sex after their divorce.

But his house was empty when he got home, and he found himself wandering from room to room aimlessly. He tried to go to bed, but his thoughts were full of Kate. Almost angrily, he went down to his workshop, but even that project was about her. He couldn't escape.

When he got to work midmorning the next day, he was glad she wasn't working until the dinner shift. He was able to concentrate on scheduling, the bane of his existence, and calling the linen company. But he kept getting phone calls about the festival, and he gradually realized it was getting bigger than he'd imagined. She'd lined up at least five bands and multiple sponsors. Tony's Tavern had never done anything like this before, and much as he knew this would definitely increase his business, he didn't like feeling beholden to her.

She'd always been ambitious, and he'd learned it was just a part of her. She could never slack off on anything. When the festival had gone from being four hours in the evening to six or seven hours, starting in the afternoon, he'd accepted it, because he knew how she was.

But . . . maybe letting her take over meant that at last he'd really forgiven her, that he could let go of the past. Coordinating the event honestly seemed to be fun for her, and he couldn't change who she was.

And then she came in before four, and every thought in his head faded away as his blood rushed south. She was wearing a cropped top, short skirt over tights and high boots, and her short blond hair was wild about her head, styled to look like she'd just gotten out of bed. Was she doing this just to tease him?

And then he remembered the bachelor party and the concert.

"No, you're not serving or dancing or whatever at the bachelor party," he said when he was finally able to talk.

Her throaty laugh almost made him shiver.

"Don't worry. I just want to fit in at the concert. The Dead Can Sing play to a young crowd. I'm kind of old, but—"

"You're not old," Ted Ferguson said reverently, before holding up a mug of beer to salute her.

She kissed his cheek. "Aw, thanks, Ted."

"We might be needing a lawyer soon," Ned told her.

"You guys just give me a call."

When the bachelor party guests started arriving to play poker, they demanded that Kate be one of their servers. Tony saw her blushing, and he didn't have to say anything as she held up a hand.

"No, no, guys, I'm out of here soon."

Adam Desantis, the groom, shook his head. "Damn, Tony, you're crazy to have her here. She must drive you wild."

Will snorted and put an arm around Tony's neck. "We can only imagine." For Tony's ears alone, he added, "When you're done with her just—"

Without thinking about it, Tony shoved him a little too hard, and Will almost stumbled over an empty chair. Voices died as people turned to see what was going on. Adam looked curiously at Tony, and even Kate frowned from the table she was waiting on.

Will grinned. "Sorry, stupid joke, my fault."

Adam exchanged a glance with his future brothers-in-law, Nate and Josh, but didn't say anything.

Tony felt like an idiot. "Go on in, guys. The tables are all set up for poker. I'll get the pitchers of beer."

As the others left, Will put out a hand and, as his smile dimmed, said, "Sorry, Tony."

Tony took it. "Don't apologize. I'm distracted. I wasn't thinking."

Will hesitated, as if he was going to say something else, then ambled into the back room.

Tony went into his office and sat down, staring at the computer screen blankly.

"Are you okay?"

He turned to see Kate leaning in the doorway, her expression one of concern.

"I didn't exactly see what happened . . ." she continued.

"It was nothing, Will and I just fooling around."

"Glad you shook on it then," she said, her smile crooked.

She started to leave, but he called her back. "So where is this concert?"

"At Chameleon in Aspen. Why?"

"Just want to know where you are if you don't come home. Ethan might worry."

She eyed him curiously. "Thanks."

In between all the poker playing and pool challenges, Tony heard his bartender Lamar say that Kate had left. He thought of her driving in winter weather conditions to Aspen. She was a mountain pro; she had a Range Rover. And then he thought of her alone in a bar, looking hot and available, and he lost card game after card game, to the delight of the Sweet brothers. Even the dancer—she was a little too tame to be called a stripper—didn't interest him. After a word to Lamar, he left the party and headed for Aspen.

He knew where the bar was, of course, though he had to park blocks away and walk through a windy snowfall to reach it. Inside, it wasn't hard to find Kate. There were a lot of flashing lights and too-loud music, and she didn't hear him approach as she sat at the bar, leaning over it to say something to the bartender.

Tony got jostled up against her by other patrons, and she started, looking swiftly over her shoulder.

Her eyes widened. "Tony."

The guys on either side of her looked pissed off. For the first time since he and Kate had started sleeping together, he was able to put his arms around her neck from behind in public and lean in to kiss her cheek.

"Hey, babe, sorry I'm late."

She glanced sideways at him, her smile slow and knowing. He could smell her perfume, and he wanted to bury his face in her neck—but not in a bar. When he straightened, she swiveled on the stool and looked up at him, elbows back on the bar in a provocative pose. The guys on either side of her gave Tony a last reproving glance and turned away.

"I'm so glad you could make it," she teased. "Couldn't resist hearing The Dead Can Sing?"

No, I couldn't resist being with you. But he wasn't saying that aloud. It was hard to even admit to himself. He leaned down so she could hear him over the music. "It's the last band on the list, right? I'll be happy to have it finalized. I got a lot of calls about the festival today, by the way."

She looked sheepish. "Hope you didn't mind too much. But I think it'll be a success."

"I don't doubt it, not with you in charge."

"What a lovely compliment."

"It's the truth."

She angled her head toward the back of the bar, where the band was playing and the fans crowded against each other. "What do you think?"

He listened for a while. "Not bad. Ethan has mentioned them before."

She stood up and took his hand. "Then let's dance."

Dragged along in her wake, he watched heads turn to stare at her as she walked by. It was hard to even think of her as the elegantly garbed, steely-eyed lawyer she also was. But there were a lot of sides to Kate Fenelli.

They danced without touching, he kind of just moving side to side, watching her as she danced with her arms over her head, her body gyrating, her eyes closed as she felt the music. God, she was incredible. He wished there'd be a slow song soon so he could feel her against him, but no such luck with this band. But the next song was a little slower in beat, and she stepped up against him, moving her hips against his in time to the music, holding onto his waist as she arched back. He let his fingers caress her exposed midriff, and it took everything in him not to make out with her right on the dance floor. It was freeing to know they knew nobody and didn't have to keep secrets or pretend that they weren't really hot for each other.

They didn't last long. Before he knew it, she was grabbing her coat and pulling him out the door.

"Where's your truck?" she asked. "It's got bigger seats."

God, she turned him on. They both started to run through the snow, holding hands and laughing.

Once in his truck, they didn't speak after she said, "Find someplace deserted. Quick."

He knew a road not too far outside of town that dead-ended near the Roaring Fork River. He was barely in park before she was out of her seat belt and wiggling out of her underwear. He slid over on the bench beneath her, and she did another little dance on top of him, swaying to silent music, moving her hips to a beat he didn't have to hear to understand. His hands roamed her body, sliding along her bare skin at her waist, then under her skirt and between her legs. He mouthed her breasts through her clothes.

She moaned and said breathlessly, "Don't make me wait."

He unbuckled and unzipped as fast as he could. And when at last he was inside her, encased in her moist heat, everything in his world was all about her, tasting her, touching her, never being able to get enough of her.

But afterward, when they were both perspiring and panting and grinning at each other, he felt his smile die as he looked into her beautiful face. He cupped it, letting his thumb rub her lower lip gently. They stared into each other's eyes, and he couldn't help thinking, *What am I doing?*

Everything Lyndsay had warned him about was coming true. It wasn't just sex anymore for him—Kate was rocking his world. He couldn't stop himself from being with her, having her. He was getting obsessed all over again, like he was still in high school.

He wasn't sure what she could read from his expression, but she slid off his lap, tugged on her underwear, and readjusted her clothing.

In a slightly forced teasing tone, she said, "Good thing I found my underwear, or with our luck, Ethan would have."

He nodded, then zipped and buckled himself back up. As he started the truck, he asked, "Can you drive home okay? I'm not sure how much you had to drink."

"Just a glass of wine. I'll be fine. I'll show you where my car is."

On the drive back into Aspen, she chatted on about plans for a Christmas cookie bake-off she'd concocted with the widows and a bake sale to raise funds for the school, all to be held at the band festival. He nodded at the right moments but didn't really have a lot to say. His mind was in panic mode.

He let her off a block from the Chameleon, just past her Range Rover.

She waved. "You don't have to follow me home. I'm a big girl."

"Good night, Kate."

As he drove away, he hoped she would still be a big girl when he broke things off with her. Because it was over—it *had* to be over, before it went too far and someone got hurt. But he hadn't been about to drop her right after sex. He might be an obsessed idiot, but he wasn't a jerk. He would find a better time to tell her.

It was only a couple of days until Christmas, so Tuesday after work, Kate headed to her mom's house for dinner and to help bake cookies. She texted Ethan to let him know what she was doing, but she wasn't going to force him to help. Although she always loved how he could take a simple cookie-cutter cookie and make it look different—like turning a gingerbread man upside down and painting it to look like a reindeer with antlers.

She beat her mom home, let a grateful Barney outside, found the meat loaf in the fridge, and put it in the oven before starting to mix cut-out cookie dough. Back inside, Barney patiently sat on the kitchen throw rug in front of the sink, waiting for scraps. Kate put the dough in the fridge and started to glance through more recipes, wondering which looked easiest, when her mom came through the door, out of breath, carrying packages. Her keys dropped to the floor.

"Damn," Christina said.

"Let me help, Mom." Kate grabbed bags and set them on her mom's small corner desk.

Christina dropped her purse on the counter, then slowly began to unwind her scarf, still breathing raggedly. "I wish winter was over." She absently petted Barney, who'd trotted over to greet her.

"Mom, that's blasphemous around here, you know that." Kate picked up the keys and set them near her mom's purse. She frowned. "You okay? You're really out of breath."

"I'm just tired. The restaurant has been packed with people too overwhelmed to do their own cooking. Though we appreciate their business, it's getting harder and harder for me to play the jovial hostess. And don't say I'm getting old," she added sharply.

Kate held up both hands. "I would never dream of it. But maybe you're not getting enough sleep."

"Yeah, there's that." She took off her coat and draped it over a chair. "Maybe I should lose some weight, too.

That would help." She sagged into a chair. "And exercise more. I guess bustling around Carmina's isn't exactly exercise."

"I'll go walking with you. Or there's snowshoeing. Tony introduced me to that. It's fun."

Christina gave her a sudden shrewd look. "When did he do that?"

Kate knew better than to look away. And she was used to hiding her emotions, with the work she did. "Last week. He let me borrow some when I complained one too many times about hating to run." And none of that was a lie; she'd just left out some facts.

The back door opened, and Kate was relieved when her dad trooped in, followed by Joe and Ethan.

"Hey, Grandma," Ethan called. "Dad said I should come hang out here, since he has to work. Something about cookies needing to be baked?"

Kate grinned and felt all mushy looking at her son. And then he noticed her, and his happy expression faded a bit.

"Hi, Mom."

He could have stabbed her and it might have hurt less. She was done wondering what was going on, waiting for him to open up. First chance she got, she was going to ask him.

They ate meat loaf and baked potatoes and peas, a favorite childhood menu of hers. The talk ranged from the holidays, to Joe's next basketball game, to a snowboarding slalom competition Ethan was thinking of entering.

"Ethan, I went to see The Dead Can Sing last night."

Joe gaped and spoke before Ethan could. "No way! How did you score tickets?"

"No tickets. They were performing at a bar in Aspen. You just have to be of age to attend, and pay the cover."

She pushed aside any thoughts of Tony and his pickup so she wouldn't blush. She'd never look at that truck the same way again.

Joe and Ethan wore identical frowns, and Kate barely kept from laughing.

She finally put them out of their misery. "You'll both be happy to know that they've agreed to perform at our band festival."

Immediately, the boys high-fived each other, and Kate's parents exchanged smiles.

"We're trying something else, too, a Christmas cookie bake-off."

"You mean a competition?" Ethan asked, frowning.

"Yep. And a bake sale, too, which we hope will benefit your school. Aunt Lyndsay wants to get you kids involved."

"You mean baking?" he asked. "I bet kids would help, since they're going to get to hear bands and stuff."

"That's a good kid," Tom said. "Always jumping right in to organize things. Just like your mom. Sometimes being driven is a good thing."

Ethan looked down at his plate and didn't say anything. Kate was getting more angry than hurt, but she kept a lid on it. And besides, even she didn't want her kid called "driven." "I think he's a lot more like Tony He knows how to take it easy."

Ethan gave a crooked smile but didn't look at her.

She didn't need to remind herself how difficult it was to compete with Tony as a parent—but it wasn't a competition. *Life* wasn't a competition, although she'd been too good at making it so.

Christina smiled tiredly. "There's nothing wrong with a child who's like you, Katie."

"Thanks, Mom." Kate hesitated. "Are you sure you're up for the cookie making?"

Christina laughed. "When else are we going to do it? Brooke's wedding is tomorrow afternoon—Christmas Eve, remember?"

"I remember. Okay, let's leave cut-out cookie dough in the fridge as long as possible. Shall I start with the fudge, and Ethan, you can make the Seven Layer Bars, and Joe, how about the Reese Bars? Dad, turn on the Christmas music."

They spent three hours baking, singing, and laughing. They laughed harder when they accidentally set off the smoke alarm and poor Barney ran upstairs to escape. Kate almost forgot about Ethan's attitude problem until it was time for him to head home.

"Hey, tell your dad to give me a call tonight, okay? We forgot to discuss how we wanted to handle Christmas with you."

"Well, it's your turn for Christmas morning, isn't it?"

He spoke with a little edge of disrespect, as if she was stupid.

"And to think I can't remember such easy things myself."

He shrugged.

"Just have him call me. And remember, you're hanging out here while your dad and I are at the wedding."

"Are you going with Dad?"

She stared at him in surprise. "No. We've just both been invited."

"Okay, good."

Joe headed out of the kitchen, and Kate's parents made a big deal out of washing dishes at the sink.

Kate lowered her voice. "Your dad and I are friends, E. If we wanted to go to another friend's wedding together, we could."

He kept his eyes on the Seven Layer Bars he was putting into a plastic container. "I think you spend too much time together already."

"Really. Most kids would be happy their parents get along so well."

He didn't answer for a moment, then looked at his grandparents. "I've got homework, Grandma. Mind if I take off?"

"Sure," Christina said, drying a spatula. "We'll rope your mom into finishing up with us."

When Ethan had gone, Kate stared at the back door. Christina came and put an arm around her waist for a quick squeeze.

"Kids don't get any easier," Christina said quietly.

Kate sighed. "No, and I certainly didn't give you an easy time."

"You know parenting—it's a life sentence."

Kate smiled, but it wasn't really funny right about now. "He hasn't been willing to tell me what's bothering him. Any clue?"

"No. At first he seemed so happy to have you here. I wonder if he's upset because the time is approaching when you'll leave?"

Kate frowned. "I hadn't thought of that. You think he's taking my departure out on me early, like he's pushing me away before he gets too used to this?"

She shrugged. "Could be. Teenagers are full of emotions."

"Okay, you've given me something that I can chew over. Thanks, Mom." Kate kissed Christina's cheek. "Now go rest! I'll finish putting everything away with Dad."

It was almost ten o'clock when Kate got home, and she didn't hesitate to call Tony. She collapsed in front of the cold fireplace and drew an afghan over her.

"You still at work?" she asked when Tony answered.

"Yep."

"Good. I wanted you to know I started talking to Ethan about Christmas, and it didn't go well."

"Damn."

"Yeah, I know. Mom thinks he might be pushing me away because he knows I'm leaving soon."

"Could be," Tony said cautiously.

"But you don't agree?"

"I don't know. Something's different."

And something was different in Tony's voice, too. What the hell was going on with the men in her life?

She sighed. "Okay, since it's my turn for Christmas morning, are you doing Christmas Eve dinner with your family and E. after the wedding?"

"Yeah, that's the plan."

"You know, since I have my own place, you could come over Christmas morning when he opens gifts."

"I don't think so, Kate."

She blinked at the phone for a moment before putting it back to her ear. "E. must have told you what he told me—that you and I are spending too much time together."

"No, he didn't," he said, drawing out the words. "I find that pretty confusing. I'm positive he doesn't know what we've been doing together."

She felt a blush at memories that momentarily distracted her.

"But I've got to tell you, he was all for finding something to keep you occupied when you first arrived. He was *glad* about you working for me. And suddenly he's not?"

"I don't think it's so sudden," she said. "It's been coming on for a while now. So I guess it makes sense why you wouldn't come hang with us Christmas morning. But . . . I'll miss you."

Oh, God, she'd really said that. She held her breath, waiting to see what he'd do.

"That's nice of you to say," he said awkwardly. "Chef needs mc. Talk to you later."

The phone went dead, and she scrunched her eyes closed and tapped the phone on her forehead a few times. *She was an idiot.* She'd asked him to spend Christmas with her; she'd told him she'd miss him. She was changing the parameters of their ex-sex relationship, and he was pulling back.

Maybe she was the only one whose feelings were

changing. Maybe she was the only one who was frightened and nervous and hopeful all at the same time.

Maybe to him she really was only a good lay in a pickup truck.

Chapter 21

The Christmas Eve wedding of Brooke and Adam took place in her riding arena—and Kate couldn't even imagine that horses ever used it. A hardwood floor covered the dirt, beautiful drapes hid the metal walls, low lighting created romantic ambiance, giant heaters kept everyone warm. With Father Frank from St. John's officiating, the happy couple stood under a gorgeous little gazebo to say their vows. Monica had festooned the gazebo and tables with beautiful displays of bare white branches amidst evergreen boughs, vases filled with glittering pinecones, or candles with berries. Potted poinsettias stood on shelves and tables of different heights behind the gazebo, along with potted evergreen trees twinkling with white lights.

Monica stood at her best friend's side, and both Thalberg brothers stood up for Adam. Along with everyone else, Kate sighed with happiness as the stalwart cowgirl wiped away tears throughout the vows.

Kate didn't sit with Tony, of course, because they weren't a couple to anyone, not even themselves. He and his sister sat with Will on the groom's side, and she sat behind the bridesmaids, Emily and Whitney, and made happy faces at little Olivia whenever she could. The baby dress matched the bridesmaids' Christmas red, and she wore the most adorable poinsettia headband.

It was hard not to look at Tony, hard not to wonder if he was looking at her. This had gotten so complicated—as she'd worried it would. Every so often she'd catch Lyndsay's eye, and they'd smile at each other.

When at last the "You may kiss the bride" announcement was made, there was much cheering and celebrating. After the kiss, Brooke, dressed in a simple white cocktail dress rather than a full wedding gown, grinned at her new husband, then they each folded up their chairs and tucked them under their arms before leading the way down the small aisle to the tables at the far end of the arena, where pillars of candles brightened each table. Laughing, the guests all brought their chairs with them, too.

Kate was assigned to the same table as the widows and Mr. De Luca, and as they were eating dinner prepared by Heather's catering company, Mrs. Thalberg, on Kate's right, chatted on about the plans for the bake sale, and how the middle school was excited that people were interested in raising money for them.

"They need to refurbish the cafeteria," Mrs. Thalberg said. "And doesn't a bake sale just go hand in hand with that?"

"Emily's goin' to help, too," Mrs. Palmer said.

"She's goin' to open up her bakery kitchen for an hour here and there so kids can sign up to learn to bake to make the treats for the event."

"Wow, that's really generous of her," Kate said.

"Ethan is already textin' all the students—he didn't tell you?"

Kate gave a bright smile. "He must have forgotten."

"Renee offered the boardinghouse for baking lessons," Mrs. Ludlow said, "but I convinced her we don't have the room, not compared to an industrial kitchen. But of course we'll be there to help."

"I'd love to come, too. I baked Christmas cookies with my mom last night," Kate confessed, "but every year she has to walk me through it."

When Mrs. Palmer and Mrs. Ludlow started discussing what kind of baked goods they should focus on, and Mr. De Luca chimed in with his opinion on Italian cookies, Mrs. Thalberg leaned closer to Kate and said softly, "Maybe you and Tony can come, too."

Kate glanced at her, trying not to look too curious. "Well, if Ethan wants his parents there, sure."

"Come, come, Kate, that's not what I'm talking about. You are both very good at secrets, but apparently one of your neighbors saw Tony sneaking into your backyard."

Kate shot a shocked glance at Mr. De Luca and the other widows, but luckily they weren't paying attention. And it was pretty loud, with all the discussions and the music. "Maybe he saw a burglar."

"Everyone knows Tony, my dear—and apparently you still know him quite well."

Kate's face heated up, and she took a quick sip of wine.

Mrs. Thalberg touched her arm gently. "I am not chiding you, Kate, my dear. I am not surprised in the least that with prolonged contact, the two of you would be drawn to each other. Does this mean you will be reuniting?"

"I—I don't know." Kate glanced swiftly at Tony's table. He was laughing at something his sister had said. He looked so handsome in his suit that she was startled by the sharp ache of need.

"Ah, so it's like that," Mrs. Thalberg said. "I told Mario that—"

"Mr. De Luca knows?" Kate whispered urgently.

"Who do you think your neighbor told when he saw Mario's own son sneaking around?"

Kate closed her eyes and willed herself not to groan aloud. "He must be so upset. After all I put Tony through nine years ago . . ." Kate bit her lip and finally looked at Mr. De Luca, but he was eating his steak with determination as the other two widows talked.

"Mario knows Tony is an adult, and he certainly re-members how you and Tony felt about each other."

"Our relationship is not the same, not really."

"Relationships are never the same, my dear, not from moment to moment, let alone year to year. The two of you have changed, but if you found your way back to each other . . . how wonderful that would be."

"I . . . I don't know what will happen, Mrs. Thalberg. We don't plan to be together again, not really."

"But my dear, I look into your eyes, and I think regardless of what you thought weeks ago, things have changed."

Kate felt the stinging of tears.

"There, there, don't worry—and don't force anything. Just be patient, and though it's a cliché, I'll say what was meant to be, will be. Now go ahead, finish your dinner. You'll need the strength for all the dancing!"

When the dancing began, Tony stood beside the bar and pretended not to notice. He had lots of company— many men only danced because their women liked it. But he didn't have a woman to worry about.

And as if on cue, his gaze went to Kate. She was dancing with his traitor sister. Couldn't Lyndsay have made Kate sit in a corner and talk? But no, he had to watch Kate move in the green dress that only covered one shoulder and showed off her curves and her long, bare legs. Her short blond hair was styled sleekly against her head, making her look exotic.

And as he well remembered from the other night, she could dance.

You're breaking up with her, he reminded himself, taking another sip of his beer. You'd think he'd have had enough of her by now, but maybe she was like a drug in his system: The more he had, the more he wanted. Time to go cold turkey.

"Tony, you should be on the dance floor."

Tony smiled as his dad approached. "That's okay, Dad, no date to impress."

"Well, I know why you didn't bring a date."

Tony eyed him suspiciously. "Enlighten me, then."

"Well, you're looking at her. And you never stop, you know."

"Looking at who?"

Mario sighed heavily. "Kate, of course."

Tony frowned. "She works for me, Dad. I can't help seeing her."

Mario rolled his eyes to the heavens. "Am I so blind then, your own father? And Charlie Bombardo saw you sneaking into her house one night through the backyard."

Tony almost choked on his beer.

Mario patted him on the back. "Secrets never stay secret for long in Valentine Valley. What do you plan to do?"

"We don't have any plans. We're just having fun."

Mario eyed him. "Will it be fun when Ethan finds out?"

"He won't be finding out, Dad. We're ending it, and she's leaving."

"Ending it?"

"This hasn't been a relationship, Dad, no commitments, nothing."

"But she's the girl you've loved your whole life."

"Not for the last nine years, I haven't," Tony pointed out patiently.

"Neither of you has remarried in all this time. I think nine years is long enough to show you what you've missed, to show you that you've both changed."

"Dad, I'm done talking about this."

"Fine, I've said my piece. Now go dance with her."

"I'm not dancing with her. That would be—obvious."

"Because you have feelings for her?"

"Hey, focus on your own love life."

"That's what I've been doing."

He playfully elbowed Tony, who winced.

"You and Mrs. Thalberg are official?" Tony asked.

"Well, that's a mighty strong word. We're enjoying each other's company on an exclusive basis."

"Next thing I know, you'll be moving in with her."

"Now that I won't do. Can you see me at the boarding-house?" Mario shuddered. "But you—you have an empty house a certain woman could move right back into."

"Walking away now." And Tony did, his dad's chuckles grating on him. After everything Kate had put him through, Tony was shocked his dad thought that miracles happened and they could somehow get back together. That wasn't going to happen.

For the rest of the reception, he avoided the dance floor—and Kate. But he was restless and upset with himself for making decisions because of her, even dancing decisions. He was almost relieved when Brooke and Adam left in a sleigh for a moonlit ride before heading to the bunkhouse for their wedding night. In the morning, they would be off to New Orleans so Adam could show her where he'd lived after leaving the Marines, then the Caribbean.

At last Tony could go home and spend Christmas Eve with his son.

But of course, his dad and sister would be there, too, looking at him knowingly. Damn.

Kate lay in bed Christmas morning and thought of how magical and romantic it had looked last night when the wedding couple had ridden off in their sleigh festooned with bells and greenery—and tin cans, which hadn't made much of a sound dragging in the snow but had banged against each other merrily.

For the first time in a *long* time, she thought of her own wedding. She'd been pregnant, of course, so they hadn't had time to plan anything elaborate. But it had been summer in Valentine Valley, and though St. John's had been booked solid, they'd been able to exchange vows in front of their family and friends in the Rose Garden, the block that the Four Sisters B&Bs were all stationed around. She remembered the smell of the roses climbing the trellis above them as they'd said their vows. Roses always made her think of Tony, and how he'd looked at her that day, as if his every dream had been coming true. And though she'd had no doubts that she loved him, she remembered mostly being overwhelmed and frightened of the future. She'd only been nineteen years old, and worried she'd derailed every plan for her life.

But Tony had believed in her. Though she'd had a full scholarship, Tony was really the one who'd made it possible for her to go to school and still be a mom. He'd even dropped out himself after a while because he hadn't had a clue what he wanted to major in, and he'd wanted to be with their baby during the day, then work evenings to support them. Those early undergraduate days had been filled with the joy of being together, of furnishing their little apartment with homemade or secondhand things. She'd studied hard, yes, but she'd still loved her life. Law school and worries about Ethan's future had changed everything—had changed their marriage.

At last Kate tired of remembering . . . and worrying and wondering what she should do now, in the present. She got into her bathrobe, started a fire, put on some Christmas music, and actually had to wake Ethan up, first time ever on a Christmas morning. He really was growing up. She drank coffee while he opened his gifts, and of course, the best one was the smartphone she and Tony had decided on.

"Awesome, an iPhone!" he said, looking at the box.

"You know you have to set aside a lot of your baby-sitting money to contribute to the plan, right?"

"I've already been doing that," he insisted. "And Dad says next summer I can get a real job. You're okay with that, right?"

She laughed and ruffled his messy hair until he ducked away, but it was an *Aw shucks, I'm too grown up, Mom* duck, rather than something that showed resentment.

"Your dad and I talk about everything. I'm cool with it."

"Your turn!" he said.

The big box had intrigued her, and inside she found a beautifully made wooden bookshelf that would stand on her desk.

"Ethan, it's incredible! Did you make this?"

He reddened. "With Dad's help, yeah."

"Thank you. This is the best Christmas present I ever got."

"Oh, I got you one other thing, though I forgot to wrap it." He came back from his room and handed her a music book. "Look, it's for the trombone. It has Christmas stuff in it, too."

"That is a thoughtful gift, E. Thank you. Should I try playing something now?"

"Uh . . . maybe later."

She laughed.

Ethan continued to look at her, then under the tree. "So . . . you didn't get anything for Dad?"

Though she'd considered and disregarded it, she only said, "No, of course not. What makes you think I would?"

He stood there, hands in the pocket of his flannel sweatpants, looking gawky and uncomfortable.

She patted the sofa beside her. "E., come talk to me. We haven't done enough of that lately."

He sat down with obvious reluctance and looked at the fire rather than at her.

Gently, she asked, "Why would you think I'd get your dad a present when I haven't since the divorce?"

He shrugged. She said nothing, waiting.

"Because you two are friends now," he finally said, his voice a grumble. "Or something."

She didn't try to read anything more into his words than their obvious meaning. In everything she'd ever read about a child's reaction to divorce—and she'd read a lot—the child was almost always desperate for the parents to get back together. But not Ethan. "Why don't you want us to be friends again?"

He gave another teenage shrug. She waited.

"I don't really remember much of when you were together," he finally said, speaking slowly.

"You were only four when we divorced."

"I remember . . . being sad. It was really sad."

It took everything in her not to apologize or burst into tears. She swallowed a few times until she trusted her voice. "It was a very sad time. We were confused more than we were angry. And though we *were* angry, we never fought loudly. We discussed and just couldn't seem to come to an agreement."

"Well . . . I don't want you to be sad. I don't want any of us to be that way. We're happy like we are, right?"

At last he looked right into her face, his expression so wistful and full of hope. He might not have known the details of what was going on between his parents, but he sensed that *something* was different. "Oh, Ethan, I've always said only you can make yourself happy. You can't wait for another person to do it for you. But then again, nothing in life stays the same. Something could change tomorrow and we'd have to adjust to it and learn a new kind of happiness. But can you trust that whatever happens, your dad and I always want to make sure you're happy?"

He studied her face for a long moment. "Yeah, I get what you're saying. I know you love me and all that."

He brushed that sentiment aside like it was so taken for granted—but she understood. "So you aren't trying to get me to leave earlier or anything?"

His brown eyes widened. "Mom, I wouldn't do that! Well, okay, I probably haven't been too nice lately."

She arched a brow.

"I didn't mean to hurt your feelings," he said, his shoulders slumping.

She touched his knee. "I'm glad to know it. It's okay to try to figure out why you're feeling bad. Next time, remember that I'm happy to help talk things over. So should we start getting ready to go to Grandma and Grandpa's?"

"Aren't we going to watch *It's a Wonderful Life*?"

She laughed with happiness. "I'll make some French toast while you get the DVD going."

Her morning was complete when together they read out loud the winning stories for the *Gazette*'s lost reindeer writing competition and picked their favorite. Okay, her son hadn't entered—but he'd finally told her what was wrong, and her shoulders felt so much lighter.

The day after Christmas, snow fell steadily all day. Kate worked the busy lunch shift at Tony's, then spent several hours on the phone or the computer, dealing with suppliers, sign makers, and the company from whom she'd rented the stage and the portable heaters. Emily sent a note about how the baking sign-ups had gone, and the widows e-mailed about the various churches contributing baked goods for the school. Kate's list kept growing, and she was starting to wonder how she'd get it all done, but she knew she would.

Tony leaned against the doorjamb. "So when do I get my office back?"

"Oh, sorry!" she said, jumping up.

"I'm kidding. I want the festival to be as much a success as you do. Do what you need to."

"Wait, please, I wanted to tell you about my conversation with Ethan Christmas morning."

He pulled up a chair from out in the hall and sat across from her. "A serious one?"

"Yeah, it seems he hasn't been hoping to get rid of me—he's worried about the relationship between you and me changing. He thinks we've been happy—he's been happy—and he's worried about it all."

"He doesn't have to worry about that."

"That's what I told him." Tony seemed so . . . dismissive of Ethan's worries that their relationship might change. It set her nerves on edge, but she put that aside. "I told him about each person making their own happiness, not relying on someone else—well, you get the point."

He slapped his thighs as he rose. "Sounds like you handled it."

"Uh, yeah." Though she didn't mean to, she thought about their steamy encounter in the pickup and how, since then, he'd seemed distant. "Tony—"

"Josh!"

She heard their friend's name called from several voices in the bar. Tony smiled and turned his head toward the hall.

"Go ahead," she said, shooing him with her hand. They really needed to talk, but obviously the tavern wasn't exactly private. She grabbed her bag and coat and followed Tony out. Josh was still standing at the front door, rubbing his arms up and down, making no move to remove his big coat. His nose was red, his cheeks white, and he stomped his booted feet.

"Let me guess," Tony said, leaning against the bar. "You're cold."

Ned and Ted looked at each other. "Last time we got that cold," Ned said, "we were working in a house where the heat was off for days."

They shuddered in unison.

"What are you up to?" Tony asked. "And do you need help removing your coat?"

"My fingers are probably that numb," Josh said, between chattering teeth. "Coffee?"

Kate rushed to the wait station to pour a mug. When she returned to the bar, Josh was sitting on a stool, his coat still on, but his heavy gloves and hat off. He held the coffee mug between his pinched white hands and gave a relieved sigh.

"I forgot to bring a thermos of coffee on the run," he said, then took a slow sip.

"What run?" Tony asked.

"Brooke and Adam left on their honeymoon, and I volunteered to help run the sleigh back at the ranch for the tourists and the wagon here in town for the holidays. Today was the last day in town, thank God, but we've had so much snow today, I was able to bring in the sleigh."

"The sleigh—" Kate began, then she hurried to the window, cupping her hands beside her eyes to see outside. Dusk had settled over the valley, and big flakes of snow still fell gently. "The sleigh—and the horses—are in the parking lot!" she said with excitement.

"The horses are fine." Josh inhaled the coffee steam. "They spend most of the winter outside. I'll only stay a minute."

"I didn't realize the wagon rides were just for the holiday," she said, her voice disappointed. "I meant to go and just ran out of time."

"If you want, you can ride back to the ranch with me," Josh offered.

"Oh, I don't want to put you out . . ."

He smiled. "Well, I've got to go back, don't I?"

"I'll feel kind of silly riding alone."

"Tony'll go with you," said a deeper voice.

They all turned to see Chef Baranski standing near the entrance to the kitchen. He was eyeing Tony meaningfully. Kate couldn't even speak for fear he might reveal the kiss he'd seen. What did he think he was doing?

"Sure, I'll go," Tony said, as if it meant nothing.

But for some reason, her heart started to pound. He wasn't keeping his distance now—but then, Chef had forced his hand.

Josh drank the rest of his coffee and had a hamburger before bundling up again. "Layer up," he warned her. "Although I do have blankets in the back."

She put on an extra sweater, then her high furry boots, along with her parka. Tony came out of his office in a heavy coat, a knitted hat, and thick gloves.

"Have fun!" the twin plumbers called in unison, and then snickered.

"Yeah, I'm a sucker," Tony murmured.

"You don't have to go," she said.

"I'm going."

After dumping her bag in her Range Rover, she walked around to the front of the sleigh to see the horses, petting their noses and running her hands along their sleek necks. Snow settled softly into their manes, like it did in her hair. She admired the elegant lines of the sleigh, the way it seemed to cup the riders before curving up beneath the driver's seat.

"Josh, is this an original sleigh?" she asked.

"From my grandfather's time. We fixed it up."

Tony eyed the bench behind the driver's seat. "Looks like new leather you might have worked on."

Josh grinned. "I might have done some tooling."

They climbed inside, and Tony spread a thick blanket over their legs. She felt the warmth of his thigh along hers, but she didn't dare snuggle beneath his arm as Josh climbed up in front of them.

The sleigh gave a little jerk as Josh started the horses down the length of the parking lot and out the far entrance onto Nellie Street, but after that they glided smoothly. Sleigh bells softly jingled from the horses' harnesses.

"Oh, that sounds lovely," she said, glancing at Tony. "We must look like a Christmas card."

Josh concentrated on his driving and let the silence work its magic. As they turned north on Seventh Street, the wind picked up. Kate shivered and tucked the edge of the blanket under her legs. But when they turned onto Main Street two blocks later, she found herself distracted by all the lights.

"Oh, Tony, isn't it beautiful?"

There was something about the quiet ride of the horses, with just the clopping of their hooves and the jingle of the bells, that made it all seem so peaceful. Cars were few and far between the day after a holiday. And then she shivered again.

To her surprise, Tony put an arm around her, drawing her tightly against his side. Instantly she felt protected from the wind.

She glanced up at him. "Is this wise?"

"Keep your hood up and don't call attention to us. They'll all think we're tourists anyway."

She nodded, biting her lip to keep from smiling. With a happy sigh, she leaned against his chest and relaxed. The nineteenth-century buildings moved past slowly, their windows circled in lights, or with wreaths spotlighted in each. The breeze ruffled her bangs, but she was no longer cold, warm and safe instead in Tony's arms.

She truly was safe, she realized. Safe and happy and content, feelings she hadn't known in . . . over nine long years. She realized then that she was fighting her feelings for nothing—that she just had to let go and face the fact that she still loved Tony. The sleigh bells continued to jingle as they drove down Main Street, past the three-story Hotel Colorado. She'd forever associate those bells with the realization that even though she couldn't change the past, she was well on the way to changing her future—their future. She didn't want to leave him—she *never* wanted to leave him again. His place was here, in Valentine Valley. And suddenly, as if blinders had been lifted from her eyes, she knew she wanted to stay here, too, with him. Her career in a powerful law firm hadn't led to the happiness she'd once imagined. She'd lost too many years figuring out that Valentine was really where she belonged. She belonged with her son and her family—she belonged with Tony.

These realizations were overwhelming and scary, and she didn't know how to tell him. And what if she said she loved him and it just pissed him off, because he'd wanted sex with no complications?

"You're awfully quiet," he murmured.

She practically jumped, and she felt his chuckle vibrate through his chest. "Sorry, I'm just thinking how beautiful it all is, especially with the snow!"

At town hall, the snowflakes fell through the spotlights that highlighted the beautiful stone tower. They took the turn north on First Street to swing by the Sweetheart Inn, where dozens of rooms had a candle in each window. They jingled past the Rose Garden, admiring the Four Sisters B&Bs, all of them outlined in strings of white lights highlighting their Victorian architecture.

They drove into a more residential area, and she straightened to look past Tony at all the lights along the stone bridge and the trellises in the Rose Garden as they faded into the snowy scenery behind them.

Tony was looking down at her, his eyes intent. She leaned up and kissed him, cold lips to cold lips, and felt like she'd come home. On her part, the kiss was full of all the love she didn't know how to say.

He lifted his head at last and stared down at her, his

expression inscrutable, just as the sleigh pulled up in front of the tavern. She sprang away from Tony.

Tony cleared his throat and called to Josh. "What's going on? I thought we were heading out of town."

"I didn't want to strand you at the ranch. I'll just go home from here."

"Thanks so much for the ride!" Kate called, smiling brightly as Josh gave her a tip of his Stetson before lifting her down by the waist and setting her on her feet.

She laughed. "You're a charmer. I know why Whitney married you."

"Well, there might have been a baby involved—but then you know how that is." And he winked.

She did.

"I liked having an excuse to get her down the aisle faster," he added, grinning. "See you guys at the band festival."

She stood beside Tony, watching the horse-drawn sleigh disappear into the shadows of a side street. The bells jingled long after they were out of sight. She sighed with happiness.

"Uh, Kate, can I talk to you for a sec?" Tony asked.

"Sure." She faced him, her smile dying as she tried to figure out what was in his voice.

He looked into her face. "There's no easy way to say this, but I think it's time to end this . . . thing we've got going between us."

The cold chased up her spine so suddenly that she shivered, and all she could do was stare at him while all the warmth and excitement of her newfound realization of love drained right out of her.

"You'll be leaving in a couple weeks," he continued, "and with Ethan sensing—whatever—I think it's better not to risk getting caught. We've had our fun, right? You okay with this?"

She opened her mouth, and for a moment she feared she might not be able to speak. All the emotions she'd just been feeling were welling up inside her, desperate to break free, desperate to make him see that she still loved him.

But it was obvious he didn't love her.

She wet her lips. "Sure," she answered, a little breathless. Oh, please let him think it was just from the winter ride.

"Okay, that's good." He smiled. "I'll see you tomorrow."

And he walked back inside, leaving her out in the cold.

Chapter 22

Tony didn't bother going home for dinner like Kate had. He was relieved to have a couple hours break from her before she returned in time for the evening's festival work. The widows descended on the tavern to coordinate the first delivery of bake sale items. Tony stared in bemusement at the big table set up along one wall in his back room, which now made his place look like a bakery. Even the pool table was covered, to the good-natured disgruntlement of a couple of cowboys.

He watched Kate bustle about with the widows, trying to look cheerful, and probably succeeding to most people in the room. But not to him. Every smile looked forced, and her eyes had lost that gleam. Was she focusing so intently on the festival that nothing else mattered? Or was she thinking about their split?

He certainly was. He'd thought of nothing else all evening. He'd been trying to find the right time to end things, and the motivation had been that stupid sleigh

ride around Valentine. He'd pulled her against him—
what had he been thinking? He *hadn't* been thinking,
not with his head, that's for sure. He'd stopped thinking
the moment he'd challenged her to work for him. On
the sleigh ride, she'd made such adorable sounds looking at the Christmas lights, like she'd never seen them
before. And when she'd looked up at him, the lights had
reflected in her merry eyes. If she hadn't kissed him
first, he would have kissed her.

And then—the breakup had just spilled out of his
mouth, and it was like he'd watched Christmas die in
her eyes. He'd known from the beginning that someone
might get hurt, but he was frankly shocked it was her.
At least . . . he told himself it was only her. But how
to account for the frozen hole where his heart should
have been? He'd existed in a depressed daze the last
few hours.

Oh, he'd rationalized everything: of course she felt
bad, they'd been having a good time; the breakup probably reminded her that real life was returning fast, and
she'd be leaving.

And then he'd ask himself, Why would she be sad to
be leaving? It was what she wanted—wasn't it?

She escorted a man with a box into the back room,
directing him where to set it. When she saw Tony, her
smile faded just a bit, and he felt like he'd kicked a
puppy.

And then his dad came in with Mrs. Thalberg, carrying a few bags. Huh, his dad and Mrs. Thalberg. Still
seemed . . . surreal. But he was glad they were both
happy. Christina Fenelli arrived next, and Tony sud-

denly became more alert. She was breathing heavily, though she was only carrying one small bag. Her face looked pinched with strain.

"Kate?" he called, not wanting to alarm Christina.

But whatever was in his voice, Kate responded to it fast, shooting a glance at him. He pointed to her mom, and he saw Kate literally drain of color before his eyes.

"Mom? Hey, Mom, give me that." She took the bag, and then she took Christina's arm.

Sounding breathless, Christina said, "Kate? What's wrong?"

"I don't know, you tell me. Come on, sit down."

Tony pulled a chair right up behind her, and Christina gave a little "oof" as Kate made her sit.

Christina forced a laugh. "I'm just tired from the holiday."

"Mom, you don't look just tired. You're breathing heavily, and all you did was walk in from the parking lot."

"Well, yeah, I do feel a little light-headed and queasy."

Kate squatted in front of her. "Okay, I'm calling an ambulance."

"No! I don't need an ambulance, I'm just fighting a cold or something."

"You've been strangely out of breath a few times this last month. It's not just a cold. Tony?"

He already had his phone out of his pocket, and he dialed 911.

"Kate, this is silly," Christina insisted. "Let's just go to Doc Ericson's. He'll see me."

"And he'll tell you to go to the hospital. Mom, if it's nothing serious, then we can all have a good laugh after. But if it's serious—Mom, it's a half hour to the hospital in Aspen. We can't afford to wait. Now let's open your coat a bit so you don't overheat."

Without being asked, Tony next began to call Kate's dad and brothers. She noticed what he was doing and thanked him with a warm, tremulous smile. He watched her show no fear to her mom; Kate just teased her to make her relax. Kate was the kind of woman who handled emergencies well, and he'd always admired that.

The fire department was only a few blocks away—like everything in Valentine—and the ambulance arrived so quickly that Kate barely had time to unbutton her mom's coat. The paramedics worked with efficiency and an easy calm, as if nothing bad would happen.

Tony saw the way Kate had her arms folded over her chest. She was clutching her elbows with white fingers. He put a hand on her shoulder and she gave him a distracted, thankful glance. She was trembling, and he wanted to wrap her in his arms and bear the burden of her fear if he could.

As they began to roll the stretcher through the front of the tavern, Kate fell in line, asking if she could ride with her mom. Tony grabbed Kate's coat and handed it to her as she turned around.

"Did you call Ethan?" she asked.

"He's next on the list. We'll see you at the hospital."

"He doesn't have to come. It might be frightening or boring or—I don't know."

"You're babbling."

"I know, I'm sorry."

He kissed her forehead. "It'll be okay. Whatever it is, you caught it early and did the right thing."

Her eyes shone with tears as she gave him a grateful smile before jogging along in the stretcher's wake.

At the hospital, the waiting room quickly grew crowded. Jim beat everyone there, since his restaurant was right in Aspen. Ethan didn't leave Tony's side; he just stood with his hands in his pockets while his frightened gaze darted around. Tom Fenelli came in with his three other sons, pale and mumbling how it should be him and not his wife as he shuffled past Tony to the receptionist. A nurse took him away and soon Kate appeared, her expression calmer. Tony took a deep, relieved breath.

"I thought Mom and Dad needed some time together," she said to her brothers, who immediately gathered around her.

Walt, who'd been pacing, now frowned. "I knew this festival would be too much work for her."

Kate blinked as if he'd slapped her.

"Take it easy," Tony said mildly. "Christina's been having some symptoms for a while, but they were easy for all of us to explain away."

Walt shot him a look, then seemed to sag. "Yeah, you're right. Sorry, Kate. I'm just—worried."

Kate stepped into Walt's arms, and they stood there

a long time, just holding each other. Then she suddenly looked up. "Oh, God, I didn't even say the important news. She hasn't had a heart attack."

The relief that went through the family circle was like a breeze ruffling through their clothes, as they all sagged and shuffled and took turns hugging each other.

"What is it? What happened?" called Mrs. Palmer as the three widows and Tony's dad came through the door.

"Everything's okay," Kate said. "Well, it's not okay, but it's not as bad as it could have been. Apparently, she's been having some occasional discomfort that was actually angina."

"It's so hard for women to read the signs of impending heart problems," Mrs. Ludlow said solemnly.

Kate nodded. "They're discussing what to do next right now, but it's looking like they'll perform an angioplasty if the blockage is bad enough." She glanced at Ethan. "That's when they open up a blocked artery with a little balloon they thread into her heart. They don't even open her chest up. It's pretty miraculous."

Ethan nodded, eyes wide with confusion, and Kate put her arms around him and just held on. Tony so badly wanted to be in the circle of their arms that it was painful.

This was his whole family, and he knew how lucky he was. Right in front of him were two people that meant the world to him.

And he'd just told Kate he didn't want to be with her.

Was he making a mistake? Or was the mistake imagining he could revive a relationship that had been killed nine years ago?

The angioplasty procedure was finished successfully at around midnight. Kate stood with all her brothers, and she wasn't ashamed that the fear of the day was released with tears flowing down her cheeks. Dave stood with Jessica, Jim kept an arm around their little brother Joe, Walt had Diana—and Kate would have given anything to walk into Tony's arms for the comfort only he could give.

But he didn't love her.

She'd watched him through the long evening as he'd played cards to distract Ethan. Oh, she knew Tony now considered her a friend, and she knew she'd always be important to him. But she wanted to be loved like he'd once loved her, the love she'd let her worries and fears and narrow-mindedness and ambition throw away.

But she had her family, these wonderful people she might occasionally fight with—she glanced with fondness at Walt—but the people who'd love her regardless. She had her mom, thank God, for many more years. Kate was determined to find an exercise that she and her mother could enjoy together.

She hadn't realized how much she'd missed being with them on a regular basis until these last few weeks. She wanted that closeness more than anything. She wanted to come home, even if she couldn't be with Tony.

But looking at him from afar, watching him date and maybe get married—these were all things she'd thought not to have to watch from Denver or Vail. She would have to be strong, so strong, to give him up with grace.

And then she looked at Ethan, who watched his uncles celebrate the good news with high fives. She wanted to make sure he felt the same closeness with her as she felt for her own mother. And much as she'd done her best these last nine years and knew he loved her, she wanted more. He was almost fourteen. There were only a few short years until he would go off to college. She didn't want to waste another moment.

And maybe if she was in Valentine, Tony might begin to realize they should be together . . .

As the room grew quiet with the glow of relief and joy, Jim suddenly said, "Well, it looks like I'm going to take back that stand mixer I got Mom for Christmas and replace it with a treadmill."

They shared happy, relieved laughter.

Tony watched Kate spend the morning of the band festival at a brisk but calm pace. She oversaw the stage setup in the parking lot, the hanging of the sponsors' banners, the open-sided tents to shelter the food. She sat down for only a moment in the tavern to have a quick coffee break while she still worked, asking about stage techs switching out the bands' instruments. When she heard the front door open, she looked past Tony, and her face brightened with recognition and curiosity.

"Michelle?" she called.

Tony turned around to see a plump African-American woman with close-cropped hair and a cheerful, round face. She was dressed casually in jeans and a big oversize sweater beneath her open coat. Tony looked back at Kate with interest, even as he rose to his feet.

"Kate! So glad I found you this easily."

Kate stood up. "Tony, this is Michelle Grady, a colleague at Clements, Lebowitz, and Yang."

Michelle shook hands with Tony. "Nice to meet you. Are you the owner?"

"I am."

"Well, I think this festival is a great idea. I know a lot of people who are planning to come from Vail."

"That's quite a trip, thanks." With Kate running the show, even Denver was probably plastered in posters, just like the storefronts in Valentine Valley.

Michelle grinned at Kate. "It's quite the lineup of bands. When you announced that you were coordinating it on your Facebook page, how could I not come?" Then her voice lowered. "But I do have some business to discuss. Do you have a minute to talk privately?"

Tony stepped back. "You ladies go ahead. I have a beer truck due any moment."

Tony couldn't stop glancing at Kate and her work colleague, who talked seriously together before breaking for lunch. They were discussing work, which meant that Kate was one step closer to leaving. All this time he'd been telling himself this was for the best, that this was what Kate wanted.

But it wasn't what *he* wanted. He'd been miserable, distracted, and blown away by how much he'd wanted to be the one Kate had leaned on during her mother's illness.

Was he really still in love with her, after all this time?

"Dad, who's that with Mom?"

Startled, Tony turned to find Ethan coming out of the back room. "She's a coworker of your mom's from Vail."

"Oh, I thought I recognized her. She dropped off some files once or twice at our place."

Tony nodded, but he didn't take his eyes off the two women.

"Guess it's not that much longer before Mom heads back."

Tony grunted his response, then realized Ethan was watching him closely. "Something wrong?"

"I don't think you want her to go," Ethan said slowly.

Tony gave his son his full attention, debating what to say. "It's been nice becoming friends again after all these years. Are you okay with that?"

Ethan sighed. "Mom told you what we talked about Christmas morning, didn't she?"

"No, not everything. We've both been worried about why you've been upset. She thought things were better between you."

"Yeah. Seeing Grandma sick like that—and seeing Mom go through it kind of by herself, well, I guess I've been thinking about things. She's usually so strong, you know?"

Tony leaned back against the bar. "I know."

"Maybe she needs somebody. Maybe you asked her to work here because you need her, too. Have you thought about that?"

Tony hid a smile. "Yeah, Ethan, I've been thinking a lot about that. But thinking isn't the same as it being true. I don't know what's going to happen. It might not be happily-ever-after. Sometimes we just have to take the risk. Things have always been good with our families, but maybe they can be great if I stop playing it too safe. Do you know what I mean?"

They looked at each other. Ethan would be his height soon, would be a man far too quickly for Tony's peace of mind.

His boy finally smiled. "Yeah, I guess you gotta take risks or you never get something you really want, right?"

Tony grinned. "Right."

"Well, I gotta get back to the bake sale stuff."

Tony briefly put his hand on Ethan's shoulder and squeezed. "And I'm gonna see what my parking lot looks like."

By three o'clock, the light snow had stopped, and the sun peeked lazily out from behind the clouds. Tony's normally grungy parking lot was *not* full of customers ready to rock and eat; instead, it was full of senior citizens. He loved the widows as much as the next person, but had word of the festival only spread to their friends? Had Kate's vaunted social media brought no new customers—hell, not even his regulars? Tony threaded through them, looking for Kate.

"Lovely day for a festival, Tony!" called his dad's elderly receptionist.

"Rock on, Tony!" said an old man wearing leather and shaking his cane over his head.

Tony thought he might be the patriarch of the local funeral home. "Kate?" he called anxiously as he got near the bake sale booth.

She heard him and turned around. Her expression told him of her guilt.

"What the hell's going on?" he whispered.

She winced. "I didn't know how to tell you. I didn't have the heart to refuse, and you really didn't pay attention to the lineup, which meant you trusted me and I appreciate that—"

"Ladies and gentlemen!" the loudspeakers boomed.

Tony turned around to see Will Sweet on the stage. It hadn't taken much effort on Kate's part to coerce him into being their announcer. He always loved to be the center of attention.

"Fresh from a Christmas Eve gig in Denver, it's time for . . . Frankie Rudinski and the Polka Dots! Let's polka!"

The senior citizens let out a big cheer, and Tony felt his mouth dropping open. The accordion started to play.

Kate tugged on his arm so he'd bend for her to speak into his ear. "The widows were so excited that the Polka Dots were in Denver. They've done so much for us— how could I refuse to invite one of their favorite bands? Mrs. Ludlow's husband was in the army with Frankie Rudinski. And a polka band played at Woodstock!"

"Woodstock?"

"Well, Woodstock 1999, anyway."

He found himself chuckling. "Thank God they're on in the middle of the afternoon. Maybe we won't scare away every rocker in town."

Kate looked relieved, and he patted her hand on his arm. She'd been trying to please everyone, mostly him.

"You've done a great job, Kate!" he yelled so she could hear over the sounds of "Roll Out the Barrel."

She briefly leaned her head against his arm. "Thanks for saying that—I wanted this to be a success for you."

"I know you did."

They smiled at each other, and for a moment, he saw the sadness deep in those purple eyes, the shadows beneath, as if she hadn't slept enough.

"Kate—"

She backed away, blinking too fast. "Oh, I almost forgot. I promised my mom I'd take videos. Better get to it!"

As he watched her hurry off, he felt another tug on his elbow, only to find Mrs. Thalberg there, looking smart in a winter parka with a big fur-lined hood.

"Tony, you have to buy a selection of cookies and vote for the best one."

"Sure, Mrs. Thalberg."

"And then you have to go find Kate and tell her you love her."

She'd had to yell, and surely all the widows could hear, but they were looking at him expectantly as if they'd known all along.

"It's not that simple," he began.

Mrs. Palmer, who wore earmuffs clamped down on the center of her big blond wig, said, "Nothin's simple, boy! If we waited for things to be easy, we'd never do anythin'!"

He waved and escaped.

Hours later, Kate was tired. The sun had long since set, and so many people kept telling her what a great time they were having. She even saw Vince, her lonely customer who'd told her that Double Cyn was his favorite group. For once he wasn't wearing a suit, and he didn't take his phone out of his pocket. He stood kind of rocking back and forth as they performed their hit "Tell Me Another One."

Kate stopped beside him. "Hi, Vince!" she yelled into his ear. "Having fun?"

"This is the best!" he yelled back. "I haven't been to a concert in years."

She smiled up at him, and for just a moment, she let happiness wash over her. She hadn't done much beside talk to Vince about music, but it felt good to help remind him that there were other things in the world beside sorrow. She thought of Tony, doing that every day for people.

She knew she helped people as a lawyer, too, but for some reason, this felt just a little more special, personal, a small step she'd helped Vince take.

When Toke Lobo and the Pack were performing, Ned and Ted actually found her in the crowd and made her dance with them to "Full Moon Lady." They were sweetly disappointed when that was the last number of their favorite band and the stage techs started dismantling their equipment. She promised to dance with them later. She had a feeling the three of them might be the only non-teenagers dancing during The Dead Can Sing.

She was just watching the tarot-reading booth,

where Mrs. Palmer was reading the cards for an enthralled Chef Baranski, when she heard the speakers give a loud screech. Too loud. She rushed forward, threading her way through crowds who were standing around waiting for The Dead Can Sing. There were more teenagers there than during the polka band, that was for sure.

The speakers gave an even louder screech just as she got near the stage. To her surprise, Tony got there at the same time she did. He gestured for her to go first. She went around behind the portable stage, through the security guards, until she reached the lead singer, who she remembered from the concert. He was standing offstage, urging a sound crew member to turn the speakers up louder.

"Hey!" Kate shouted. "I'm running this event, and my permit says you can't play that loud. Please turn it down to the level we'd agreed on."

The singer was a cute young guy, with a tattoo on his neck and a ring in his lip, but he had a little sneer going on that amused her more than anything.

"Lady, this is what my fans want," he said.

He didn't flinch when someone strummed a guitar so loud that she felt it clear down to her belly button.

"Well, the fans can't have it."

"Then we don't go on."

She thought of Ethan's excitement for this band, and how he'd gotten all his friends to help with the bake sale with the reward of enjoying this silly group.

"Look here, kid. If you turn it all the way up to eleven—"

"Hey, that's from *Spinal Tap*," he said, laughing.

"No kidding, but if you turn it up, I will sue you back to the Ice Age."

"Yeah, well, your lawyer ain't here."

"*I'm* my own lawyer—Kate Fenelli."

She saw Tony out of the corner of her eye. He was barely keeping a straight face, but he let her do the talking.

"Well, talk to my manager." The kid pointed to a guy standing by the fence out back, smoking a cigarette.

"*You* talk to your manager and see what he says."

With a loud sigh, the kid went down the stairs, and Kate and Tony followed.

Tony took her arm when she would have joined the conversation. "Maybe we should give the manager a minute to talk sense."

The taped music had been turned off in anticipation of the band taking the stage. Crowds of people milled and talked and laughed, but Kate had no problem hearing the manager say, "Kate Fenelli? She's the chick who represented the performing arts center I told you about—the one who sued Billy's band. She's a terror. Turn down the music before we get fired."

The kid tried to argue, then ended up stomping past Kate. She resisted the urge to smile in triumph; instead, she looked up at Tony and said, "I'm a terror. Did you hear that?"

To her surprise, he slung an arm around her shoulder. "Tell me about it."

And suddenly, her throat closed up and she started to tremble. Will, who was heading up onto the stage for the next announcement, did a double take when he looked at them. She wasn't sure what he saw in her face, but she tried to get a hold of herself.

"What is it?" Tony asked in her ear.

"I just . . . I just didn't want to fail, not again, not for Ethan, not for me. God, I feel like an idiot," she said, dabbing at her eyes.

"Fail? The great terror, Kate?"

But her lips trembled as she looked up at him. "I failed too much, Tony. You trusted me with this, and that's important."

"Kate—"

"I know, I know, it's just a band, and everything's going great and I'm worrying for nothing, but—"

"Kate."

To her surprise, he put his arms around her. Though they were backstage, they could be seen. She stiffened and tried to pull away.

"Tony, don't—"

But he wouldn't let her go. "I failed, too."

She felt a flash of hot disbelief. "You? Tony, you never failed. You might not have known what you wanted right away, but you made your dreams happen, one step at a time."

"Then I learned that from you. And I was able to do it with your help, even after the divorce. When we were married, I failed to even ask about our future, just assuming we'd always want the same thing. And I took it so personally when that wasn't true."

Her eyes widened. "No, oh, Tony, no! I was so focused on what I thought was right, how desperately worried I was about our family's future. It wasn't right of me to assume that my way was better, that only some big degree could provide a future for Ethan. But I was so scared, so afraid I couldn't make it work—that I'd fail you. I didn't mean to make you think I didn't trust you—I did everything wrong—" Her voice broke, and she covered her mouth on a sob. "God, why am I saying all this now, when it doesn't matter? I'm so sorry. I need to—get away before people wonder what the hell is wrong with me."

She turned and ran, past security, out the side entrance, away from the festival. She went in the back door of the tavern through the kitchen, where the line cooks stared at her.

She tried to close herself in Tony's office, but to her surprise, Tony grabbed the door and forced his way in.

She groaned and backed away. "I don't want to do this now. I never should have brought it up. But I can't stop thinking, can't stop remembering, now that any chance for us is over." She sank down in his office chair and covered her face.

He pulled her hands away and held them between his, dropping to his knees. "I don't want it to be over. I love you, Kate. I've never stopped."

Her eyes flooded again. Tears spilled down her cheeks, and she stared at him as if trying to read the truth in those warm brown eyes.

"But . . . but you said . . . last night—"

"Yeah, I broke it off. I was afraid of feeling too much, of feeling like I did nine years ago."

"When I left you," she whispered, her stomach roiling.

"But I left you first," he said. "I took Ethan and came back to Valentine Valley when you were still in law school, instead of working through our problems."

"But we agreed on that! Ethan was so upset in Denver, and so much happier in Valentine. I had to study too much, and I was afraid he'd think me a terrible mother—"

"Stop it, please. You're making me feel even worse, that I let you think of yourself that way. You were never a terrible mother. Never once. Yeah, we stupidly didn't talk about our plans, and I was so proud and self-righteous when I thought you might be leaving me behind."

"Leaving you behind?" she whispered, aghast.

"I know, it was stupid. I always thought I was perfectly prepared for marriage because of my love for you, but I wasn't. And neither were you. We were young and stupid, but we've got to stop beating ourselves up for the mistakes we made back then. The point is—can we put them behind us?"

"I . . . I want to, but Tony, we haven't even discussed what we'd do—"

"I don't care what we do, as long as we're together."

The flare of hope shocked her. "But Ethan is worried his life will change—"

"We haven't raised a dummy. He already suspects we've been trying to be together again. He's okay."

"Are you sure?"

"Am I sure about Ethan? Of course. I need you to be sure that I love you, Kate Fenelli, that I don't ever want to be apart from you again. Last time my heart broke leaving you, and this time, it would be ripped out of my chest if we can't be together. God, I can't believe I just said something so sappy," he added, shaking his head.

"Oh, Tony," she whispered, then flung her arms around him and kissed him through tears and laughter and desperation. Then she cupped his face in her hands and stared into his eyes. "I love you, too. I want to be with you. I'm resigning from the firm."

Now it was his turn for his eyes to go wide, then search hers. "Kate, I'm not demanding you move back here. We'll find a way to make it work. I saw the way you were with Michelle—your job's important."

"No, you don't understand. Remember how the partners wouldn't let me ask GAC Biochemical about the file I shouldn't have seen? Turns out after all the angst, the disagreements between me and the senior partners, the way they thought they were punishing me with the sabbatical—well, GAC just voluntarily let the firm know they'd accidentally included a file from a different research project. Can you believe it? All I wanted to do was ask, and everything would have been easily explained."

Tony's eyebrows lowered. "But I don't understand—why wouldn't you go back if your problems are cleared up?"

"Because this sabbatical is the best thing to ever happen to me. Without it, I wouldn't have moved back with my parents, I wouldn't be here with you. I wouldn't have rediscovered the joy of falling back in love with you. My life and my priorities have completely changed. Never have I missed home so much as being here these last few weeks. Being with Ethan and our family, and with you—my God, with you most of all. I don't ever want to go back to working fifteen hours every day, living my life for the brief time with our son. Sure my company will take me back—but I don't want to be with people who don't trust my judgment. I—I didn't tell you, but Cal Carpenter offered me a partnership, said he'd been holding it open just for me." She said it almost shyly, waiting for his answer.

His growing smile was like the spring sun rising after a long winter. He leaned forward and kissed her so sweetly, so tenderly. "I don't want to waste another minute," he said. "I want to be with you."

"But how do we tell people? They'll all be shocked."

He pulled her forward, sat in the chair in her place, and pulled her back to his lap. "Well, I bet lots of people won't be surprised at all, not if they knew us then. My dad and the widows already know, and so does Ethan."

"My parents," she began.

"We'll go to the hospital first thing in the morning and tell them. They'll be happy."

She curled up against him, head on his shoulder as she looked up at him, and just sighed with happiness.

"Will and Lyndsay already know," he said.

Kate laughed. "It's starting to look like everybody closest to us knows. Oh, probably not my brothers."

"They'll be fine. But me—I won't be fine, not until we're together. Let's get married again."

"What? Don't you think we should take some time to make sure?"

"Kate, I've never found another woman who makes me feel a tenth of the way you make me feel."

"Oh, Tony," she said, wondering if she was going to run out of tears at some point. She never wanted to leave his arms.

"If you want to wait, I can wait until spring or summer, or whenever. But say you'll marry me again."

She laughed. "I'll marry you."

Just as they were about to kiss, the door opened.

"Dad—? Oh."

Kate would have jumped up, but Tony held onto her. Ethan stared at them, but his expression didn't look so much upset as exasperated.

He rolled his eyes. "You're missing The Dead Can Sing."

Kate and Tony glanced at each other and started to laugh.

She stood up, still holding Tony's hand. "Uh, E.—"

"Yeah, I'm not blind. You two better not screw it up this time."

"We won't," Kate said, looking up at Tony, hoping he could see the love and determination in her eyes. "I'm moving back to Valentine. You cool with that?" But she wasn't really looking at her son.

"Oh. Yeah, that's cool." He sounded brighter. "Come on, let's go. They're going to close with my favorite song, I know it."

And they followed him out, holding hands.

When the band was finished, fireworks started, and Kate gaped up at the night sky from the center of the roaring crowd. "I didn't order this!"

"I did," Tony said, holding her from behind. "I was hoping it would be a celebration of your accomplishments. Who knew it would mark a new beginning at the same time."

She turned around and kissed him.

"Kate! Tony!" Lyndsay's voice was an astonished scream.

"Time to tell the relatives," Kate said. "You ready?"

He took her hand. "More than ready."

Epilogue

They got married again under the same trellis in the Rose Garden that summer, and this time, Kate wasn't scared or worried or overwhelmed. She was marrying the man she'd loved since she was ten years old, and she was confident that he felt the same feeling of rightness, of belonging.

They had the blessings of their son, who gave them a bird feeder he'd made as a wedding present, saying with the exasperation of a teenager, "Mom, don't you get it? You can't have a bird feeder at a condo, but you can at a house. Our house."

She got it.

She was determined to do everything right this time, to talk over every detail. Tony was already a little sick of talking all the time, but he'd come around.

But the number one thing she wanted to do in the normal old way of newly married couples?

Get pregnant on the honeymoon.

Give in to your Impulses!

**These unforgettable stories only take a second
to buy and give you hours of reading pleasure!**

**Go to *www.AvonImpulse.com* and see what we
have to offer.**

Available wherever e-books are sold.

AVONIMPULSE

IMP 0811